PRAISE FOR *LEGACY (*

MW00593265

An immersive, masterful work of altern:
Dick and Robert Harris will love.–*BestT*

The legacy of World War II meets the complexities of the 1950s Cold
War in this globe-hopping thriller, as a small group battles their personal
passions to prevent a revival of the Nazi regime. Maitland-Lewis has assembled an interesting cast. However, character development is not the
main focus of the book, which is mostly action, and the author keeps the
story moving at a nice clip, with a variety of tense set pieces in exciting
locales. The book concludes with a battle scene that reveals a strong eye
and ear for how a battle is actually fought. Maitland-Lewis brings the
same skills to bear on outlining the horrific Nazi experiments continuing
in the Americas, potentially sensational material that he handles with hu-
manity and respect. The final showdown with a traitor is both tense and
cathartic, and readers of smart international thrillers will appreciate that
the book leaves the door open for further adventures. –*BookLife Review*

Full of high drama and exciting twists, *Legacy of Atonement* is a page-turn-
ing thriller which reimagines the events from the Second World War and
its immediate aftermath. –*IndieReader*

This fast-paced thriller has a plethora of unexpected twists and turns that
will keep readers guessing to the end. Fans of historical fiction will appreciate the fact that the author has obviously done his research on World
War II, the Holocaust, the fleeing of many Nazis to Argentina in the aftermath of their defeat, and the conspiracy theories surrounding Nazi
leader Adolf Hitler and his wife, Eva Braun. Did they really die in that
bunker in Germany as the Allies closed in on them? As each layer of this
mystery is peeled away, frightening revelations and possibilities come to
light. Devotees of World War II fiction, especially those familiar with the
questions surrounding Hitler's death, will undoubtedly relish this book.
–Glenda Vosburgh, *US Review of Books*

PRAISE FOR *LEGACY OF ATONEMENT*

Legacy of Atonement is a novel of perfection . . . so many incredible twists and turns, and every page reveals an incredible step forward in this harrowing journey. Stephen Maitland-Lewis has crafted a story that touches the pulse of our world today. A must-read that leaves you breathless.
–**Jann Robbins**, Award-winning best-selling author of *Hope and Honor* and *Harold & Me*

Maitland-Lewis hits the jackpot with fast-paced suspense in *Legacy of Atonement*, a Cold War thriller linking the shadowy world of global banking to traitors in high government. Complex family ties sunder as protagonist Daniel Lavy unmasks a horrific coda to the Nazi reign of terror. The finale of this bravura alternate history is sizzling with action and surprises. This is, however, far from a tall tale: the moral is evident—that fascism and antisemitism then and now, is fueled by untraceable fortunes. –**Michael Findlay**, author of *The Value of Art* and *Seeing Slowly–Looking at Modern Art*

This book is a riveting rollercoaster of action set post-World War II. It has a compelling alternative history at its core. Mr. Maitland-Lewis imbues his characters with wit and savvy as they travel from one international locale to another. A smart, fun read from start to finish. –**Peggy Scott Laborde**, New Orleans-based author, talk show host, and Emmy Award-winning documentary producer

Stephen Maitland-Lewis has once again provided us with one of his fascinating, international page-turners. He takes us on a fast-paced journey back to the post-Second World War era, and to a chilling scenario which might have changed the world we live in today. –**Mike Burstyn**, Award-winning stage & screen actor and director

Stephen Maitland-Lewis has returned with arguably his most provocative work amid a succession of compelling page turners. Maitland-Lewis is a man of the world, and *Legacy of Atonement* is a testament to his talent of coupling his prodigious writing with his uncommon ability to tell a story.
–**Jim Engster**, President Louisiana Radio Network

PRAISE FOR STEPHEN MAITLAND-LEWIS'S OTHER TITLES

HERO ON THREE CONTINENTS
A moving, complex and well-crafted fictional biography... Maitland-Lewis renders the multitudinous cast of characters with marvelous detail ... a touching read, with a fictional character to admire. **–Kirkus Reviews**

EMERALDS NEVER FADE
A poignant story of two men whose lives are forever altered by a period of history that should never be forgotten. **–Robert Dugoni**, *NY Times* Bestselling Author

I couldn't put it down until the end. It is a page-turner – greatly enjoyable and informative. Perfecto. **–Connie Martinson**, TV Host of *Connie Martinson Talks Books*

AMBITION
This financial thriller rocks and rolls with sex and skull-duggery and more money than Midas can count. It's un-put-downable. Chilling. **–Kitty Kelley**, seven times *NY Times* Bestselling Biographer

Ambition creates the excitement of free-fall – it's difficult to put down. Who said financial institutions were dull? A wonderful book and a great reading experience. **–Mickey Kantor**, former United States Secretary of Commerce

BOTTICELLI'S BASTARD
Botticelli's Bastard is beautifully written and to its further credit impossible to categorize. Part thriller, part intriguing mystery, this book is compulsive reading. Above all, it is a first-class novel. **–Sir Ronald Harwood**, Oscar® winning writer

Botticelli's Bastard is a fascinating complex and completely compelling novel. It is everything I love, history, art, suspense, intelligence and creativity. I am captivated. **–M.J. Rose**, International Bestselling Author

My interest in collecting important art came together with my love of thrillers. Stephen Maitland-Lewis' *Botticelli's Bastard* is a great read. **–Arnold Kopelson**, Oscar® and Golden Globe® winning producer

DUPED
A realistic and engagingly descriptive novel. **—Kirkus Reviews**

DUPED delivers the excitement of a heist film with the exotic adventure of a globetrotting spy tale. While Maitland-Lewis' dialogue-driven writing makes for fast-reading, well-crafted adventures through portions of Africa, Europe and California will please the travel-starved masses. **—BestThrillers.com**

In *DUPED*, author Stephen Maitland-Lewis has written a novel of high-stake schemes, suspense and sex. A deftly crafted, impressively original, and inherently riveting read from first page to last. **—Midwest Book Review**

PRAISE FOR STEPHEN MAITLAND-LEWIS'S OTHER TITLES

Stephen Maitland-Lewis has secured his place as a supremely gifted writer of the cunning, courage and evil residing within the human spirit. With his special talent of developing characters capable of both heroic and treacherous acts, Maitland-Lewis relies on his wits to create another fabulous book. *DUPED* ranks as another masterpiece from this writer with a hugely impressive body of work. —**Jim Engster**, President Louisiana Radio Network

Maitland-Lewis delivers a sophisticated, high-stakes, international thriller that will make you grateful for the life you have, providing you aren't already caught in a web of corruption and deceit in the sweltering Nigerian streets. Be thankful you're a reader and not a character in this haunting tale of desperation, greed and power. —**Stephen Jay Schwartz**, *LA Times* bestselling author

MR. SIMPSON AND OTHER SHORT STORIES
Personal connections, and our failure to make and tend to them, dominate this entrancing collection of irony-infused short stories, set mostly in postwar Europe and America. The greatest lure of the stories are the characters. Maitland-Lewis (*Botticelli's Bastard*) sharply limns the foibles of the well-heeled and privileged. The decisions Maitland-Lewis's characters make haunt them forever, and the characters themselves will haunt the readers. Takeaway: The community of characters—the good, the desperate, the greedy—will grab readers' hearts and make them care, story after story. Great for fans of: Graham Swift, Julian Barnes –**BookLife** - *Publisher's Weekly*

5 stars (out of 5) Stephen Maitland-Lewis' *MR. SIMPSON AND OTHER SHORT STORIES* include tales that range from droll slice-of-life to high-octane suspense. Maitland-Lewis brings a dry British wit to many of the tales contained in the book. IR Verdict: Stephen Maitland-Lewis wows with *MR. SIMPSON AND OTHER SHORT STORIES*—a triumph of alternative history featuring humor, action, romance and an eclectic mix of characters, genres, and moods—from an exemplary storyteller with a unique voice. –**IndieReader Review**

Stephen Maitland-Lewis, author of the pulse-pounding financial thriller *Duped*, is back with a collection of suspenseful stories that succeed wildly in chronicling the relentless pursuit of success, status, and survival. Prepare to squirm as Maitland-Lewis reveals one dark secret after another. Deliciously ruthless predators rule in this collection of stories about deceit, deception, fraud and power. Highly recommended. –**BestThrillers.com**

These stories are wonderfully cosmopolitan. The range of characters really reflects the ways of the world, its successes, and its failures. An up-to-date Somerset Maugham is announced, you might well think. –**David Pryce-Jones** - Author - *Fault Lines, Signatures,* and *Closed Circle*

This book makes for a great nighttime read. It is the author's first collection of short stories, but his international and business experience helps to make the stories realistic and believable. –**Seattle Book Review**

PRAISE FOR STEPHEN MAITLAND-LEWIS'S OTHER TITLES

I admire authors who sit down with their vocabulary and place words in an order that I never could—whether to evoke an emotion, unearth a bygone era, or capture a unique slice of the human spirit. Stephen Maitland-Lewis is one such writer and he accomplishes it time and again in Mr. Simpson and Other Short Stories. This book is great. I'm also certain that he knows more words than I do. **–Alan Zweibel,** original *SNL* writer/Thurber Prize winning novelist

An entertaining smorgasbord of short stories that pay tribute to the masters of the genre. With an arch sense of humor and a delicious dash of irony, Stephen Maitland-Lewis follows an intriguing cast of characters—including a philandering banker, a blackmailing florist, a failed musician, and a disenchanted spy—through clever plot twists and surprise endings that never fail to satisfy. **–Tom Sancton,** Author of *The Bettencourt Affair and Sweet Land of Liberty - America In The Mind of The French Left 1848-1871*

LEGACY OF
ATONEMENT

LEGACY OF ATONEMENT

STEPHEN MAITLAND-LEWIS

Hildebrand Books
NASHVILLE, TENNESSEE

Copyright © 2023 Stephen Maitland-Lewis

This book is a work of fiction, using research from public domain and free information readily available. All incidents and dialogue, and all characters with the exception of some well-known historical figures, are products of the author's imagination and are not to be construed as real. Where real-life historical figures appear, the situations, incidents, and dialogues concerning those persons are entirely fictional and are not intended to depict actual events or to change the entirely fictional nature of the work, with the exception of factual descriptions of the actions of said historical figures. In all other respects, any resemblance to actual persons, living or dead, events, or locales is entirely coincidental.

This book does not represent personal or political views. It was written for entertainment. regardless of race, religion, or country of origin.

All rights reserved. No part of this publication may be reproduced, distributed, or transmitted in any form or by any means, including photocopying, recording, or other electronic or mechanical methods, without prior written permission, except in the case of brief quotations embodied in critical reviews and certain other noncommercial uses permitted by copyright law.

Hildebrand Books an imprint of W. Brand Publishing
j.brand@wbrandpub.com
www.wbrandpub.com
Printed and bound in the United States of America.

Cover design by designchik.net

Author Photo by Darien Photographic

Legacy of Atonement – Stephen Maitland-Lewis first edition

Available in Hardcover, Paperback, Kindle, and eBook formats.
Hardcover ISBN: 978-1-956906-52-3
Paperback ISBN: 978-1-956906-53-0
eBook ISBN: 978-1-956906-54-7

Release date: June 13, 2023

Library of Congress Control Number: 2022923401

Dedicated to the Memory of Three Wonderful Friends

Michael Cogswell, Jerry Chazen, and Budd Friedman

In the spring of 1959, a seemingly minor mistake in a wire transfer at a Swiss bank leads to the discovery of a plot by the CIA to launch a nuclear attack on the leaders of the USSR and China and to install Hitler, who is still alive and hiding in South America, as the leader of Western Europe.

CHAPTER ONE

Geneva, Switzerland
Tuesday, March 24, 1959

"**D**amn it!"

Daniel Lavy slammed his mug of Lowenbrau down on the coffee table in front of him, levered himself up from the black leather couch, stomped over to the television set, and turned up the volume full blast against the fierce late-winter sleet storm battering at his living room windows.

The noise from the storm was drowning out the television announcer's coverage of the championship soccer match between Bayern Munich and Real Madrid being played in Munich. The teams were tied one-one, and as usual, he and Guy had drawn straws to decide who would get which team. Daniel had drawn Spain, and if they lost, he would be out a hefty sum.

He was backing toward the couch, his eyes fixed on the teams scrimmaging in front of Spain's goal, when the doorbell rang. He wheeled around at the unexpected noise just as pandemonium erupted on the television screen. The Germans were shouting for their home team and hugging one another while the announcer bellowed, "*And Bayern Munich has just scored! Two-to-one with five minutes remaining!*"

And he'd missed it!

The doorbell sounded again.

"Go away!" he shouted.

No answer, but he knew that whoever it was would not be able to hear him through the heavy door. He went to the door and called, "That you, Guy?"

Silence.

He edged the peephole open and saw the face of a young woman, her face half-hidden under a sodden black beret, wiping rain from her face.

"Go away!" he barked. "You've got the wrong address!"

He glanced back at the television set. Play was about to resume. He slammed the peephole shut so hard that it bounced open. He grabbed it to try again, but she pushed her index and middle fingers into the opening.

"Uncle Daniel!" she stammered. "Please . . ."

He stared at her for a moment, feeling the poignancy of "uncle" which was how she had always referred to him despite the actual relationship being cousins by marriage.

"Giselle?" he said uncertainly.

She nodded.

"I have nothing to say to you," he snapped. "So just go back to wherever you came from." After a moment, she pulled her fingers away and her face disappeared. He closed the peephole but remained at the door listening.

The old bitterness rose up. *How dare she show up again?*

He eased the door open. She was at the end of the hall tapping the elevator call button. Her shoulders hunched, her hair dripping in tangles down her back, her tan wool coat mud-colored with rain, and her shoes leaving saturated footprints on the carpeting.

"Wait!"

She turned, her face blank and cold. "Don't worry! I'm leaving!" Her words were defiant, but he sensed that bravado was all she had left.

"Come back," he said with a sigh. "I can't let you go back out into that." He hurried down the hall and reached her just as the elevator doors slid open with a soft chime. Before she could step inside, he reached in and slammed the emergency stop. The doors froze.

She studied him for a moment, then marched past him and down the hallway into the apartment. He followed wondering what the hell he was getting himself into.

As soon as he closed the door behind them, she swung around to speak, but he held up his hand. "Exactly what made you decide to show up here tonight?"

She shivered. "I had nowhere else to go," she whispered.

"So–" he snorted, interrupted by the announcer screaming over the roars of the crowd. *"It's Munich in the last eight seconds! Final score is three-one!"*

"Hell!" He strode to the television and turned it off.

When he turned back to her, he saw that she looked panicked by his anger. He reined himself in and managed a tight, perfunctory smile. "You're drenched. Go on in and dry your face . . . you may still remember where the bathrooms are."

She nodded and walked unsteadily but unhesitatingly down the hallway to the second door on the right. The bathroom tiles flashed white as she switched on the lights. The door closed.

He sat down on the couch and wondered what in hell she wanted. Still, he owed it to himself to at least be civil. And even now, at twenty-three, or however old she was, she seemed so young. Still so much like the grieving thirteen-year-old whom he and his then-wife Claudia, her cousin, had taken in ten years earlier, after her parents died in a car accident. *Why hadn't he let her leave?* But he hadn't, and now he was going to have to deal with it. All of it. All the history.

By the time she came out of the bathroom combing at her hair with her fingers, having apparently tried to towel-dry it, he had managed to control his irritation.

"Please." He gestured at the leather armchair next to the couch. She perched on the edge of the seat.

"Where's your coat?"

"I hung it up in the bathroom to dry."

"Fine." He waited for her to speak, but she remained silent and uncomfortable. "So?"

She twisted her hands in her lap, unable to look at him. "I'm . . . I was just let go from my job, I have no money, and I've been locked out of my flat. I didn't know where else to turn."

"So you came to me? Of all people?"

She couldn't look at him but nodded.

He studied her. "And when was the last time you had anything to eat?"

She looked confused. "I don't remember."

He hauled himself to his feet and headed toward the kitchen. "All right. Suppose I get you something and then you can tell me what this is all about."

When he opened the refrigerator door, he saw that his housekeeper had left it well stocked as usual. He loaded a tray with several pieces of roasted chicken, a baguette, some butter, a glass of wine and one of water, cutlery, and a cloth napkin, and took it into the living room, where he placed it before her on the coffee table.

"Thank you," she whispered, and reached for the napkin. He returned to the couch and watched her. She was clearly ravenous but still had the manners she had learned as a child. When she had eaten a little and touched the napkin to her lips, he asked quietly, "Are you up to telling me what's been going on?"

She pushed the wineglass away and took a sip of water. "I thought that maybe you could help me get my job back."

"I had no idea you were even back in Geneva!"

She straightened up and pulled her shoulders back. "Why would you have? Since we both know that all you wanted was to get me out of your sight for good."

"And what I did was cover your entire secondary school education, as well as your four years at university."

"And without ever doing me the courtesy of allowing me to thank you!"

He said nothing. She was right. He had made it clear that he was writing her off entirely.

"I came back three months ago," she said. "One of my classmates helped me get the job at the bank. And with your business . . . I thought you might be able to talk to someone . . ."

"Which bank?"

"Desbodiens."

He was stunned. "Desbodiens! You mean the Schmidts?"

He saw that his vehement reaction had not registered with her because she just nodded and continued, "Yes. Banque Debodiens. But they let me go even before I'd completed my probation . . ."

"And just what did you know about them?"

"Not much. Antonia helped me. My classmate. We were best friends. I was desperate. I'd been searching for two months, but she set it up and saved me. And I thought everything was fine. Most of the people were nice, and the president's nephew, Francis Schmidt, even said he would take me to lunch sometime. But then that woman showed up, and that was that."

"Who was she?"

"Elisabeth Martin. They introduced her to all of us yesterday. But when I came in this morning, they'd given her my desk. And then they told me I'd made a huge mistake on a wire transfer and were dismissing me immediately. They made me get my coat and hat and purse and had a security guard walk me out to the street. Right in front of everyone."

"And then?"

She bowed her head. "And when I got back to my flat, the manager had padlocked it. Because I was behind with my rent."

"By how much?"

"Three months. I'd been living on the rest of my money." She hesitated. "The rest of what you had settled on me, but ..."

"And I'm sure you never frittered anything away when you were in school."

"You mean you never spent any money having fun when you were a student."

When he was a student. Yes, sent away to learn all about commodity trading in England in 1933 when he was eighteen. Away from his parents and younger sister. He pushed the thoughts away.

"In any case, I can't help you with the Schmidts and never would." His voice rose. "I can't believe you're asking me that! Don't you know that Desbodiens is the nastiest, most cutthroat bank in Geneva? And that the Schmidts are vicious anti-Semites?"

She stared at him.

"Everyone in Geneva knows it! And if you'd done any checking at all, you would've known it too."

"It was the only thing I could find! And I was so grateful to Antonia—"

He gestured for her to stop. "So you're, what? Twenty-three?"

"Twenty-four next month. You've probably forgotten."

"No, I haven't! It's been eight years! And six since I've seen my boys! And—"

She jumped to her feet. "And I was only fifteen! And you blamed me!"

"I blamed you for not telling me!"

"I didn't even understand what was going on! How could I have told you something I didn't know?"

"I don't believe you didn't know! You should have come to me! I took you in when Claudia asked me to! And paid for your entire education, which I hoped would prepare you to make something of yourself without ever needing to see me again! Much less show up asking me to help you get your job back with Desbodiens, of all places!"

She stood and smoothed her skirt.

"Where are you going?"

She ignored him and went back into the bathroom. When she came out, she had her coat draped over her shoulders and her purse tucked under her arm. She went to the front door without looking at him.

"Wait." He stood. "I'm sorry." He glanced at the windows. "It's too treacherous for you to go back out there."

"If you think," she replied, "that it was easy for me to come here . . . I know you still hate me, but I've always been grateful to you."

"Just for tonight. Please. You can have your old room."

He reached for her coat, and after a moment, she handed it to him, walked to the room past the bathroom, and then closed the door behind her. *How many times had he seen her do that after he and Claudia and she and the twins had all wished one another good night?*

A few minutes later, he went to knock on her door but stopped when he heard her sobbing. He felt torn between sympathy for the straits that had forced her, as a last resort, to turn to him and resentment that her reappearance in his life was forcing him back into the past, to the ruins of his marriage, and the loss of his boys.

He decided to let her cope on her own with what she was going through, so he took the tray of food into the kitchen and was placing it in the sink when the wall phone rang. He snatched it up.

"Yes, Guy! I know! You can stop crowing!" he snapped. "Yes, I know exactly how much I owe you! I have to go. I'm in the middle of a drama here . . . No, nothing like that . . . Stop by my office in the morning and I'll settle up . . . Yes, with a smile. Don't I always, damn you!"

Daniel returned to the living room knowing what he could no longer avoid doing but fearing he lacked the courage. After pacing back and forth along the wall of rain-streaked windows for several minutes, he went to the door across from the bathroom and eased it open.

A tiny nightlight in the shape of a candle cast a dim glow on the furnishings. The twins' cots, still made up with the patchwork quilts that his grandmother had sewn for him and his sister, Felice, and that the boys had inherited. The matching patchwork cushion sat on the rocking chair where she used to sit and sing to him. Their favorite toys, a huge stuffed elephant seated on its hind legs and holding a teddy bear between his front ones, were positioned neatly on the boys' battered but still colorful painted chests labeled "Michael" and "Matthew". Both toys shabby from much toddler love. He remembered the boys squabbling over them at their third birthday party.

And against the far wall, his and Claudia's carved-oak credenza, the marvel of antique Italian woodworking that both sets of parents had presented to them on their wedding day. He and she had vowed to treasure it forever. But six years later, after Claudia and her new husband had robbed him of their boys, he realized that the only way he could go on would be to bury all the memories as best he could. So, he had moved the credenza into the boys' room, draped his grandmother's fringed shawl over it, set out a few of the faded family photographs that had survived the war, and finally closed the door behind him.

He had not opened it since. He did not know whether his housekeeper ever went in to dust. He had not wanted to know.

He sat in the rocking chair and picked up one photo that he had been seeing in his mind's eye since Giselle had reproached him about his own student days—an oversized print of him and his mother, father, and baby sister, Felice, who was only twelve. On the summer day in 1933, they had seen him off to London to study banking, trade, and commerce. How young he had been. A smiling, optimistic boy-not-quite-man, barely eighteen but topping his father by an inch, with the same dark-brown hair but his mother's hazel eyes and finely modeled chin. The last time they would be together.

He heard a sound and set the photo down. The door opened and Giselle peered around. She gasped when she saw him.

He sprang to his feet. "Get out!"

She tried to pull the door shut, but he slammed it against the wall and stormed into the hall after her.

"What the hell were you . . . you had no business . . ."

Terrified, she ran into her room and locked it behind her.

He was shaking with rage. *How dare she come back and resurrect all of it?*

He returned to the boys' room. Reluctantly, but knowing he had to face the inevitable, he sank into the rocker and, for the first time in eight years, let it all flood over him.

Why hadn't Giselle come to him and told him? How could she have been that naïve? How could she not have known that Claudia had begun an affair with Luciano Moretti, a wealthy Argentinean diplomat? He had suspected nothing until the day

Claudia had demanded a divorce. And then, what made it even worse, as soon as they had married, the shattering blow when they manipulated the legal system, and she was granted sole custody of the twins. Immediately after which, she and Luciano took the boys to Rome, and then half a world away to Buenos Aires as Luciano rose in the diplomatic ranks. All of which had made it so easy for them to keep his children from him. Six years now.

And with one knock at his door, Giselle—damn her!—had rekindled all the pain and bitterness he had tried for six years to repress.

He opened the top drawer of the credenza and riffled through the few family documents and photographs that had survived the war until he found an unframed color snapshot of a grave, gawky twelve-year-old with dark-blonde hair and blue-green eyes. Giselle, still a child herself, in a light summer dress in a park with Matthew and Michael clutching her hands. The way they used to hold his.

He touched a finger to their faces and studied the photo more closely. After the accident, after he and Claudia had taken her in, she had found her place as a loving "big sister" to the boys.

Studying her face at twelve, he realized that even after three years with them, she had still been grieving her parents, and that his and Claudia's bitter divorce had destroyed her fragile sense of safety again. He had lost Claudia and the twins, but so had she. But out of his pain and rage and his need to find someone to blame, he had spent six years holding her innocence against her. She was right; she had been caught up in something she was much too young to understand, much less handle. He had been so blind, so wrong.

And now?

He set the photo aside, went into the hall, tapped on her door.

No response.

He kept his voice low and soft. "Giselle?" He sensed that she was at the door, but it remained closed. "I promise I won't hurt you."

Silence.

"I want to tell you . . . I've never told anyone."

Silence.

"I know that if my parents hadn't sent me to England, I would have been able to save them. Somehow. And my sister."

Silence.

"I begged them not to send me away, but . . . and then the world changed, and I wasn't able to come back. They died, and I've always felt it was because I wasn't there. I know they sent me away to keep me safe. But . . ." His voice broke. "But why didn't they send Felice too? Because they thought she was too young? She was only twelve. Your age when you came to us."

Still silence.

"You kept telling me that you were only fifteen. That you didn't understand what happened with her and Luciano. I know now you're right. And I've wronged you in my thoughts and treatment of you and in every other way for the past six years. Even the money I threw at you was because I blamed you and wanted you gone."

Still silence.

"I'm going to go back to the boys' room now. I'll stay there. You won't have to see me. If you don't feel safe here and want to leave, I understand. I don't expect you to forgive me. But I promise you that I will help you, in whatever way I can, now and for the rest of your life. Even if you never want us to meet face-to-face again."

Silence again. Then the click of the lock. The door opened. She had her coat wrapped around her and her purse under her arm, and she was wiping at her eyes with a handkerchief. "Please . . . their room."

He gestured for her to precede him, and when they entered, he indicated the rocking chair, but she shook her head and sat on Matthew's cot near him.

She sighed. "It looks the same. Except for the credenza."

"I had to put it away. It was the only way I could close the door on everything."

He took some photos out of the drawer and placed them on the shawl. She hesitated, but he assured her, "I can't hide any of this from you any longer. You're part of my family. And I'll tell you whatever you want to know."

She reached for a color photograph of Claudia holding the newborn twins in her arms and beaming at the camera.

"I took that," he told her. "We had just brought them home from the hospital."

"So beautiful."

"Yes."

She reached for another photo, a faded black-and-white formal portrait of his parents and sister and himself when he was sixteen and Felice was ten.

"They gave it to me the day they sent me away," he said. "July 14, 1933. Bastille Day. We were picnicking in the Bois de Boulogne. Before you were born. It's the only one I have left. Everything else was lost."

She held out her hand and then studied the picture he handed her. Hesitated. "Where?" she asked. "No one ever told me. No one ever talked about it."

"I found out after the war that they were all slaughtered at Auschwitz in 1943. Just sixteen years ago."

After a silence, Giselle reached for another photo, turned it over, and showed it to him. It was a shot of him and Guy in a forest clearing. Both a good eighteen years younger, in rough clothing, sporting unkempt beards, arms slung around each other's shoulders, rucksacks and rifles at their feet.

"We met in the Free French forces. I joined in 1941. I knew I had to do something, so . . ." He set the photo down. "He saved my life more than once. He's based mostly in Geneva now, so we stay in touch."

Giselle looked around the room. "Being here in this room again. Reading them bedtime stories. Even their bear and elephant . . ." She buried her face in her hands and sobbed.

Daniel's throat tightened. He dared not touch her to try to console her. He tried to swallow his own tears but finally gave way to them, and side by side they mourned. Loss after loss after loss.

At last, she wiped her eyes and touched his arm.

He asked, "Do you want to leave now?"

"No. How could I? This has changed everything."

She stood and left, easing the door shut silently behind her. He replaced the photos in the drawer of the credenza, slid it shut, and let the silence and the dim glow of the nightlight soothe him. It reminded him of a Sabbath candle. Although he and Claudia had not been observant, she had apparently placed this small reminder of their Jewish heritage in their sons' room. The grandsons neither his nor her parents had ever met. He wondered what more he might have learned about his and Felice's heritage had his parents survived. The heritage that had caused their deaths and millions more.

CHAPTER TWO

D aniel hardly slept that night and by morning was feeling drained but oddly at peace. He barely scanned the newspaper report on the soccer match and was sipping on his third café au lait when Giselle emerged, pale with exhaustion. The housekeeper, Madame Pougatch, had not met Giselle before so Daniel had informed her that she was his cousin and staying with him. Madame greeted her with a warm, "Welcome, Mademoiselle!" and poured her coffee before retreating to the kitchen.

Their new footing left him feeling awkward and unsure of himself, so nodding at the paper he remarked, "Apparently it was one of the best matches of the past three seasons."

She looked uncertain, so he added, "I'm sorry. This is . . ."

She summoned a smile. "Well, you know that my showing up had nothing to do with them losing!"

He laughed. "After you have something to eat, can we go over what happened one more time? I need to know the whole story so we can figure out what to do."

She nibbled some toast. "They claimed I'd made a big mistake that had cost them a lot of money. But it isn't true!"

"Still, you were on probation. Was there anything else that they could have used as an excuse?"

"No! I knew I couldn't afford to make any mistakes. So, every day I recorded everything I'd done in a notebook and reviewed everything again at home that night. There were never any problems until that Elisabeth showed up."

"And who was she, exactly?"

"Someone said she was related to some important clients. I knew the name because of some transfers I had done."

"To?"

"Diessen's."

His stomach lurched. "Diessen's!"

"Yes. Why?"

"I'll tell you more later. Go on."

"That's all. But if I show them my records, won't they see that they were wrong to let me go?"

"No—it's actually much more likely that Francis and Elisabeth are involved with each other, and they wanted you out of there. And that's a battle that you never would have won."

"Still," she insisted, "I need to know for my own sake!"

"Suppose we start out with the rent issue. How much are we looking at?"

She hesitated. "Fifteen hundred francs."

"Done. Cash, I assume. Given how landlords are."

"I just feel ashamed. Especially after what you said last night."

"That was then. We all make mistakes. So let's start fixing yours. First, we'll go to your flat. I'll cover your arrears and some extra to tide you over. Can you be ready in fifteen minutes?"

As he entered his study next to the living room, the phone rang. "Lavy here . . . Hello, Guy. Sorry about last night—"

"I'm not sorry! Since I won!"

"Do you remember Giselle?"

"Claudia's little cousin? The one who—"

"Yes, but it's complicated. Last night she came to my door, drenched and sobbing. After all this time. Right at the end of the match."

"Is she all right?"

"She's lost her job and been locked out of her flat. She's almost twenty-four now but . . ."

"So what happened?"

"She'd had trouble finding a job and finally secured an entry-level position at Desbodiens—"

"Those damned lowlifes!"

"Yes. Something about a mistake in a wire transfer that they claimed had made them take a big hit."

"I'm surprised that they even hired her. I mean, if they had checked her out at all, they would've learned about the Jewish connections."

Daniel sighed. *Would the hatred never end?* "I suspect that the wire-transfer issue was an excuse, and the real problem was that young Schmidt was after her—until some new young woman came onto the scene and caught his eye. But Giselle insists that she was set up. That's all I know right now."

"Sounds as if you're willing to help her out. But I'm surprised she dared to come to you, given how you treated her."

"I can't believe that until last night I'd never realized . . ."

"Listen, DL, we've been friends for a long time, but frankly—I know how hard it was on you—if I'd been fifteen and orphaned and taken in by relatives and then gotten caught up in what happened with you and Claudia and Luciano . . . She always seemed like a sweet kid. Smart, too."

"I know that now. I have to think it through. In any case, come by my office around noon? Maybe we can come up with some ideas for her."

"Good. Actually, DL, I'm surprised she dared come to you at all."

"Yes." He didn't add that he had lain awake most of the night reliving it all.

CHAPTER THREE

An hour later, Daniel parked his Porsche Cabriolet across from Giselle's dilapidated pre-war apartment building. As they got out of the car, a balding middle-aged man in shirt sleeves and bright red suspenders sitting at a desk in front of the office window saw them and stood up.

"That's Monsieur Schnabel," Giselle said. "He's actually not so bad most of the time."

"Good. Let's get this over with." Daniel slipped an envelope of banknotes into his suit jacket pocket and walked around to open her door. The manager came out onto the sidewalk.

"Good morning, Miss Faber." His manner was polite but businesslike. "I saw you arrive. At least the storm is over, and the weather has cleared up." He gave Daniel a curious glance.

"I'm Daniel Lavy, Mademoiselle Faber's cousin," Daniel said. "I hope we can clear up this unfortunate matter as well. I understand that she owes you three months' rent."

Schnabel ushered them into his office. "That is correct, plus an administrative fee for the eviction notice. And of course, the matter of the padlock."

Giselle, her cheeks flushed, stood to the side, and studied the floor.

Daniel handed Schnabel the envelope. "Then this will cover all the arrears, plus an additional two months' rent as a personal thank you for your help."

"Yes, thank you, Monsieur Schnabel," Giselle murmured.

Schnabel counted the notes, placed the envelope in the top drawer of his desk, pulled out two sets of keys, locked the drawer, and led them up to Giselle's flat. He removed the padlock and stood aside. She unlocked the doorknob lock, pushed open the door, and gasped.

The dingy flat was in a shambles, with bedding, clothing, kitchenware, books, and overturned furniture strewn everywhere.

"My God," Daniel said quietly.

Giselle burst into tears. "Who did this?" She wheeled on Schnabel. "How could you let this happen?" She buried her face in Daniel's sleeve. He didn't know what to say or do to calm her, so he turned to Schnabel. "How in hell could anyone have got in if you had padlocked it?"

The manager shoved his hands into his pockets and studied his shoes. "Last night, a man came here who showed me a letter of introduction and an identification card from Banque Desbodiens. He said he needed to see Mademoiselle Faber because she hadn't been at work for three days and her employers were concerned. I told him she was out, but he insisted on checking, so I went up and took off the padlock. Then I gave him the door key and came back down to my office."

"My notes!" Giselle cried. She pulled away from Daniel and ran into the bathroom.

"So this man," Daniel said, "apparently ransacked the apartment, locked it again, returned the door key to you, and told you that everything seemed to be in order. Why the hell didn't you stay up here and keep an eye on him?"

"I should have, but . . . the Munich-Madrid match . . ."

Daniel grinned in spite of himself. "I hope you bet on the winning team because I sure as hell didn't. So you came back up and padlocked the door again later on? Without checking inside?"

"Yes. It was very careless of me . . . When you've finished here, please tell me what you and Miss Faber intend to do, and I'll give you a receipt."

As he headed down the stairs, Daniel shouted after him, "And where's that letter?"

"I placed it in her file."

"Get it out! I want to see it!"

He went into the bathroom. Giselle was pulling a small black notebook out from behind the water tank above the toilet. He reached for it, but she held it away from him. "These notes are confidential! I should never have made them in the first place! The bank secrecy laws—"

"How would they know you were keeping notes? I know how upset you are, and this is the worst thing yet, but how can I help you if you won't let me?"

Reluctantly, she handed it over and he began leafing through it.

"Where are your notes on that wire transfer?"

She turned to a page toward the back. He read out, "'Twelve million US paid to Asian Commodities, a Hong Kong corporation, at their bank, Bank of East Asia, by Diessen Corporation, Argentina, out of their account, number 874589 at Banque Desbodiens, in respect of a shipment of copper from Hamburg to Hong Kong. Also, one million US to Banco de la Nacion in Buenos Aires.' You don't say for what."

"Apparently a monthly transaction for fertilizer. They've been sending it out for years. I know because it's being debited every month from a company called Panto, a Desbodiens' client, and I was studying the files during my breaks. To learn as much as I could . . ."

"Perhaps you should start getting your things together," he said gently.

While she picked through the debris, he scanned more pages. "And here's another twelve million US transfer, for copper and fertilizer. And one for rubber. Quite a lot of business. Actually, business I wish my companies were getting. But why are they using a broker in Hong Kong to buy fertilizer for use in Latin America?"

She balled up some clothing and tossed it into a worn but high-quality suitcase. "Probably to support large-scale agricultural development in South America. Based on the reports I've come across in the financial newspapers."

Her offhand comment startled and impressed him. She might have been up against it in terms of learning how to support herself, but she had obviously been learning as much as she could.

When she was ready to leave, Daniel locked the flat and they returned to Schnabel's office. He apologized again and handed them the receipt and the letter, which Daniel scanned and tucked into his pocket. "And I hope," he added, "that the additional sum I added to what Miss Faber owed will motivate you to be more careful in the future."

CHAPTER FOUR

B y the time Daniel and Giselle arrived at his office, Guy was waiting for them. Every time they met, Daniel was both glad to see him and envious of his apparent ability to avoid any signs of encroaching age. Daniel was six years older than him. Guy was two inches taller with clean-cut features, gray eyes, fair hair, and a wardrobe tailored to show off the athletic build he maintained with demanding workouts, a routine he had never relinquished since his days playing college football at his alma mater, the University of Wisconsin. Approaching forty, he had maintained the same weight since those college days.

Before Daniel could introduce them, Giselle exclaimed, "I remember you! Daniel showed me a photo of you last night. You used to come and visit."

He smiled. "And I remember you, even though you're all grown up now."

Daniel cut in. "Let's go to my office." He led them down a long, carpeted corridor lined with contemporary paintings and into an office that offered a dazzling view of Lake Geneva. When Giselle saw that his desk faced into the room, she asked, "How can you possibly turn your back on that view?"

"Because I can't afford to get distracted," he replied, and ushered them to the conference table at the far end of the room.

As soon as they were seated, Guy turned to Giselle. "Daniel told me a little about the problems you've been having. I'm not sure if I can help, but—"

Daniel broke in. "Things have changed since you and I talked earlier." He recounted the visit to Giselle's flat and ended by handing him the letter from the "bank representative." "Does that name ring any bells?"

Guy scanned it. "Gottfried Gadicke? No. But give me a phone and about five minutes."

"Ask Madam Gilly to give you an outside line in one of the other offices."

After Guy left, Daniel said, "I've been thinking about what to do about your flat."

She shivered.

"Obviously you can't go back there, but I was hoping you'd stay with me until we know more about what's going on. For your own safety."

She studied him. "If I had thought twenty-four hours ago that we'd ever be able to talk like this . . ."

"I know." He paused. "Well, we can store your things there for the time being."

"What's left of my things," she said with a wry smile.

Guy returned holding a page of scribbled notes. "Interesting. Gadicke's a lawyer. German. No big client list, but my contact said he's known to handle all the Diessen's business in Europe. Which would be substantial."

Daniel turned to Giselle. "How often did you see Diessen's transactions occur?"

She considered. "Perhaps twice a week. Sometimes three times. And never less than two million US each."

"Do you remember any talk about them at Desbodiens?"

"Only that they were important clients. But I don't remember ever seeing much about them in the newspapers I was researching." She frowned. "And of course, Elisabeth Martin was related to them. Who are they?"

"They have their tentacles all over Europe," Daniel explained. "And in Latin America as well. There were rumors about them playing both sides against the middle during the war, but they covered their tracks too well for anything to be pinned on them."

Guy went on with his notes. "Apparently Gadicke's office consists of just him and his secretary."

"So now what?" Daniel asked.

"Daniel has said I can stay with him," Giselle told Guy. "So, we need to go back to my flat and clear it out."

Daniel turned to him. "Will you go with her? I don't think she should go there on her own."

"I agree." Guy smiled at her. "Perhaps we can even have lunch afterward."

"How kind of you!"

Daniel turned to her. "Can you give us a few minutes? Madame Gilly can bring you some coffee if you like."

As soon as the door closed behind her, he spat, "Any time I hear 'Diessen's,' my skin crawls!"

"Yes. There've been ugly rumors about them since the '20s."

"Gang of fucking war criminals! Damn them to hell!"

Guy gave him a few moments. "So we look into Gadicke? A visit to his office?"

"The sooner, the better. Tonight?"

"I'll get the full range of gear together. Eight thirty? Do you think we still have the knack? It's been a long time since this was routine for us. Actually, it should be easier than when we were with the Free French; we have better equipment."

"Good." When Daniel stood to walk him to the door, Guy also rose but remained where he was. "And our debt of honor . . .?"

Daniel took out his wallet, counted out a number of banknotes, and handed them to him.

"Thanks. And now, next week? France and Italy?"

"Italy again? Oh, all right." He started to open the door but closed it again. "By the way, about Giselle." He stopped.

Guy waited for him to continue, but Daniel felt unsure what to say. He finally shook his head. "I just can't . . . Looking back . . ." He could not bring himself to talk about what he and she had shared and settled for, "I spent most of last night thinking about how I'd treated her. And feeling like shit. Maybe I'll be able to make it up to her."

Guy patted his shoulder. "It was a hellish time. All of it. But—" He grinned. "—I saw your face when I mentioned lunch and figured you were going to warn me off her."

"I know you better than that. I think."

Guy pocketed the bills. "In my eyes, she's still a kid, and anything but 'Uncle Guy' is out of the question. All I'm really interested in right now is finding out what Gadicke's up to vis-à-vis Diessen's."

CHAPTER FIVE

J ust before eight thirty that night, Daniel parked the Porsche behind Guy's mud-splattered black two-door Opel Rekord around the corner from Gadicke's office. Most of the businesses on the street had closed as usual at five, so the streets were deserted. The cold from the lake, only a few hundred yards away, was bone-chilling.

He spotted Guy, hands buried in his coat pockets and fedora tilted low over his forehead, leaning against the wall of an alley across from the two-story brick building that housed the lawyer's office. Daniel grinned to himself and thought he should tell Guy that he looked more like a stalker than the industrial espionage expert he had turned himself into after the war. When Guy saw him, he crossed the street and popped open the trunk of his own car.

"With any luck," he said, "we may get everything we need in this one trip. I reconnoitered, and everyone in the other offices has left." He pulled out a camera and flash unit, tucked them into the capacious pockets of his overcoat, and pulled out two large black satchels.

"In case we decide to take any evidence instead of just looking at it. Gadicke's office is on the second floor." He handed Daniel a ring with two keys. "Duplicates. The janitor left at seven thirty, so we should be fine. And . . ."

He pulled a pistol out of his coat pocket and handed it to Daniel. The weight of the firearm in his palm made him feel queasy because it was an instant reminder of their fighting days. All the killings. All in the name of survival, and the hope that the war would somehow, someday, lead to peace.

Daniel tucked it into his pocket. "What's the office layout?"

"Two rooms. The secretary's office and reception area and Gadicke's office." He closed the trunk. "The blinds are lowered, but there's some light coming through the slats."

They hurried around the corner and into the shadows of the building's portico. Daniel unlocked the front door and eased it shut as soon as they were both inside. Although the lobby and hall lights were off, the streetlamps were bright enough that they were able to move quickly and silently up the stone staircase and along the short second-floor hallway.

When they reached Gadicke's suite, Guy tapped Daniel's arm and indicated that he should leave the satchels just outside the office door. He then pulled out two pieces of black fabric and handed one to Daniel.

"Hoods? Good call."

After they slipped them on and adjusted the eye and mouth holes, Guy pulled out his camera, attached the flash, and gestured. Daniel slid the key into the office door lock, opened it two inches, and stopped.

"What?" Guy whispered.

"Music. From the inner office."

"What is it?"

"Fucking Wagner!" he hissed. "Fucking *Tristan und Isolde.* I loathe—"

"Maybe they forgot to turn off the radio."

They listened. Daniel tried to tamp down his rage, so he didn't endanger both of them.

"I don't hear any voices," Guy said.

"No."

They crept through the door, leaving it ajar to avoid any sound. The door to the inner office was half open, and dim light from a lamp inside made it easy for them to navigate past the secretary's desk. The only sounds were the music and the voices of the soprano and tenor soaring in their "Liebesnacht" duet. Guy and Daniel peered around the door and saw a man and woman, naked and entwined in each other's arms, asleep on a duvet spread over the carpeted floor.

Guy focused the camera and nodded at Daniel, who flung the door open. The crash when it hit the wall startled the couple awake. Guy began clicking off shots nonstop. Blinded by his flash, the woman screamed and pulled the duvet over herself. The man crouched and covered his genitals. He tried to speak but could not get any words out.

Daniel waved the pistol at him. "Stand up!"

The man staggered to his feet and grabbed at the desk to steady himself. His movement knocked a riding crop lying on the leather desk blotter to the floor. Daniel and Guy exchanged raised-eyebrow glances.

"Turn around!" Guy ordered him. The man obeyed, and Guy aimed the camera at the welts on his buttocks.

"Who are you?" Daniel demanded.

"Gottfried Gadicke," the man stammered.

Guy jerked his head at the woman. "And her?"

"My secretary, Frau Sigrid Harmsdorf. But who are you?" He glanced around wildly, and his voice rose. "Surely we can work something out—"

Guy scoffed. "Of course! The cheating spouse's attempt to save himself!"

Daniel turned the pistol on the woman. "You, too! On your feet!" She started to pull the duvet closer around her, but he shouted, "Drop it! Let's see what you have to offer!"

Her eyes filled with tears, but she reluctantly let it fall around her feet.

"Turn around!" Guy ordered her. She obeyed.

"Nice ass!" he jeered. "Clearly you're the one who did the punishing? But why didn't you make him return the favor?"

"Please!" she begged, wiping her eyes. "What do you want of us?"

Guy studied the two of them for a moment, then motioned to the lawyer. "Go and stand behind her! Grab her tits. And you—grab him with your left hand!"

Helpless, they obliged. The flash went off again several more times.

"On your knees!" Daniel ordered her. "Facing him! Put it in your mouth!"

She looked as if she were about to faint but sank to her knees.

"Good!" Guy clicked off another shot.

Daniel moved closer so he loomed over the terrified couple. "Get dressed! Now! We have a lot to do here before we leave."

As the two fumbled into their clothing, Gadicke protested, "But what do you want from us?"

"Everything you have about one of your clients."

"But my list of clients is confidential!"

"Diessen's."

Frau Harmsdorf let out a moan and Gadicke looked as if he were about to faint.

"I said everything, and I mean it! Where are their files?" He handed the pistol back to Guy, who stationed himself behind the lawyer and held the gun to his ear.

Gadicke gestured frantically at two filing cabinets. "Practically every file there. They're our only client. We work full time on their business."

Daniel tugged at one of the file drawers. "Unlock them!"

Gadicke nodded to his secretary. She tottered over to his desk, took a key out of the top drawer, and handed it to Daniel. He unlocked the top drawers of both cabinets, which also opened the ones below. "Where are your files relating to their dealings in Hong Kong?" he shouted.

She stammered, "The Panto files—"

"Sigrid! Shut up!" Gadicke shouted. "Keep your big mouth shut!"

Guy and Daniel exchanged glances. "Panto," Guy whispered. "You told me that our young friend had mentioned that name."

"Yes." Daniel flipped through the files. He pulled out several folders, each more than an inch thick, and set them down on Gadicke's desk with a *thud*.

"What else?" he shouted.

"He told you!" the secretary faltered, weeping. "All the files are Diessen's!" She saw Gadicke glaring at her and pleaded, "We're at their mercy! What can we do?"

Guy held the pistol aimed at the couple while Daniel continued searching the file cabinets. He gathered two stacks, each about two-feet high. "This should do," he told Guy. "Keep them covered." He hurried out to the front door and came back with the satchels.

The couple continued watching him in speechless horror as Daniel packed the files into the satchels. When he was finished, he told the secretary, "Go to your typewriter. I'm going to ask you some questions, and you'll type each one, followed by your answers."

She crept to the typing table and inserted a sheet of blank paper. Guy positioned himself nearby, his pistol still on Gadicke.

"No," Daniel told her. "On your company letterhead."

"Why are you doing this?" Gadicke broke in.

"Obviously, for possible use in the future," Daniel retorted. "First question: Who owns Panto? And read us all your answers."

Trembling, she typed for a few moments, then hesitantly read out the answer: "Herr Gadicke owns ninety percent of the stock as holder of power of attorney for others. The remaining ten percent is owned by Mr. Gadicke's son, Fritz."

"Good," Daniel said. "Second question: For whom does Herr Gadicke hold power of attorney for the ninety percent?"

"Sigrid!" Gadicke shouted. "I forbid you to answer!"

Guy aimed the gun at him. "Shut up, old man!"

The secretary stammered, "I don't know!"

Daniel turned to Gadicke. "Then you tell me!"

"It is true, she does not know. Only I do, and I will never reveal that information to you, or to anyone! You would have to torture me, but I would die rather than tell you!"

"All right," Daniel continued. "Now, it appears that the sum of 100,000 US dollars is being sent every month to a bank in Argentina and that this has been going on for a number of years. Where is the money coming from, and to whom is it being sent?"

She shook her head. "You have taken the Panto files. It's all in there."

He turned to Gadicke. "And what about the twelve million that came in from Hong Kong?"

"I've already told you! Shoot me if you will! I will never talk!"

Daniel looked over at Guy. "I think we've finished for this evening." He took the paper out of the typewriter and set it before her. "Now please sign and date it."

As she complied, Gadicke asked hesitantly, "And may we please have the films you've taken? Since you have what you came for?"

Guy laughed. "Not right now. But perhaps we'll send you a set of prints once we've had them developed."

Daniel closed and picked up the satchels. "And you needn't bother to show us out."

When they reached the door, Guy turned back to them. "You may now wish to continue your evening's pleasure. But take care that Frau Harmsdorf rubs some cream on those welts before your wife sees them." He followed Daniel into the outer office and closed the door forcibly behind him, but it didn't close totally due to the carpet's pile.

"Let's wait and see what they do next," Daniel whispered.

"Who were they?" they heard the secretary sob. "And what are we going to do?"

"Jews or Israelis," he replied. "Who the hell else but those scum would know or care what we're doing?"

"Gottfried, I'm terrified!"

"So am I. But I must notify the others about this immediately."

Guy and Daniel heard him dial a number. "Yes . . . burst into my office . . . two . . . wearing hoods . . . at gunpoint . . . yes, she was still here . . . Diessen's . . . dozens of files . . . Panto, Hong Kong . . . a satchel . . ." He listened for a few moments. ". . . we did our best, but . . . yes, of course . . . goodbye."

He hung up. "We're to wait here. Someone will come straightaway to help us. They said less than an hour."

Daniel heard her break into fresh sobs as he and Guy slipped out of the office and silently closed the door behind them.

CHAPTER SIX

A s soon as Guy and Daniel reached the lobby, they stuffed their hoods into their pockets and hurried around the corner to their cars.

"We should put the satchels in your car since you have more room," Daniel suggested.

"And then wait and see who shows up."

After loading the satchels into the Opel, they crossed back to the alley, where the overhanging second story protected them from the bitter wind.

Daniel scanned Gadicke's office windows. The lights in both rooms had been turned on, and he glimpsed shadows passing behind the blinds. "I almost feel sorry for those two," he muttered. "God only knows what they've gotten themselves involved in."

***

Forty bone-chilling minutes later, they heard car engines and peered out to see a black Mercedes sedan and a medium-sized cargo truck pull up in front of Gadicke's building. Three men in overcoats got out of the Mercedes and waited on the sidewalk while two men in overalls got out of the truck, opened its rear doors, and unloaded two large moving dollies. One of the men opened the office building door with a key and they all went inside.

Guy pulled out a card and jotted down the license numbers. "I'll get my police contact to tell me who the owners are."

They waited, shivering, for another fifteen minutes before the office building door opened again. The three men from the Mercedes pushed Gadicke and Frau Harmsdorf into the back seat. Two of the men got into the front while the third stationed himself in the back between the lawyer and his secretary.

"How about this?" Guy said. "We should switch cars. You follow the Mercedes. I'll wait and follow the truck—obviously they're planning to take the filing cabinets, but that will take some time. If the Mercedes heads away from the city, the Opel will be less noticeable. If they all stay in the area, it won't matter which of us follows whom, but we need to consider every possibility."

"Good idea. Let's move the files into the Porsche. You can take them to my flat and we'll meet up later—"

He was interrupted by the sound of the Mercedes engine starting up.

"No time!" Guy hissed. "They're taking off! Hurry or you'll lose them!"

By the time they exchanged keys and Daniel jumped into the Opel, the Mercedes was halfway down the street, but he had no trouble staying a good two hundred yards behind it. The streets were deserted, and the driver was staying at a steady thirty miles an hour, halting at every stop sign, and obeying all the traffic signals until he reached the city outskirts, when he sped up.

Daniel continued to follow at a safe distance for about thirty minutes, when it turned right at a T-intersection. After Daniel made the turn, he kept well behind and switched off his headlights to avoid being spotted in the Mercedes' mirrors. Because he hadn't seen any oncoming or following traffic since the turn, he didn't think it was a big risk.

He recognized the narrow road, which was bordered only by farmlands and the occasional barn, as leading to Avully, a small agricultural village. There was no traffic, so he slowed to leave even more distance, but seconds later the Mercedes took a sudden right turn and disappeared. He stopped and crept along until he spotted a narrow unpaved lane that led him into a forest of tall sycamore trees crowding the edges of the lane so densely, he could barely see thirty feet ahead of him.

He almost missed the red glow of the other car's tail-lights about two hundred yards ahead of him but braked and eased the Opel into an even narrower tractor trail off to his right. He drove until he was deeply hidden among the trees. After turning off the engine, he found that he was still close enough that he could hear the Mercedes' doors open. Its interior lights went on, reminding him to switch off the ones in the Opel. He crept out, leaving the door open an inch to avoid making any noise, and picked his way through the trees until he had a clear view of the other car.

The two men in the front seat, both holding revolvers, got out, opened the rear doors, and prodded Gadicke and Frau Harmsdorf out of the back seat. The third man, also armed, followed them out. The three forced the couple deeper into the forest.

My God, Daniel thought, *this looks bad.*

Since he no longer had Guy's revolver, it would have been suicide to try to pit himself against the three armed kidnappers. He waited and listened for several minutes, then crept back to his car. Wanting to turn it around so he could follow the Mercedes, but knowing he was trapped because the others would probably hear his engine, his only choice was to stay hidden and hope he could move quickly when he needed to. If they found him, they would also find the files in the trunk.

Moments later, he heard the sound he had been dreading—two loud gunshots—followed instantly by a sudden deafening outburst of raucous squawking. Just above his head, almost making him cry out in surprise, was a small flock of buzzards flying out of a nearby tree; their huge wings almost brushing him as they soared over his head. Trapped, he waited until he heard the three men return to the Mercedes. He held his breath as the driver turned around, drove past the lane where he was hiding, and returned to the main road.

He stayed where he was until he could no longer see or hear the Mercedes. *What should he do? Go searching for Gadicke and Frau Harmsdorf—or rather, he had no doubt, their bodies?* That would be like looking for two needles in a haystack.

The dank woods around him took him back to his years of tactics when he was with the Resistance during the war. The bodies he and Guy and the others in his team had found had been maimed and tortured by the Germans, and sometimes even by French and Swiss collaborators. He thought of Giselle again; something around her sudden reappearance in his life seemed to be reawakening too many memories, too many flashbacks. *What was he supposed to do? Would he ever be at peace?*

Even though confessing his feelings of guilt and blame with her the previous night had assuaged some of the pain, he knew that it was not over. It was not going to be that easy. He had lived with all of it—his family, Claudia, the children—for too long for it to heal through one short, halting conversation.

Still . . . he realized that he could not leave these woods without trying to find Gadicke and the secretary. He knew that the men who had killed them were professionals, up to God only knew what. But however corrupt Gadicke had been, he still felt he needed to try to find them.

The woods were utterly silent. The buzzards had settled themselves in their nests again. He moved as quietly as he could toward the area where the Mercedes' lights had been. His night sight finally came back, which made it easier, and the clouds were thinning, which allowed some streaks of pallid moonlight to filter through the trees.

When he reached the clearing where the Mercedes had parked, he crouched and circled it looking for footprints. The faint impressions he saw led to another path through an even deeper stand of trees. He crept along for several hundred feet, wary of the danger that he might stumble over a tree root or branch and end up stranded and injured in the depth of the woods, when he reached another small clearing.

Small enough that he immediately saw the two crumpled bodies splayed out on the drenched leaves and twigs. The killers had not even tried to conceal them. He overcame his nervousness and knew he had to approach them, touch them. Remembering how matter-of-factly he and Guy and the others on their team used to operate during their skirmishes and battles, their hatred of the enemy overcame any squeamishness about taking their lives.

But that was years ago when he was younger and more fit and now, he was here alone in the trees with these two dead bodies. He did not know how to deal with the mingled anger, hatred, and pity shaking him—how to reconcile humanness and evil. And these two had, he knew, in their own ways, been doing some kind of evil. He stood immobilized for several moments letting it all wash over him before deciding that all he could do was gather what information he could, get back to his car without hurting himself, return to Geneva, and tell Guy so they could decide what to do next.

Reluctantly, he crouched over them. The dark shadows on the ground under their heads told him that they had probably each been shot once in the back of the head. He remembered the synchronic sound of the shots and found himself hoping that their deaths had been simultaneous so neither of them had to watch the other die.

There was nothing he could do, not even cover their faces to protect them from the possible predations of the buzzards, so he made his way back through the sleeping woods to the Opel.

CHAPTER SEVEN

I t was almost two in the morning by the time Daniel returned to his flat. He was surprised that Giselle, though
looking tired, was still up and that she and Guy were
comfortably settled at opposite ends of the couch chatting.
His warning to Guy flashed through his mind again, but he
pushed it aside and set the satchels on the coffee table with
two resounding *thuds*.

"We were starting to worry," Giselle said.

"I'm fine. Just a lot to tell you."

"Ditto," Guy replied.

Daniel poured himself a cognac and sank into the armchair across from them. "You first," he told Guy.

Guy stretched his arms along the top of the couch. "Fairly
straightforward. I followed the truck along the lakeside road
for about thirty minutes, dropping back to let cars get between us for more cover. They drove to a residential area
in Nyon and pulled up to a chalet-style house with all its
lights blazing. As I drove past, a young man and woman, I'd
guess in their thirties, hurried out. The man yelled for the
driver to pull into the driveway. I drove to the end of the
street, waited for a bit, and drove back. The man was help-
ing unload the dollies with the filing cabinets. I noted the
street address and hightailed it back here. I've already left
a message for my police contact, who I hope will get back
to me first thing in the morning. Finding out who owns the
Mercedes and the truck won't be a problem. And you?"

Daniel was reluctant to speak in front of Giselle. "Aren't you exhausted?" he asked. "You look as if you need some sleep."

"I'm part of this too!" she objected. "After all, if it weren't for me . . ."

"It may be more than you'd want to hear. Are you sure?"

"Yes."

"Fine." He turned to Guy. "You're going to have a lot more to tell your contact about than just getting those names." He related what had happened in the forest. When he told them about the gunshots, Giselle gasped, but Guy just nodded. "I thought that might be how it would play out. Did you find them?"

"Yes. Both of them. Shot in the head." Giselle hunched forward and squeezed her eyes shut.

"I'm sorry," he told her.

"No. I want to know everything."

Guy continued, "Gadicke's wife and her husband will report them missing before long, if they haven't already. The police will launch a search starting, of course, with the office and both couples' homes. It'll be obvious that the filing cabinets have been removed. I'll tell my contact as much as we think I should, up to and including the approximate location of the bodies. And in return, he'll tell me who owns the Nyon house and the two vehicles."

"You can't let him know that we were ever in the office," Daniel warned. "Also, if they do retrieve the filing cabinets, how would they know that anything's missing?"

"They'd probably call in forensic experts," Guy replied.

"But look at what we have here!" Giselle gestured at the satchels. "For all we know at this point, if we want to find out what's really going on, these files may be the only way. So why don't we become our own experts?" She stood, wobbling a bit with fatigue. "May I?"

"Go ahead," Daniel told her.

She opened the satchels, stood the files on end so the tabs were visible, and riffled through several. "About five reams altogether, maybe two thousand plus pages. But I already have some ideas about how we can tackle this, which I'll show you first thing in the morning! Good night." She bobbed her head at both of them and went down the hall and into her room.

When she was out of earshot, Guy laughed. "She's so eager to get her hands on them that I bet she'll have trouble sleeping tonight. I've never seen that 'wheels turning' side of her before."

"Me, neither. Do you have any sense of what might be going on at this point with all this?"

Guy shrugged and reached for his jacket. "Too soon to say. But early though this all is, it may well be a lot bigger than anything you've brought me in on before."

CHAPTER EIGHT

A s soon as Daniel got up the next morning, he called his office, canceled his appointments for the day, and told Madame Gilly that he would be working from home until further notice. Minutes later, Guy called. "I reached my contact at home an hour ago and asked him if there'd been any missing persons' reports filed overnight. That woke him up fast. I'm heading over there right now."

"Giselle's already at work on some kind of system that she says will let us get the most out of the files in the least amount of time."

"Why am I not surprised?"

***

By the time Guy arrived three hours later, Giselle had commandeered the dining room table, set out writing tablets, pens, pencils, and adding machines, and begun sorting the files into stacks.

Daniel drew Guy out onto the balcony so she wouldn't hear them. "So where are we?"

"We've probably saved them hours of time. I told my guy that I had information about two possible murders. He wanted to know how I knew, but I said that keeping my informant—you—out of it was the quid pro quo for me telling him where the bodies were. He balked for a while but finally gave in. I told him you'd followed the Mercedes and seen the two being taken out of the car and that you'd heard shots, but not that you'd found them. The crime scene team got there within an hour and located the bodies. I also, of course, gave him the car and truck plate numbers."

"And?"

"Banque Desbodiens owns not only the Mercedes but also the Nyon house. Which is leased to Francis Schmidt. I've asked him to call as soon as he knows anything more, day or night."

"So they're in this up to their necks." He glanced inside. Giselle was poring over the files. "Let's go help her," he told Guy.

As they went inside, he felt apprehensive about what they were getting themselves into, and that Giselle was involved as well. Two murders already. If it hadn't been for her coming to his door two nights ago, none of this would be happening. On the other hand, if she hadn't come to him, they would still have been locked in the old history between them.

He had to push those thoughts and feelings aside. When they sat down, she handed each of them a stack of forms. "Based on my initial overview, I've made up these forms so we can organize and then analyze what we find."

Daniel and Guy studied the forms, which listed "Name of File", "Document Date", "Payment Amount", "Paying Bank", "Receiving Bank", "Beneficiary", "Reason for Payment", and "Other", and exchanged approving glances.

"And for now," she added, "any correspondence we come across should go into a separate pile with a note in the upper-right corner about which file it came from."

"Good work!" Daniel complimented her. She smiled her thanks and he set to work, feeling a small glow of gratitude for their new, if fragile, comfort with each other.

***

They worked almost nonstop, fueled only by Madame Pougatch's sandwiches, until after nine o'clock that night, when Daniel shoved back his chair and studied the summary sheets that Giselle had compiled.

"Fifty-one analysis sheets and one hundred thirty letters," he said. "Maybe we should stop and pick up again in the morning."

"No," Giselle said. "Based on what I'm seeing here, we need get through this as quickly as we can."

"What do you mean?"

"I'd gotten a head start on my quota of files and finished while you two were still working on yours, so I started on the correspondence."

"And?"

"Numerous references to visits by various Diessen's executives and other parties that the bank has dealt with. Also, notes by Gottfried Gadicke about meetings he attended. Letters and telexes back and forth from a number of companies, including Asian Commodities in Hong Kong. Remember that I had them listed in my notebook? Plus, correspondence about payments to Diessen's offices in South America."

"Where?"

"Brazil, Uruguay, Colombia, Argentina, and Paraguay. All on the eastern side of the continent, by the way. I've also listed all the individuals mentioned, but by and large the correspondence appears routine, typical of globally active companies."

"What about bank statements?"

"No," she replied. "Which is odd."

Guy frowned. "And probably important, given how many files we took."

"Well," she continued. "Let's do the summary forms. Line by line."

"Line by line?" Daniel asked. "However long it takes?"

"Line by line. However long it takes."

After another three hours of inspecting each entry on every line of every report sheet, Daniel yawned and rubbed his aching neck.

"So it appears that over the last almost fifteen years, starting in 1945 and up to as recently as a month ago, something like $25 million USD *has* been sent from Hong Kong to be deposited at Banque Desbodiens, and that $12 million, at the rate of $100,000 USD each month, has been sent to Argentina from Diessen's. And between 1952 and 1955, payments totaling close to $100 million have gone to Desbodiens from Hong Kong."

The phone at Daniel's elbow rang. He picked it up, listened, replied, "Yes," and handed it to Guy.

Daniel and Giselle waited impatiently while Guy questioned the caller. After he hung up, he said, "That was my man with an update on Nyon. He and his people were about to go to the house when the local police called a report that a man who lives next to the chalet was complaining about smoke and ash blowing in through his windows. When the locals investigated, they found the remains of a bonfire in the back garden. My guy's team sped out there and found the house empty, the filing cabinets empty, and the bonfire still smoldering. Clearly someone, presumably the couple I saw, had burned all of Gadicke's remaining files and fled."

"And they were . . .?"

"Young Schmidt. And Elisabeth Martin." Daniel couldn't help glancing over at Giselle, who caught his look and gave him a slight, sad smile.

"The Alfa was still in the driveway," Guy went on. "The neighbor saw them leave in a gray Audi driven by a man who helped them load up a number of suitcases."

"Any idea where they were headed?"

"My guy will get back to me as soon as they know more."

"Has anyone talked with the older Schmidt? The head of the bank?"

"He's apparently at a conference in Belgium."

Daniel surveyed the stacks of files and worksheets. "At this point, I suggest we leave the murder investigation, finding the Mercedes, locating Schmidt and Martin, and all of that to the police and focus on what we have here. Let's start again in the morning and take a fresh look at it all."

After Guy left, Daniel saw that Giselle could scarcely keep her eyes open. "I don't know where we'd be right now," he told her, "if you hadn't come up with this approach to the files."

She smiled and yawned but added, "Seeing all the names of the people at Desbodiens reminds me of that terrible meeting I had with Francis's uncle two weeks ago."

"What meeting?"

"One day when Francis and I were chatting, I mentioned that you and I were related and that you might be an excellent client for the bank. I was puzzled when he replied, 'I think not,' but didn't feel comfortable pursuing it. In any case, the next day, I was told that Herr Schmidt wanted to see me in his office.

"I'd never spoken to him, just seen him in the corridors. But I'd heard about how he terrorized the people under him and that all he cared about was pandering to the board of directors and especially the controlling shareholder."

"Diessen's?"

"Obviously. I know that now because of what we've seen in the files. But at the time I had no idea, and also everything there was so secretive . . . I was so nervous that my hands started shaking even before his secretary led me into his office. He looked like a disgusting old toad sitting there behind his desk hunched over his papers. He didn't even invite me to sit down, just scowled at me."

She tucked her chin into her chest and mimicked, "'Mademoiselle Faber, Monsieur Francis tells me that Daniel Lavy is a relation of yours. Is this true?' I told him you were my cousin by marriage. He clearly knew that you and Claudia had divorced because he asked, 'And the former Mrs. Lavy was a Jew.' I said yes, and that you were as well, of course.

"'And yourself?' he went on. I told him that my mother was, but my father wasn't and that I had not been brought up in any religion. 'Do you see much of Mr. Lavy?' he asked. I wanted to tell him that his questions were outrageous and offensive but didn't dare, so all I said was no.

"'And you think,' he went on, 'that Mr. Lavy would be a good client for Banque Desbodiens?'

"'Yes, sir.'

"'Mademoiselle Faber,' he rasped. 'Mr. Lavy is not the sort of person whom the bank would want as a client. Or the sort of person I would expect any employee of mine to have any association with.' This made me furious even though you had written me off so long ago."

He felt overwhelmed with remorse. "How will I ever . . ."

She waved that away and went on, "But then he said, 'He and his kind stick to their own. And there are still enough Jew banks in Geneva to cater to his needs.'

"That made me so angry that it . . . that it just burst out of me, 'So Banque Desbodiens would rather have Nazis as clients than Jews?'

"His face turned purple with rage. 'I will do my best to forget what you have just said! Now get back to your desk!' And two weeks later to the day, they fired me."

"But why on earth would you even say that?"

"I don't know. I had been so desperate. I had no idea what they were really like. Francis was the only person there who ever spoke with me, and he seemed all right. Knowing what they're really like . . . I'm ashamed of how naïve I was. But the war . . . last night . . . you made it all real for me. But now, having heard him say that . . ."

He held up his hand to stop her. "Do you know how many Swiss businesses made fortunes dealing with Germany, all the while mouthing 'neutrality.' Especially banks like the Schmidts'. Moving money around so it was impossible to find out where it had come from and where it was going."

"Impossible?" She waved her hand at the stacks of files and worksheets. "How do we know that the answer isn't right here?"

He shook his head. "I'm in awe of your confidence. Let's hope so."

After she went to her room, he went on studying the files until he dozed off with his head pillowed on a stack of them.

***

When Daniel emerged yawning and stumbling from his bed at dawn after a mere three hours of sleep, Guy and Giselle were already at work.

"I made some more notes after we stopped last night," he told them as he poured his coffee. "The deals on fertilizer alone, but I've seen lead and other minerals as well, are staggering. Why would Argentina be importing millions of dollars' worth of fertilizer from half a world away rather than from their immediate neighbors? There must be fertilizer plants in Argentina. Or Brazil. Or somewhere in Latin America."

Giselle looked up. "If it's really fertilizer."

Daniel and Guy looked at each other, eyebrows raised.

"A code word," she went on, "for something else? Or a number of somethings?"

"Yes," Daniel said. "There's something about all this that we're missing." He took his coffee out to the balcony, where he spent several minutes gazing out at the lake before rejoining them.

"These transactions," he said, "aren't quite making sense to me, but my gut's telling me that there's something important here."

"And you've come up with a plan," Guy said.

Daniel grinned and turned to Giselle. "That's what happens when you spend four years literally fighting a war next to someone. You end up being able to read one another's mind. Yes, I have a plan. To go where the money's been going."

"Hong Kong?" Guy asked.

"Because of Asian Commodities and the South American connection?" Giselle asked.

"To start with. Giselle, who's been signing off on the transactions to Hong Kong?"

"A Jonathan Sharpe. He's been listed on the paperwork for the past three years and through to the most recent records we have, from a month ago."

"All right. I want to leave as soon as possible."

Guy and Giselle both looked stunned. Guy exclaimed, "You're talking about dropping a small fortune in money and time based on what your gut's telling you?"

"Not just that. I guess I haven't mentioned it to you before, but for some time now I've been considering expanding my operations into Asia."

"For some time now?" Guy mocked.

"Well, you must admit it'll be great cover. So, are you in or out?"

"When have I ever not been in?"

"Wait a minute!" Giselle jumped to her feet and planted her fists on the table. "And you're just going to leave me here?"

Daniel pretended to consider. "You're right. Since this really is all your fault, you're just going to have to put up with coming along." He studied her for a moment, her youth and intelligence and energy, and again felt the wave of emotion that swept over him each time he remembered the twins' room and what they had so recently learned they shared as part of the same family. The only two members left of their family.

He dropped his teasing tone. "Besides, these past few days . . . the murders . . . there's something that's already turned deadly. But we'll keep you safe. I swear it."

CHAPTER NINE

"Wake up! Daniel, wake up!"

Giselle's urgent voice, and her hand tugging frantically at his shoulder, roused him from the jet-lagged stupor that had overtaken him on the final leg of their seemingly endless journey east to Hong Kong from Geneva. Three days and nights of takeoffs and landings, of lurching through air pockets, and landing in thunderstorms to the roar of plane engines, had taken its toll.

"Look!"

She shrank back in her seat next to the window so he could look out onto a stomach-churning view of a strip of green-painted concrete barely twice the width of their plane's wingspan jutting out into Victoria Harbour and drenched by the turbulent swells of the South China Sea. The distant streets of Kowloon were still in morning shadow, but he glimpsed traffic signals and hurrying residents already bound for work.

"We're landing *there*?" She looked terrified.

He took her hand. "We'll be fine!" But he didn't know whether he was trying to convince himself as well. They squeezed next to each other and stared as the plane descended so close to the waves lapping at the runway that when he felt the slight jolt of their safe landing, it took him a moment to believe it.

"Are you all right?" he asked her.

"I think so." But she kept her eyes on the runway markers flashing past them under the plane's wheels.

"We're here now. And safe," he reassured her, squeezing her hand.

"For now."

He knew she was thinking about all they had left behind. "And that's why we're here. I have some ideas, but first we all need some real rest, in real beds."

"Ideas you haven't told me?" she pursued. "Or you and Guy haven't told me? Even though you brought me along? Is it only to keep me safe from harm's way in Geneva?"

"No! The three of us are in this together, whatever it is. We know that something's going on, and we're each bringing something different to our investigation, and you're just as important as we are. Don't ever think otherwise." He hesitated. "And remember what I promised? About you and I being family again?"

"Yes. But it's still so new." She couldn't look at him. "Sometimes I don't trust it."

He felt his heart constrict. "We just have to try." He looked at her and smiled.

She leaned forward and looked across the aisle at Guy, who had been slumped in the window seat dead asleep and snoring slightly for the previous five hours. He yawned and opened his eyes. "So we've survived the notorious 'Kai Tak Heart Attack' runway? What did you think, Giselle?"

She grimaced. "That the guidebook you gave me was right. 'Once experienced, never forgotten.'"

***

Four hours later, after tossing and turning and trying to sleep in his fifth-floor suite at the Peninsula Hotel, Daniel gave up trying and decided to shower and look for breakfast. Although he had traveled extensively in Europe, surprisingly he had never been to Asia. Was the total disorientation he was feeling jetlag? Or was he overwhelmed at the swarms of work-bound adults and children heading to school and hawkers and businesses opening their doors that their taxi had passed on their way from the airport to the hotel? One of the most famous symbols of British colonial rule in all of Asia.

On his way to the elevator, he passed Giselle's suite, across the hall from his, and Guy's, two doors down from hers. He almost knocked on Guy's door but decided not to disturb either of them. And although Giselle had almost twenty years of youth on him, even she had been smothering yawns when they had finally reached their rooms and closed their doors on one another.

When he stepped out of the elevator into the glittering, high-ceiling lobby, he realized how exhausted he still was, and he was glad that he had taken Guy's advice and booked them into that hotel.

No sooner did he reach the lobby than a young Chinese waiter in crisp black trousers and a starched white shirt greeted him. "May I show you to the dining room, sir?"

Daniel replied, "Please," and followed him to a spacious room with dazzling late-morning sun streaming through its windows. It was so late that only a handful of tables were still occupied, perhaps by other late-night or early-morning arrivals, but the serving tables along the far wall were still set with breakfast specialties.

After the waiter invited him to sit wherever he pleased, Daniel took a closer look around and was startled to see Guy, partially hidden behind a column, seated at a round table at the far end of the room with another man. Guy spotted him, waved him over, and said something to the other man. The two stood as he approached.

"Glad you came down. I didn't want to wake you up," Guy said. Daniel noticed that he was shaved and looked fully rested. "I'd like you to meet Jaime Monteverde. He's a reporter with the *Hong Kong Courier*. Jaime, Daniel Lavy of Daniel Lavy International."

Monteverde, a middle-aged, dark-haired man with intelligent brown eyes behind wire-rimmed glasses, held out his hand. As they shook, Daniel said cordially, "Mr. Monteverde. Very happy to meet you."

"Thank you. And I as well."

Daniel noted with curiosity that Monteverde had a slight but unidentifiable European accent. He gestured that the other two should take their seats and sat down himself. A waiter carrying a silver carafe on a silver tray approached and asked Daniel if he wished to order the English breakfast. Daniel eyed the remnants of what looked to have been two very appetizing dishes on the table and realized how hungry he was. "Yes, if that's what all this was. And coffee, please."

After the waiter left, Monteverde said, "Given your very early arrival, I had planned to wait until later today to try to reach you, but then I happened to meet Mr. Broussard and we've been chatting."

"And you're a journalist. How the devil did you know about our arrival?"

"Because I'm a journalist, and that's what we do. We find things out. I cover banking and business for the *Courier*, so when someone as prominent as you arrives in the colony, I seek them out. I'm hoping you'll let me do a story on you."

"And you learned that I was here?" Daniel smiled.

Monteverde shrugged. "As we say, we have our sources."

"Such as the front desk staff at hotels, I would imagine. I was hoping to keep this trip low-key."

"It's hard to be low-key in Hong Kong," Monteverde replied, "especially when you arrive at dawn accompanied by two colleagues and check in at the Peninsula. But also because, more than anything else, Hong Kong is a small town where everyone knows—or wants to know—everything about everyone else. Particularly when it comes to business and money. So if you wish at some point to tell me more about the purpose of your trip . . . I do accept going off the record."

Daniel saw the waiter steering a cart with his breakfast toward them. "Of course we can talk with you more . . . later."

Monteverde gave him a knowing look but remained silent until the waiter had moved away before commenting wryly, "Sources can be found everywhere."

"So, in short, I decided," Daniel told him, "that it was time to explore whether I should expand into Asia by establishing an office here."

Monteverde reached for a leather portfolio lying on the chair next to him and pulled out some mimeographed sheets. "Good timing! You have a first-rate opportunity to acquaint yourself with our community this very evening. Without even leaving the hotel. The Hong Kong Business Alliance is holding their monthly reception and dinner tonight." He handed the sheets to Daniel. "Our membership roster. You'll see that I took the liberty of adding your and your colleagues' names, on the off chance that you might be interested and available."

"I can't think of a better opportunity. I like your modus operandi."

"And I can guarantee," he added, "that our members will be falling all over themselves trying to meet you." He took three embossed invitations out of the portfolio. "One for each of you, and another for Miss Faber."

"You *have* done your homework." Daniel skimmed the alphabetical list, with Guy looking over his shoulder. He saw that Asian Commodities was listed near the top with a star preceding the company name. However, the executive director was listed as a "Victor Singleton," not the "Jonathan

Sharpe" whose name they had seen in the Gadicke documentation. He and Guy exchanged glances.

"Very impressive," Daniel said. "I should think that most of your members are of long standing? Or is there a lot of turnover, given that the Colony's stature in international business and finance is expanding?"

"It varies," Monteverde replied, "but at each meeting we seem to greet a half dozen new members and bid farewell to another half dozen. Tonight, we have three new members. They're marked with a star. Actually, one is what you would call a 'returnee.'"

"Oh?"

"Yes. Victor Singleton. He returned two weeks ago to take over at Asian Commodities. He and his family were here when the Japanese occupation began. His wife and daughter were evacuated, as most family members were, and they spent the rest of the war in South America. But Singleton was interned in the dreaded Stanley Internment Camp and was among the many men who were subjected to torture. He rejoined his family after the war and went to work for a subsidiary of a large commodities firm based in South America. We were delighted to learn that he was returning to take over the AC office here. We will be welcoming him back tonight with the red-carpet treatment, not just as a business associate but also as a war hero."

"And AC is involved in commodities? Then I'm even more eager to make his acquaintance as soon as possible. And that of as many other international traders as possible."

Monteverde laughed. "They'll all be here. But even if you had missed tonight's event, all it would take for you to meet most of them would be a short trip across the harbour."

"Meaning?"

"The majority of our commodity firms, including Single-ton's, are based in and around a small section of Central. Near Des Voeux Road."

"I guess it *is* usual," Guy put in, "for similar businesses to cluster together."

"Where is it *not* usual?" Monteverde replied. "Don't we all like to keep an eye on our competitors? Certainly, we do in journalism. That's how 'scoops' come about, isn't it? Speaking of which." He pushed his chair back and stood. "I'm on deadline for another story. I do hope to see all of you this evening."

After he left, Daniel, despite his earlier hunger, was still too tired to eat and had only picked at his breakfast, and Guy took the elevator to their floor. "I have to say," Guy commented in an undertone after the elevator doors closed, "clever how you pumped him about Asian Commodities. When I saw them on the list, I was wondering how you'd pull it off."

"Thank you, but I'm surprised that I was able to get one coherent sentence out."

Guy yawned and unlocked his door. "I'm at that point as well. I think the breakfast did me in."

"Then let's just plan to rendezvous again tonight at the reception. I'll leave a note for Giselle."

Daniel unlocked his door, wondering whether to wake Giselle. He saw a chambermaid come out of another room and went over to her.

"The young lady. My niece," he told her.

The woman nodded. "Yes, sir. They tell me."

"Is she still asleep?"

"Yes, I knock one time before, she ask return later. Very tired."

Daniel thanked her, handed her a banknote, and returned to his suite, where he scribbled a note telling Giselle about the reception, that she should buy herself something to wear. He added that someone named Victor Singleton had replaced Sharpe at Asian Commodities. He folded the note around a stack of banknotes, tucked it into an envelope, and slid it under her door.

He returned to his room and studied the view of Kowloon of Central from his windows for several minutes before going back down to the front desk, where he changed some banknotes to Hong Kong dollars.

He asked the clerk, "Can you please call a taxi to take me to Central?"

The clerk looked startled. "I am so sorry, sir," he replied with an embarrassed smile. "You may not know that to go to Central, the only way is the Star Ferry. The government has plans to build a tunnel, but for now—" He spread his hands in apology.

Daniel felt even more embarrassed than the clerk for having forgotten that section in the guidebook.

"The terminal is very close, only a few minutes' walk, but if you wish a taxi—"

"Thank you, no. I'll walk." Maybe the exercise would chase the cobwebs from his brain.

CHAPTER TEN

The moment Daniel left the Peninsula behind, he found himself swallowed up in the chaotic world of Hong Kong street life with its hordes of people constantly on the move. He picked his way toward the Star Ferry Pier past huge burlap sacks of rice being tossed from carts, farmers haggling over squealing piglets, barbers wielding cutthroat razors on trusting businessmen, squatting cobblers. And above it all, competing with the reek of trash flowing through the gutters, was the rich aroma of roasting ducks and the cacophony of shouted Cantonese.

When he reached the ferry pier, he paid the fare for the twenty-minute trip across the harbour to Central by holding out some of the Hong Kong dollars he had exchanged at the hotel so the clerk could choose the correct amount. Once on board, the only free seat he could find on the wood-slat benches was next to a tiny, ancient Chinese woman in a black tunic and trousers who held a covered wicker basket that emitted occasional squawking noises.

He tried to focus on the panoramic view of the harbour, but the passengers' shrill conversations above the thrumming of the ferry's engines made him feel as if he were still traversing the turbulent streets. He considered joking with Monteverde later that night that instead of being translated as "Fragrant Harbour," the Colony's name should actually be translated as "Noise and Confusion."

***

After the ferry docked, Daniel found his way to Connaught Road, where he approached a Chinese constable in a kiosk, showing him the address that the hotel clerk had written out for him. The constable pointed to a street that veered off to the left and up a slight incline.

"It's a bit of a distance to walk, sir, about twenty minutes. I'd recommend a taxi." Daniel was impressed. The constable's English was impeccable.

"Yes." Even the short walk from the pier had thrown him into another fit of exhaustion, but he knew he couldn't turn back.

Before the constable even blew his whistle three times, a dusty, aged taxi swung around the corner and pulled up. The constable gave the driver the address, touched his cap, and returned to his post.

The taxi bumped across tramway tracks and up the hill along streets that, though crowded, struck Daniel as less rough-and-tumble than the bedlam on the Kowloon side. His destination turned out to be one of the many multistory office buildings with faded colonial façades that lined the street.

After letting the driver choose the amount of the fare and adding a tip, Daniel went to the double front doors, which opened onto a tiled lobby. It was deserted but lined with office doors. All were shut and he heard only vague voices and the faint ringing of telephones. The building directory, in English and Chinese characters, listed Asian Commodities in suite 518.

When the elevator finally arrived, he pushed five. It creaked upward, it stopped, the doors slid open—he was dumbfounded to see Giselle standing there.

"Thank God!" she exclaimed. "I was afraid I'd miss you!"

"What in *hell* are you doing here?" He stepped out into the hallway as the elevator doors started to close. "I'm furious that you left the hotel without telling me."

"*Shh!* There are people all around! Your note!" She pulled it out of her pocket. "I tried to call your room, but you'd left. I had to tell you about Victor Singleton!"

Daniel was puzzled. "Yes, the Gadicke files listed Jonathan Sharpe as the manager, but it turns out that this Singleton has just arrived to replace him. Which could be important—"

"It's more important than you realize! You couldn't have known, but Victor Singleton is Antonia's father!"

"Her *father?*"

"*Shh!*" She gestured at the closed office doors and led him around a corner. "I know I mentioned her once or twice," she whispered. "But she and I were so close that I never realized until I saw your note that I'd always just referred to her as 'Antonia.' I can't believe it—that he may be involved in all this! I mean, with what he went through in the war—"

"But we know," he replied, keeping his voice low as well, "that AC is involved somehow, so why on earth did you come tearing over here?"

"How else was I supposed to find you and tell you who he is? What if he had been here and you'd met him?" she retorted.

"I'm sorry," he said after a pause. "But perhaps it's Sharpe who's actually involved, and Singleton knows nothing about it. In any case, we need to get out of here."

He turned back toward the elevator, expecting her to follow, but she edged closer to him and whispered, "Don't worry. The office is closed for the day. There's a sign on the door."

She led him down the hall to 518. He glanced at the typed notice and put his ear to the door but heard nothing. "Still," he said, "someone from one of the other offices might see us and say something."

However, they reached the lobby and the street without encountering anyone.

Daniel looked around. "We need someplace quiet where we can talk. A restaurant or—"

"But we have no idea who might be around us," she objected. "Or what languages they might speak or understand. Maybe a park or someplace where we can see all around us."

They followed Robinson Road for several blocks. While they were waiting at an intersection, he saw her studying a beautiful, dignified white building across the street. Its façade had two round turrets.

"This must be the Oleh Leah Synagogue. I've been reading about it in the guidebook. It's a landmark," she added.

He imagined it would be perfectly quiet. "That looks ideal."

They walked up to the double front doors, but they were locked. He gestured to the stone bench in front of the building.

She sat. "Antonia's father? I never imagined . . ."

"Nor I. Listen, I know we're both still exhausted, but I need you to tell me everything, starting with when you woke up."

"Yes. Two people have already died." She dropped her gaze. "I woke up and found your note and knew I had to find you right away. I knocked on your door, but you'd already gone, so I got dressed and went to the front desk and said you'd asked me to meet you, but I'd forgotten the address. The same clerk who had helped you wrote it out for me. I was afraid that if I didn't find you and head you off—"

"How did you find your way here?"

"The guidebook." She grinned. "Which I had lots of time to review while you and Guy were snoring away on our flights."

"Why didn't you get him up and tell him?"

"I did go to his door, but the 'do not disturb' sign was out, and the maid said she had looked in a few minutes earlier but he was still sleeping. So I went back to the desk and gave the clerk a note for you in case I missed you and told him you had to get it as soon as you came back. Then I took the ferry across."

"And then asked that constable for directions and then took a cab?"

"So we must have just missed each other. But in any case, it's moot because Guy already knows about Singleton, but not that he's Antonia's father."

"What do you mean?"

"A journalist he and I met at breakfast. The one who invited us to the reception."

He recounted the discussion at breakfast with Guy and Monteverde, seeing Singleton's name on the business group's roster, asking Monteverde what had happened to Sharpe, and what the journalist had said about Singleton's history as a war hero.

"Antonia told me about that," Giselle exclaimed. "She and her mother went to Argentina, and he joined them after the war."

"And now he's back here, but where are they? Still in Argentina?"

"I think so." She looked troubled. "But I can't believe that he could be involved in any of this."

"Whatever 'this' is . . ." He heaved himself to his feet and held out his hand to her. "Let's get back. I'm too tired to think anymore."

***

By the time Daniel and Giselle arrived back at the Kowloon ferry pier, the street markets were even noisier and more congested than they had been earlier in the day. By that point, Daniel was dealing with a blinding headache and was so groggy that Giselle had to grab his arm when he almost stepped in front of a taxi.

The moment they arrived at the Peninsula, the desk clerk handed him Giselle's note and one from Guy saying that he was going for a massage and would meet up with them at the reception.

"And I think we should meet up later as well," Daniel told her as they reached their floor and headed for their rooms.

CHAPTER ELEVEN

The buzz of voices coming from one of the reception rooms near the lobby met Daniel when he got out of the elevator. Guy was waiting for him and was lounging against the wall just outside the reception.

"As soon as Giselle arrived, the company wives adopted her," he said. "This is such a tight little community that everyone falls all over newcomers—"

"Just a second," Daniel said. "I went to the AC offices this afternoon—"

"And ran into Giselle," Guy interrupted. "She's already told me all about it. And about the small-world surprise about Singleton being her classmate's father."

"Is he here?"

"Not sure. Jaime didn't supply me with a mugshot. Let's go see."

The reception room, like every other Peninsula space Daniel had seen so far, radiated luxury. Thick carpeting, glittering chandeliers, tables of hors-d'oeuvres, a crowded bar, plush leather armchairs surrounding white-draped tables decorated with tall vases of orchids and plumeria. And the crowd was the most diverse business gathering he had ever seen, not just in age, ethnic background, and manner, but also in dress—the men fitted out in either custom-tailored suits, as he was, or in national costume. He was struck by how agreeable it was to hear the sound of the two hundred or more guests speaking so many different languages. It was a group both homogeneous and heterogeneous. *Everyone there,* he thought, *having ended up, for the short or long term, working and living in one of Britain's last remaining major colonial outposts.*

"The world of expats," Guy commented.

"Quite a contrast with Geneva."

Guy gestured at the far corner of the room where several tables of women, all gowned in what Daniel knew had to be the height of fashion, were chatting, sipping drinks, and picking at hors-d'oeuvres. "See? She's over there, being made much of."

Giselle, in a simple but striking dress with a slight Asian flavor about it that he could not identify, glanced over, gave them a big smile, and indicated with a wave that she would join them later.

"She deserves it," Daniel replied. He could see that she was enjoying herself. He realized again how young she still was, and yet so intelligent and perceptive. Looking back over the past week, he found it hard to believe he had lived with such bitterness toward her for so many years. And he wondered whether there were other people in his life whom he had resented and misjudged simply because he had been so consumed by grief and loss and pain. But none of this was anything he could share with Guy, so he settled for adding, "She certainly bought herself a decent dress."

"Decent indeed, unfortunately," Guy said with a smirk.

"How many times—"

"What do you expect when you keep on giving me chances to get a rise out of you?"

Daniel rolled his eyes, scanned the room again, and spotted Monteverde, in the same suit he had worn at breakfast, making his way toward them with his portfolio in one hand and a tall glass in his other. As he approached, an idea struck Daniel that he realized he needed to share with Guy immediately.

The journalist greeted Daniel warmly. "Everyone's been asking to meet you!"

"I'm totally at your service," he replied. "Or rather, I will be in just a few minutes, but something's just come up that Guy and I need to deal with."

"Of course."

Guy gave Daniel a puzzled look but silently followed him into the lobby and to a secluded alcove that contained a table and four small armchairs.

"So, what's the emergency?" Guy demanded as soon as they sat down.

"Monteverde. My brain's still mush, but I just realized that he may be exactly the person we need here. An insider in the business community. Of course, he's always on the look-out for a story, but there's something about him that I trust. What do you think?"

Guy considered. "On the up and up, as far as I can tell. But to do what? Or to not do what?"

"The only reason we're here is to find out what's going on with Debodiens. Does he know anything about the ship-ments? Or possibly even the bank transactions?"

"Or Singleton."

"Yes. Or can he tell us how we can find out?"

"And then we give him the story. Also, it would probably be child's play for us to catch him out if he started playing games."

Daniel stood. "I want you with me on this but for you to let me do most of the talking for now."

"Agreed. Make clear who's in charge."

When they returned to the reception, Daniel spotted Monteverde greeting an apparent new arrival—a tall, rangy man in his fifties with sandy hair and a neatly trimmed goatee. The journalist waved Daniel and Guy to join them.

"Daniel . . . Guy . . . I want you to meet Major Victor Singleton, our recently returned war hero—"

"Please!" Singleton put up his hand up as if pooh-poohing the journalist's words.

Monteverde went on, "You may find that you have much in common. Daniel's companies are leaders in the European commodities markets, and"—he turned to Daniel—"I believe you said you're here for a week?"

"Possibly longer."

"Still, we must arrange a meeting as soon as possible," Singleton responded affably.

Monteverde chuckled. "A lunch cruise on our company yacht?"

"Perfect," Singleton agreed.

Monteverde turned to Daniel and Guy. "You do realize, of course, that these kinds of gatherings in no way imply that our business and media spheres are interlinked."

His playful comment reinforced Daniel's sense that he and Guy should sound him out.

Singleton cast a glance across the room and a look of surprise came over his face. "If you'll please excuse me." He bowed, hurried toward the tables of women, went straight to Giselle, and spoke to her. She looked astonished, then sprang to her feet and shook his hand enthusiastically.

Monteverde looked surprised, but Daniel and Guy both knew exactly what she was up to.

"Daniel," she burst out as they approached her table. "You'll never guess! This is Major Singleton—Antonia's father! My classmate!"

"I thought you looked familiar," Singleton told her. "But then I remembered you from a photo of the two of you."

Daniel explained his and Giselle's family relationship and that she was assisting him with his business dealings. As they chatted, he was impressed with her self-possession, even more so because she knew that Singleton was not at all what he appeared.

She asked eagerly, "Is Antonia still in Buenos Aires?"

"Yes, but she and her mother will be returning here in a few months."

"I feel terrible—I lost her address—"

"Please give her a call! I'll arrange for my office to give you her number."

"That would be so kind! But the time zones—" She paused. "I'll need to wait until whenever it'll be at least 8 a.m. in BA."

Singleton laughed. "She mentioned that you were a wizard with numbers. Daniel, would you mind terribly if the two of us spent some time catching up?"

"By all means." He smiled at Jaime. "I can see that you're champing at the bit to introduce us around."

As he, Guy, and Monteverde moved away, Guy drew Daniel aside. "That bright smile of hers didn't fool me. She's going to pump him for anything we might find useful. Not just about Antonia."

Daniel murmured back, "What's more, we both know she can carry that off!"

Daniel turned to Monteverde. "Speaking of press-business links, we'd like to talk with you about one of the undertakings that brought us here."

"Then we should go out to one of the lobby alcoves. It's understood that meetings there aren't to be interrupted."

They settled themselves at the same secluded table that Guy and Daniel had used earlier.

"I know I don't have to say this—" Daniel began.

"—but you will anyway," Monteverde riposted.

"Will you keep everything we tell you confidential until I tell you otherwise?"

"What I said about going off the record still stands. And of course, I'd come to you immediately should I learn anything that might—"

"—require revisiting our understanding. Thank you."

Daniel told Jaime that he and Guy were trying to learn what lay behind the transactions in the Gadicke files, and especially the huge shipments of soil amendment products and other commodities being shipped through the Hong Kong region.

Monteverde interjected, "Legally or illegally?"

"They're listed in the records that have come to light, so apparently legally."

"However, even larger quantities may be being smuggled as well."

"And of course," Daniel went on, "there may well be a story in it for you. But you would come to us if you learned anything that might affect our current understanding. Or how you might want to handle any story."

"Yes, especially because there could be some dangers involved. So, in short, you want to find out what's being shipped, from where, to where, and, most important, why."

"Yes, because at this point the paper trail ends here. Literally."

Monteverde steepled his fingers. "How strange. You wouldn't know, but my photographer, Wong Shinghwa, and I are working on a major series about the worldwide economic impact of smugglers from the mainland who are using this area to move their goods and products worldwide."

"Smuggling what?"

"Everything they can get their hands on, but especially raw materials. Not much in the way of consumer goods, of course, given the economic straits the mainland is in. But it's in the billions yearly and growing."

Daniel gave Guy a nod before replying. "So we seem to have parallel interests."

Monteverde laughed. "Yes. I can tell you right now, I'm your man. If you want me to be."

"Thank you, Mr. Monteverde—"

"Jaime, please."

"And Daniel and I. When can we get started?"

"Tonight, actually, if you wish. Wong and I got wind that a ship of an unknown nation is due to be in the area around Lamma Island tonight to take on some as-yet-unknown cargo from the mainland. If you want to come along—"

"Absolutely." Daniel glanced over at Guy, who nodded.

"Wong has his own small, motorized fishing boat," Jaime continued. "We plan to set out at eleven from Aberdeen Harbour. He and I will be at the *Courier* until it's time for us to leave." He pushed his chair back. "I'm going to call him and let him know that you'll be coming with us."

As soon as he left the table, Daniel asked Guy, "Does this make sense?"

"Amazing. Out of the blue, but no way we should pass up the chance."

"What about Singleton?"

"That lunch with him will give us a chance to draw him out and see what we can find out."

When Jaime returned, they agreed that Daniel and Guy would meet him and Wong at Aberdeen Harbour. Jaime estimated that the trip to Lamma would take less than an hour each way, in addition to whatever time they spent observing the possible smuggling venture.

Daniel offered to walk him out to the taxi queue, but Guy, pleading jet lag, said he would take a quick nap and meet them at the harbour. Daniel said he would check on Giselle but would not tell her about their plan.

While he and Jaime were waiting outside for a taxi, Daniel said, "Forgive me, but something's been bedeviling me ever since we met this morning. Your accent . . ."

Jaime grinned. "Hyman Greenberg, born in Berlin,1927. The only one in my family to survive . . . Belsen."

Daniel nodded somberly.

"And afterward, I could not tolerate remaining in my so-called homeland." His lip curled. "I made it to Panama, and my name was easy to translate, which in turn made life easier . . . but you also grew up speaking German, I think."

Daniel replied that he had been born in Germany and had survived only because his parents had sent him to England when he too had been barely eighteen.

"And you and Guy are business partners."

"No, but certainly close associates. Dating back when we met while both fighting in the Free French. After the war, I too could not tolerate returning to Germany, so I settled in Geneva and began working for my future father-in law. I became a partner in the business and then after my wife and I divorced, I bought out my father-in-law. A few years later, Guy moved there too and set up an international private investigation firm. I've used him for dozens of cases, and he's never failed to come through."

When Jaime's taxi pulled up, he offered his hand to Daniel. "Until later then, fellow exile."

"Yes, my friend. Until later."

Daniel returned to the reception hoping to find Giselle and learn whether she had extracted anything of interest from Singleton, but the room had emptied, and the service workers were starting to clear the tables.

He called her room from the lobby. No answer. Uneasy, he went to the front desk, but the clerk recognized him and said, "The young lady asked me to tell you that some of the ladies have invited her to dine at a restaurant near here, and she will call you later."

Relieved that she was not still with Singleton, he went back to his room hoping to rest for an hour but found a note from her under his door: "Have booked a call to Antonia for early morning! Will report back as soon as I can."

He scribbled a quick response that he and Guy would be joining Jaime for a meeting later and that they would all catch up in the morning. After pushing it under her door, he realized he was too edgy to rest, so he left another note for Guy telling him that he was leaving early to find his way to Aberdeen Harbour. He then went back to the Star Ferry and again crossed the harbour to Central, where he knew he had plenty of time to find their meeting place.

CHAPTER TWELVE

Crouched in the stern of Wong's fishing boat, Daniel watched the night mist creep across the South China Sea and muttered every curse he knew. Guy had never shown up at Aberdeen Harbour.

After he, Jaime, and Wong had waited for Guy at the docks for almost thirty minutes, Daniel had located a phone kiosk and called his room at the Peninsula, but Guy had not answered, nor had the desk staff seen him leave. Nor had he left Daniel any message. When Giselle had failed to answer her phone as well, his thoughts had gone haywire. *Were they together?* Although Guy was still given to making joking insinuations about her, Daniel knew he was only trying to get under his skin. But he still had lingering doubts until the clerk offered to call the restaurant where she was supposed to be and reported that the women were still at dinner; then he felt reassured.

He had been furious at keeping Jaime and Wong cooling their heels, but when Jaime had asked him if he still wanted to go, he had replied instantly, "I can't pass up this chance. The hell with Guy."

So they had cast off and headed for the far side of Lamma Island.

Daniel could not work out what had gone wrong. He and Guy had worked together so many times for so many years, never with any problems. Guy had always been the thorough-going professional, always unflappable, though with that sometimes-sardonic wit. Then he remembered the murders of Gadicke and Frau Harmsdorf. *Were he, Guy, and Giselle now in deadly danger as well?* To be sure, it had all started with Giselle's reappearance in his life, but now he was in charge. The one who had decided to find out what was going on. The one who got the three of them, and now Jaime and Wong, involved in it. And now, perhaps, the one who had made a potentially deadly error by going with Jaime and Wong instead of returning to Kowloon to make sure that Guy and Giselle were safe.

Jaime crawled across the deck to him. "We're rounding the point now. Wong will kill our lights so it'll be harder for anyone to see us."

To his left, Daniel glimpsed Lamma's east-facing coast, its shoreline smudged with mist hovering over dense jungle foliage interspersed with what looked like shallow beaches. Ahead of them and to the right was the South China Sea, its waves glimmering under the light of the waning sickle moon.

"Is the shore along here even inhabited?" he asked Jaime. Despite the noise of the engine, he kept his voice down.

"The villages are concentrated on the other side, facing Central. We passed them when we were heading out. But if you're a smuggler, this side is safer by far."

Wong throttled the engine, and the boat slowed. He gestured for Daniel and Jaime to crawl over to him and pointed to a flat barge several hundred feet ahead of them. By the light of a dim oil lantern hanging on the deck, Daniel saw that it was loaded with what looked like small oil drums. A quarter mile or so beyond the barge, in the open water, he glimpsed the inky bulk of a cargo ship with so few lights burning that he could scarcely see it against the low-lying clouds.

Jaime gestured that he and Wong should huddle closer. "My sources tell me," he said in a low voice, "that in these kinds of operations, the barges probably belong to one group of smugglers and are loaded with raw materials that have been smuggled to the Guangdong coast and will be turned over to the smugglers on cargo ships in this area. That group will have arranged other transfers on the way to the final destinations so the cargo will end up being untraceable."

"I *have* to find out what they've got there," Daniel insisted. "This might be our only chance."

"Of course," Jaime said.

"I don't see any watchmen on the barge," Wong whispered.

Wong opened the throttle just enough that they were able to glide almost silently to starboard, which gave them more cover from the cargo ship. They pulled alongside and waited to see if there was any movement on board.

"No one on watch, apparently," Daniel finally said. It was getting windy, and he began to wish he was dressed more appropriately for the job at hand. He envied Jaime and Wong for having the foresight to have wrapped thick woolen scarves around their necks.

"But for all we know they have someone keeping an eye out from the ship," Jaime countered.

Wong stayed at the wheel while Daniel and Jaime clambered onto the deck of the barge as quietly as they could and crept over to the steel drums, each about one-foot in diameter and two feet high and crammed together in rows two drums high that all but filled the deck.

Daniel saw that the drums were stenciled with Chinese characters. He glanced over at Jaime, who shook his head. "I can't read characters."

"Wong," he called softly, "Can you make out what they say?"

Wong shifted the boat so he could get a better view. "*Lín féi*. Food for plants. Farm crops. Made of phosphate."

"I told you about all those references in the files to huge amounts of fertilizer being shipped from Hong Kong," Daniel whispered. "Actually, we thought it might be code for something else."

Jaime shoved at one of the drums, which let out a metallic creak but was too heavy to budge. "It must weigh at least two hundred pounds. I'd guess that they're filled with chunks of unprocessed phosphate rock that was mined in China and that they're now smuggling it somewhere to be refined and sold for farm use. There's a huge legitimate business in agricultural development products between Asia and, for example, South America. So your files might have been referring to legitimate shipments."

"But there could be a huge black market as well," Daniel replied. "As with just about anything that can be bought and sold. Does it say where they're being shipped to?"

Jaime tilted the drum in Wong's direction.

"Yes," Wong said. "*A-gen-ting.*"

"Argentina?" Jaime asked. "Anything else?"

Wong peered again. "*Buyinuosi Ailisi.* Buenos Aires."

"Maybe," Daniel mused, "the numbers and payments in our files bear no relationship to whatever was being shipped. To conceal what was really being smuggled."

"After we get back," Jaime said, "I'll check on the market values for phosphate."

"And we'll see if we can find any evidence in the files that the numbers have been including some kind of 'smugglers' premium' the whole time."

"Not only that," Jaime added, "these labels may be fake, so we still don't really know what's inside."

"Then it's all the more urgent that we get samples."

"Done!" Wong said. He pulled a crowbar out of the low seat-cupboard next to the wheel and handed it to Jaime, who began prying at the lid of the nearest drum.

"And whatever it is, we'll need something to store it in. Ideally something watertight," Daniel said. He gestured at Wong's metal camera case, which was lying on the deck under the wheel of the boat. "Like that. Is it?"

"Of course. It's a Graflex. Waterproof gaskets all around, but—"

"If anything goes wrong, of course I'll replace it."

Wong hurriedly wedged his cameras, lenses, flashes, and film canisters into the cupboard and handed him the case just as Jaime pried off the drum cover, which crashed onto the deck. Daniel held the case open, and Jaime began dumping fistfuls of the grayish rock fragments into it.

When it was full, Daniel secured the gaskets and slipped the strap around his neck so it lay against his chest. "Now let's get out of here."

But his voice was drowned out by the roar of boat engines and a shout of warning from Wong. A power boat had rounded the bow of the cargo ship and was speeding toward them. As Daniel and Jaime crawled back onto Wong's boat, he heard gunfire.

"Hold on!" Wong shouted. He opened the throttle full bore and turned the wheel so hard that the boat heeled, and he had to fight to keep it from capsizing. The sudden movements made Daniel lose his grip on the camera case, and he almost fell overboard, but he was able to drop flat onto the deck and crouch against the hull next to Jaime.

Wong steered as well as he could while squatting down at the wheel, keeping their speed up, and weaving slightly from side to side to make them a more difficult target.

"Run us aground!" Jaime shouted. "And head for the trees! It's our only chance!"

The gunfire continued as Wong steered the boat toward the beach and plowed it into the damp, dense sand. It toppled onto its port side, pitching them into the shallows. Daniel landed in the shadow of the hull out of view of their pursuers and fell onto the camera case, which knocked the breath out of him as its edge cut into his chest. Gasping with pain, he looked around for the others.

Wong was belly-crawling toward the nearest bushes, but Daniel could not spot Jaime and dared not call out to him. Before he too could scramble for cover, another volley of shots rang out. He lay still, hugging the deepest shadows.

After the shots died away, he peered out. Flickering lights and sharp rumblings were coming from Wong's boat, and he realized that the engine had caught fire. The next moment, a deafening explosion sent him scuttling into the nearest bushes. When he looked back, the boat was engulfed in flames.

He retreated farther and farther back into the thickets of bamboo and snakelike vines until he was completely hidden—he hoped. *But where were Wong and Jaime?* He lay still and listened, but the raging fire and more explosions from the boat were drowning out any other sounds. And the farther he got from the flames, the less he could see into the heavy undergrowth surrounding him.

"*Ssssst!*" a voice hissed.

Daniel saw Wong huddled in a tiny clearing. "Where's Jaime?"

"I don't know! Wasn't he right behind you?"

Without a word, Daniel turned and began crawling back to the beach. Wong followed. When the jungle thinned out, Daniel stopped. "What if they're still here? Waiting for us?"

But he heard the attack boat's engines revving and peered out from their hiding place.

"What if they've gotten him?" Wong whispered, horrified.

Daniel too was terrified for Jaime and infuriated by his own helplessness. "This is a fucking disaster! God knows what they'll do—"

"*Ssh!*" Wong interrupted.

Daniel heard the sounds of motors coming from somewhere in the jungle above them.

"Goddamn it!" he swore. "More trouble?"

Wong hushed him. "Maybe that's why they took off. There's an old Buddhist monastery on the hill up ahead. Maybe the monks saw the fire and are coming to investigate. And the smugglers saw them."

"But Jaime—"

"I don't know. But if it is the monks, I know they'll help us."

Daniel recognized the sounds of motor scooters. A few minutes later they went silent and were replaced by the rustling of men moving through the jungle and shouting "*Lai-lai! Lai-lai!*"

"It's the monks," Wong assured him, and shouted, "*Gau-mehng-a! Gau-mehng-a!*"

Four men with flashlights emerged from among the trees and bowed to Daniel and Wong, who returned the bows, introduced himself and Daniel, and began explaining their situation in Cantonese.

Three of the four appeared to be in their late twenties and were wearing long-sleeved jackets with frog-style closings, loose knee-length trousers, matching leggings, and flat fabric shoes. The fourth man, apparently a senior monk, was older and wore a robe tucked up around his waist that he loosened so it fell to his ankles as Wong began recounting what had happened.

When Wong stopped for breath, the senior monk responded with what Daniel could tell was an emphatic phrase in Cantonese. Wong turned to Daniel. "He says we *must* first search for Jaime. Perhaps he was injured when the boat exploded, and the smugglers do not have him after all."

"God, I hope so!" Daniel exclaimed as the monk called out some orders to the other three, who hurried toward the beach, and brought out two small flashlights from a bag at his waist that he handed to Wong and Daniel.

They followed him back to where the flames enveloping the boat were dying down. The monks spread out along the shore while the senior monk called out occasional commands. Daniel felt furious and helpless and at a loss for what to do. Aside from his having collected the samples from the barge, the whole expedition had been a disaster. Whatever had happened to Jaime was his fault. His alone. And he thought about Giselle and that if he were killed as a result of this night, she would have no one left to turn to. Everything had been happening so fast that he'd had no time to make any provision for her. And his boys. It was quite possible that he might die tonight and never see them again.

"A total loss." Wong sighed, looking at what remained of the boat.

"I gave you my word," Daniel reminded him.

Wong shrugged. "Camera gear . . . the boat . . . it's all replaceable. But Jaime . . ."

Daniel could say nothing in reply. Waves of guilt crashed over him. *How could he live with yet another death on his conscience?*

"Here! Here!" a voice cried in Cantonese. One of the young monks was waving his flashlight and shouting from a small spit of sand half-hidden in foliage at the far end of the beach.

Daniel felt his breath stop. He knew instantly Jaime had been found. Wong raced across the beach with the other monks and their master. Daniel followed, reluctant to face what he knew was coming. They were all gathered around the monk who had sounded the alarm. He was on his knees in the sand brushing seaweed from Jaime's body. The others knelt to help him.

Jaime lay on his stomach, his jacket rucked up to his shoulders, his feet bare. After the monks cleared away the waterlogged debris, they slid their hands under his body and gently turned him over.

Even by flashlight, Daniel could see that Jaime's face was blue. He had drowned, suffocated by the fierce seawater that had forced all the oxygen out of his lungs. *Had he realized that he was dying?* A sudden nightmare image rose up, not from his memories but rather as a horrifying creation of his imagination—the cyanotic faces of his father and mother and sister and so many millions as the Zyklon B had filled their lungs. Overcome, he had to turn away and try to quell his anguish by forcing himself back to the present. Reliving the moments when they had run aground, he realized that the sudden impact when the boat had hit the sand and capsized must have thrown Jaime overboard and into the roiling waves.

Wong bowed his head. "He once told me that he regretted not having learned to swim."

"I know you did all you could. But one thing we can be grateful for is that he wasn't carried out to sea and lost forever." He knelt, took Jaime's left hand, and felt his wrist hoping for a pulse although he knew it was futile. He rested Jaime's hand on the sand and sat back on his heels next to the body of this man who might have become his friend.

How many deaths since Giselle had knocked on his door that night? First two. Now a third. How many more might there be? If he continued to go forward, how great a toll in lives might he ultimately bear responsibility for? And would it be worth it? And for just a moment, his grief about Jaime turned to anger because had Guy been with them, this night might have turned out differently.

The senior monk motioned one of the younger men forward. "Lin Litian has much English," he said haltingly. "He will take you and your departed brother to the ferry, and you will reunite him with his family."

Daniel bowed and turned to Wong. "May we talk for a moment?" Wong rose heavily and they moved a few yards away from the gathered monks, who continued to their vigil around Jaime.

"You know how upset I was when my colleague didn't meet us," Daniel told Wong. "And now I'm worried that something has gone very wrong, and I feel I must get back to Kowloon as soon as possible. Will you stay here with Jaime and help the monks care for him until morning?"

"Of course."

Daniel pulled out his wallet and handed him a number of banknotes. "For the monks, for whatever they feel is proper because of their care of him. And when we're back in Kowloon, you must tell me what you know about his family, so I can help them. And your boat—"

Wong bowed. "You are very generous. It is sad that none of this seems important right now."

"Yes. But you must let me do this. It's all I can do now."

When they returned to Jaime's body, the monks had covered his face with a cloth. The master gestured at Lin, who said, "He says that we will call the police in the morning."

"You have a phone?"

"Yes. We will say that we found him floating in the bay."

"Then please may I try to reach my friends?"

The senior monk, who had been listening intently, replied, "Yes, yes."

Daniel bowed. "Thank you for your great kindness." He then looked at the ruins of the boat. "But the police, they will see that there's been an accident."

Lin translated again, and after a few moments, the senior monk again replied. Lin said, "He says that there are enough of us at the monastery to take this all away, even to the marks of oil on the sand. So the police will not inquire too much." He gestured at the wreckage of the boat. "He also says that good wood, even damaged, is scarce, and we will use it to build another sacred shrine."

Daniel could not help smiling at the elder monk, who smiled back and said, "*Wú jué rén zhī lù.*"

"He says," Lin put in, "'there is always a way to do things.'"

Daniel handed over almost all the money he was carrying and asked Lin to say that he regretted that the only way he could express his gratitude was with money. Wong also explained in Chinese that Daniel had asked him to remain with Jaime's body until he could be returned to his family.

"Now, because it is urgent that you try to reach your companions," Lin went on, "I will take you to the monastery. My brothers here will stay, and I will send others to conceal what happened and to bring your friend's body to the monastery later."

Daniel was too moved by the monks' kindness to say anything but, "Thank you, thank you." Lin led him through the dense jungle hillside and up to a roughly paved two-lane road where the monks' scooters were parked. Daniel had ridden scooters and motorcycles as a teenager before the war and was surprised by how easily he regained his feel for the road, and how noisy they were in the dark night silence.

Ten minutes later, they reached the monastery, a rather crude two-story building of white-painted brick that had been shaped by hand. But a light bulb above the front door proved that it was equipped with electricity.

Daniel had to conceal his overpowering impatience to find the phone. Not knowing where Guy or Giselle were or what might have happened to them, and not being able to reach them, took him back to some of the hardest and darkest days of the war when he and Guy had more than once lost touch with their comrades and had been left on their own to fight their way back to safety.

Lin seemed to sense his impatience and hurried him inside. The main hall was bare except for two scrolls, one picturing the Buddha Sakyamuni and the other Guanyin, the goddess of mercy and compassion—and a table in a corner that held the phone.

"If you wish, I can place the call for you," Lin said, "because it will be faster to speak in Cantonese."

Daniel gave him the number at the Peninsula, and after several attempts to get through, Lin shouted, "Wait a moment! *Dang-jat-haa!*" He then handed the phone to him.

At first, all he could hear was static, so he too had to shout. "Peninsula Hotel? . . . This is Daniel Lavy! . . . Daniel Lavy . . . Please put me through to Mr. Broussard . . . Broussard!"

Through the static, he heard the clerk repeat, "Broussard?"

"Yes!"

"One moment, sir!"

Daniel cursed under his breath at the bad connection until the phone clicked again.

"Broussard here."

"Thank God!'

"Daniel! Where are you?"

"On Lamma! What the hell happened to you?"

"An accident—" A high-pitched whine interrupted him, and Daniel cursed again. When the line cleared, he heard Guy shouting, "—a set-to between my cab and another driver. Police and so forth took forever! I knew I'd missed you, so I came back here—"

"What about Giselle?"

"In her room packing."

"Packing!" Daniel exploded.

"We're booked on the next flight to Buenos Aires—"

"*What the fuck?*"

"I'm serious! Let me talk! In case we lose each other! It's a good thing, because Giselle was frantic. She called

Antonia, and while they were catching up, she told her that she'd met Claudia in BA and that Claudia had said how much she regretted—"

His voice cut out again and Daniel cursed silently.

"—everything that had happened. Around the divorce. So Antonia gave her Claudia's number, and—"

"What? What?" Daniel shouted.

"Giselle called her to make amends—" Guy yelled through the rise and fall of static.

"What? Damn it, what?"

"—Claudia was crying so much that Giselle could barely understand her. I hate to . . . but she said that your boys have disappeared."

Daniel wheeled around and slammed the phone receiver against the wall. Lin ran over. "Sir! No!"

Daniel sagged against the wall. "Terrible, terrible news!" He grabbed the phone back. "Guy? Guy!"

Guy shouted, "The police say—probably being held for ransom by some goddamned bandit gang wanting to get at Luciano —"

"And where the fuck *is* Luciano in all this?" Daniel spat.

"Spending every moment pulling every string he can to find them!"

"And you really believe that?"

"All I know is that we've *got* to be on that plane!"

"I don't—has the whole world turned to shit?—"

"She begged Giselle to tell you to come as soon as you can! The next flight to BA leaves in eight hours. And I got you a ticket on the next flight." The static kicked in again and Daniel lost the next few words. "—be there waiting. Just be on it—" The line went dead.

Daniel forced himself to set down the receiver without slamming it and turned to Lin, who was standing to one side looking horrified. "Do you have enough English to have understood most of that?"

Lin nodded. "Yes, and you will be on your plane. I swear it."

CHAPTER THIRTEEN

C lutching Wong's camera case under his arm, Daniel
barreled through the main doors of the airport to the
only cab idling outside. He scrambled into the back
seat and slammed the door with a rattling thud. "Italian Embassy! It's urgent!"

"*Embajada italiana?*"

"*Si! Emergencia!*"

The cabbie nodded wearily and edged into the dense
early-afternoon traffic. Daniel slumped against the seat, exhausted from nineteen hours of plane engines seeming to
mercilessly drone, "They're gone . . . you'll never see them
again . . . they're gone . . ."

He lunged forward and shouted, "*Mas rapido!*" but was
drowned out by the blaring horn of a black sedan rushing toward them. The cabbie braked so hard that Daniel's forehead
slammed into the front seat.

The sedan skidded to a stop right in front of them. The
driver's door swung open, and Guy jumped out. "They're
okay!" he shouted. "They're safe!" He dodged a minibus and
jerked Daniel's door open, but Daniel was too stunned to
move.

"Come on!" Guy tugged at his arm. "They're probably back
now!"

Daniel shoved Guy's arm away so he could bury his face
in his hands. Deaf to the horns blaring all around them and
almost too shaken to move, he groped for the camera case

and tottered over to the sedan while Guy paid the cabbie. He tried to calm himself as Guy bulled his way into the sluggish herd of vehicles before he asked the only question he could. "You're sure?"

"Yes. Believe me. Yes."

"How the hell do you *know*?"

"Because Luciano—"

"That son of a bitch—!"

"—he went to get them. In fact, they may already be back—"

"And you *believed* him?"

"Listen. All I know is, he signed off on letting them go on some mandatory two-week camping trip with their school. Except he did it behind Claudia's back, because she didn't want them to go, and when he told her, she fell apart. This was happening right when Giselle called her. She heard Claudia screaming that she'd never see them again, and then apparently, she fainted, and he started shouting for an ambulance. Giselle was still on the line when he came back on shouting, 'The *hell* with their fucking school! I'll bring them back!' And he begged Giselle to come. So what else could we do?"

Daniel felt torn between rage and fear. "How is she?"

"Nurses around the clock. The doctor visits twice a day. And Giselle's been with her almost every minute. She says Claudia managed to tell her that they'd been fighting about the trip, but when he told her he'd sent them anyway . . ."

"Does she know that he's bringing them back?"

"He wanted to tell her, but the doctor wouldn't even let him see her at that point. He left right after the doctor and nurses took over. Giselle's sleeping in her room. She thinks Claudia's aware of her presence, and that it's keeping her a bit calmer." He stopped at a signal.

"You have no idea what hell this has been."

"And I had no fucking way to reach you after your flight took off."

"And where *are* they?"

"I'm not sure. Somewhere in the west, couple hours by plane."

"By *plane*? I can't believe . . . what the hell kind of school flies ten-year-olds off to some godforsaken nowhere?"

Guy shrugged. "The most elite boys' school in BA."

"Oh, of course! The military ones that diplomats always go for!" He turned away and looked out of the window. His boys. Not quite children any longer but not yet teens. He shifted in his seat and toed the Graflex case away from his feet. The gravel inside made a scraping sound.

"By the way," he said, "This is Wong's. We managed to grab some samples from one of the canisters on the barge just before we were attacked. He said the labels were all marked 'phosphate rock.' Which Jaime had told me is being smuggled in huge quantities from the Chinese mainland through Hong Kong to BA. He translated it as 'plant food.'"

"Really? *Fertilizer*? And huge shipments?"

"Exactly like what we found in the Gadicke files." He sighed. "Gadicke, and Frau Harmsdorf and now Jaime and Wong."

"What do you mean?"

Wearily, he filled Guy in on everything that had happened on the Lamma expedition. "And," he concluded, "just as I was leaving the peninsula, the radio reported that a photographer for Jaime's paper had been found dead. On the beach at Lamma."

"Four deaths so far," Guy said. "And all of them apparently due to what we've set in motion."

Daniel saw that they had left the heart of the city and were driving through increasingly wealthy neighborhoods. "You said he promised to be back with them around now."

"He swore it."

Moments later, Guy turned onto a wide, paved lane that wound through a lush park landscaped with century-old trees and bordered on all four sides by stately Italianate and French-style mansions, most flying the flags of different nations.

They passed a soccer field where a group of schoolboys the twins' age were kicking soccer balls, as much at one another as at the goals. Daniel's heart tightened. *Why weren't Matthew and Michael there roughhousing with them?*

Guy pulled in front of a two-story mansion flying the red-white-and-green flag of Italy. "This is the residence. The embassy's two blocks away."

The uniformed guard posted at the wrought-iron gates hurried to their car. "*Bienvenidos, señores!*" He bowed before opening both doors.

Guy asked, "Has His Excellency returned?"

"No, sir."

Guy and Daniel exchanged uneasy glances, but as Daniel dragged himself out of his seat and slung Wong's case over his shoulder, the front doors flew open. Giselle ran out. She managed to shout, "Thank God!" before throwing herself into Daniel's arms. She was shaking so much that he felt the need to hold on tighter, to secure her in a sense. Guy signaled Daniel that he was going to park the car.

"Why aren't they here yet?" he asked gently.

He felt her shake her head against his shoulder.

"And how is she?"

"Still very sedated." She stepped back and wiped her eyes.

"And where the hell is Luciano? He promised he'd be back with them by now."

"I don't know! I heard the same thing you did."

"Where is this damned camp, anyway?"

"Apparently on this huge stretch of land that some wealthy donors deeded to the school decades ago. Just across the Paraguay border."

"Paraguay? Hell of a long way away for children to be carted off to for a summer camp. No wonder Claudia—"

Giselle nodded. "The students can't go until they're in fifth grade, and then they have to go back each year before they graduate. The boys were terribly upset when Claudia said it was too far away and dangerous and refused to let them go. But after she collapsed, Luciano swore to her . . ."

"I know." He glanced back out at the park and saw the boys, possibly some of Matthew's and Michael's classmates, still playing under the trees. "They may not even remember me."

"Please don't *ever* think that!" Her arm linked in his, she led him inside and along a skylit entry hall to double doors that opened onto a sun-filled formal salon.

"I don't even want to ask whether she knows I was coming."

She gave him an apologetic smile. "Which you just have . . . all I can say is not yet. But before long, I hope. I'm so sorry." She patted his arm and walked down the hall and into a room at its far end.

He sighed and glanced around the salon. One wall near the fireplace was hung with photographs, including several school portraits of the boys taken over the five years since he had last seen them. Their images brought tears to his eyes, and all he had lost crashed over him.

Guy came in through a side door that opened onto the garden. "God knows where—"

The salon door slammed open, and Luciano burst into the room but stopped still when he saw Daniel. Like the other, more famous Luciano who came to mind—Charles "Lucky" Luciano, a deceptively handsome architect of the National Crime Syndicate—he had thick straight brows, a chiseled jawline, and a smile that entirely altered his face, changed it into something that otherwise sensible women melted for. He might not have had Lucky's patented dead-eye stare, but by default, this Luciano's expression was intense. He might be threatening to a man with much less life experience than Daniel. But Daniel was ready for him, always.

"What the *hell* are you doing here?" the man growled.

"Where are they? *Where are my boys?*"

"They wouldn't let me bring them back! They said they'd be expelled."

"They're still *my* sons."

"*Luciano!*"

Daniel wheeled around. Claudia, barefoot and clutching a dressing gown tightly around her, was clinging to the door jamb. Tears were streaming down her cheeks, her ashen face was half-hidden by the wild, curling masses of her long black hair, and he realized with horror that if not for her hair, which she had always begged him to caress when they were making love, he would not have recognized her.

She stumbled over to Luciano. "Where are they?" she whispered, then shrieked, "You promised!"

Giselle ran to her, but Claudia's knees buckled, and she fell to the floor sobbing.

Mad with rage, Daniel lunged at him and kicked his knees out from under him, then straddled him and seized him by the throat, but Luciano reared up and shoved him sideways, scrambled out from under him. Daniel dove after him. Slammed him on his back. Jumped him again, this time, he managed to shove Luciano's fists away to land a ferocious punch to his face. He heard a satisfying loud crunch, followed by the sound of Luciano screaming and the sight of him burying his bleeding face in his shirtsleeve.

Daniel pulled Luciano's arm away from his face and stabbed him in the throat with two knife-straight fingers. Luciano gagged as he tried to roll over, but Daniel threw him onto his back and locked his hands around his enemy's throat. "You—"

"Stop it!" Guy jumped him and tried to pull him away, but Daniel drove his left elbow into his ribs and threw him to the floor. He was aiming his foot at Luciano's groin when Guy scrambled back onto his feet, seized Daniel's arms from behind, and muscled him away.

"Giovanni!" Luciano roared, "*Help!*" He rolled over and curled up into a ball with one arm shielding his face and the other clutching at his throat.

A guard ran in and made as if to seize Daniel, but Guy yelled, "Stop!"

The guard hesitated, then made his way uncertainly over to Luciano. Guy dragged Daniel several feet away. "Are you *insane*?" he shouted.

Daniel went still. Despite all he had gone through during the war, he had never known that uncontrollable demons of rage were living inside him. Panting, he studied the streaks of Luciano's blood on his hands, and finally murmured, "Yes . . . I think perhaps I am." He lifted his head and watched as Giselle helped Claudia, still sobbing, to her feet and out of the room.

The moment the women were out of sight, he knelt over Luciano, still wiping away smeared masses of blood and mucus, and shoved his face almost into his. Guy stepped forward watchfully.

"What the *hell* is going on?" Daniel asked.

Luciano wiped more blood from his mouth and choked, "They wouldn't let me!"

"They're just children—what are you talking about? This is bullshit!"

"No! The school! They said they would expel them!"

"So you had no choice?"

"It was too big a risk. My family . . ."

"And what about what *she* wanted?"

Luciano tried to sit up, but Daniel shoved him back down. "No, she didn't want them to go," Luciano panted. "She hates it here. She thinks it's dangerous, that something might happen to them. But *I* make the decisions here. My government sent me here. This is my duty!"

"It also meant you could take them halfway around the world from me."

"No! She did not want to leave Italy . . ." He laid his head on the floor and closed his eyes. "Because then you could see them sometimes."

"That's a damned lie."

"No! I did not want to leave Italy, either! But *mi famiglia* . . . After my brother died, I had to take his place here. I did not want to, but my parents made it happen that way. And also . . . they were not so unhappy to see us come here. When we left, they said to me, 'We will come when you can show us real grandchildren. Keep the two from your Jew wife but give us our own, from our blood.'"

Daniel was seized with such rage that again Guy had to hold him back.

"For myself, I care nothing about blood. I love her. I love them, and I tell you that, after a time, if we had been able to stay in Italy, I would have let her invite you to see them. And even to see her because I know why you lost her. And so do you." He bared his blood-smeared teeth in a triumphant smile. "I gave her my self and my soul, but you, all you cared for was your business." He choked again. "Attack me again if you will, but you know I am right." He closed his eyes again, but his triumphant smile remained.

Daniel turned away, unable to speak. Luciano was right. It was torture to hear the truth from his enemy, but this didn't stop it from being the truth. He motioned Guy, still keeping a wary eye on both of them, to a corner where Luciano could not hear them.

"We need a plan," he whispered. "For the boys. And for her."

"Yes. But it seems they're safe, even if they're still at the camp. So if you believe him, that he defied his family for her and cares about them . . ."

"I don't give a damn what he says! Who knows what's really going on, or what he's going to do next? I want him guarded. Around the clock. And there's Giselle to think of."

"It did occur to me that she might be exhausted enough to need a break from being here. Hope you don't mind, but I reserved a suite for her at your hotel."

"Perfect." He glanced at Luciano, who lay on the carpet still, hands over his eyes.

"And him?"

"I know just the thing." Daniel summoned a grin. "As usual."

***

Ten minutes later, Daniel and Guy shoved Luciano up a set of stairs along the ivy-covered back wall of the garage behind the residence and into a simply furnished two-room apartment that smelled faintly of oily rags.

Daniel looked around. "Wait."

He checked that the bathroom had no windows, then waved Luciano over. "Don't close the door all the way. And stay in there until we tell you to come out."

Luciano, apparently resigned to his situation, lurched past them, and eased the door three-quarters shut.

Guy moved onto the landing, well out of Luciano's hearing and line of sight, and motioned Daniel over. He then pulled a small pistol out of his pocket and handed it to Daniel. "I picked up a couple of these as soon as we arrived. Just in case. I couldn't do that in HK. They're much stricter about firearms."

"Really?" Daniel commented. "Not in my experience!" He hefted the gun, enjoying the cold weight of it in his hand, before tucking it into his jacket pocket. He felt safer already. "What next?

Guy gestured at Wong's camera bag. "That?"

Daniel sighed. "It is all we have to go on at this point."

"Any ideas about who might be able to help us?"

"Where's the phone?"

Guy went inside and pulled the bathroom door fully shut. Daniel heard Luciano protest, but Guy ignored him and stationed himself in front of the door. Daniel took a phone from the table next to the front door onto the landing and then he dialed.

"Felipe? It's Daniel . . . Yes, I am . . . He's here, too . . . We need to talk."

CHAPTER FOURTEEN

Two hours after Daniel and Giselle checked in at their hotel, Daniel was back in the lobby, settled in a cheerful, flower-patterned armchair at a small wicker table with a view of the hotel garden.

Although she had made him promise to sleep, he was still feeling too edgy to try. Rest could come later. Instead, he planted himself under his shower head and scrubbed away what felt like layer upon layer of fatigue, stale airplane air, and endless time zones, grief, pain, rage.

But he could not wash away Luciano's revelations about his and Claudia's failure to have "children of their own" nor the man's triumphant skewering of how Daniel had failed her.

Daniel felt as if the Luciano he had finally beaten to a pulp after five years lived a life that was more complicated than he'd ever cared to consider. But why should he have, when his rage and loss were all he knew?

Still, he found himself wondering at the cause of Luciano's infertility—for it obviously couldn't have stemmed from Claudia. Luciano prided himself on being able to provide for her everything her previous husband had not been able, or perhaps willing, to. There being an area in which he could not rise to what Daniel had accomplished must have destroyed him. And while Daniel experienced a flicker of victory at the thought, he quickly found himself wondering if the inability to have children destroyed the man in ways unrelated to his and Daniel's constant war. He could not imagine his life without his children, even seeing them so rarely. And for all that he loathed about the man who'd replaced him, who'd burgled his family and his happiness, Luciano had seemed sincere in saying he loved the boys.

He set the Graflex case on the table and studied it. What he'd said to Guy was the truth: it was all they had to go on. *What if it was a dead end?* And even if it wasn't—even if he and Guy and Giselle managed to make sense of it all—would uncovering the truth turn out to be worth four lives?

The doorman opened the lobby door for a young, dark-haired man wearing sunglasses and carrying a scuffed leather bomber jacket slung over one shoulder.

Daniel sprang up. "Felipe!"

Felipe broke into a huge grin. "It's been so long!"

"Too long."

They embraced and clapped each other on the back, and Daniel led him to their table. He was glad to be in Felipe's presence again. The younger man had been born with an open, enthusiastic spirit he had somehow retained despite his horrifying wartime experiences.

"Too long." Daniel reached across the table and pulled at the front of the jacket. "The day Guy gave it to you, it reached halfway to your knees."

"'Here, kid!' Felipe mimicked Guy's voice. "'This'll keep your skinny butt warm!' I wonder if he remembers it."

"You can ask him yourself. He's just busy with something else at the moment."

They asked for coffee, and Felipe requested a sandwich. Daniel continued studying him as he ordered, glad to see that he was still the same Felipe but had matured into the self-possessed adult Daniel had anticipated he would. Felipe had been barely fourteen when the war ended and Daniel and Guy had taken leave of him near the French-Spanish border, Daniel to return to Geneva and Guy to the United States.

Although Daniel had fifteen years on him, their intertwined experiences in war had made brothers of them; he would have recognized Felipe on the street, even after all these years, and he didn't doubt this would always be true. To be sure, Felipe had grown two inches taller in the interim, and his formerly undisciplined mop of dark-brown hair was now cropped medium-short, but his hazel eyes and open smile remained unchanged.

When they had met, Daniel, then twenty-nine, had been fighting with the French Resistance near the Spanish border, and Felipe had been a half-starved twelve-year-old who just weeks earlier had seen his mother, father, and two older sisters massacred by Franco's forces. After escaping the slaughter, he had joined a band of similarly orphaned ten- to thirteen-year-olds who had sworn not just to survive together but also to take revenge on their enemies.

While waiting for their orders, Daniel filled him in on everything that had happened from Giselle's arrival at his door to having left Guy guarding Luciano at the embassy residence. A few minutes into his report, Felipe began taking notes.

Daniel lifted the lid of the camera case. "This is another link in the chain, possibly a major one, but we still don't know why."

Felipe rubbed some of the fragments between his fingers.

"It's phosphate gravel," Daniel said. "Have you ever heard of it?"

"No, but I know someone who might have."

"Who?"

"You'll laugh."

"All right, who?"

Felipe gave him a look, waited, and said, "My tango teacher, Tomas Maier."

Daniel laughed as Felipe had sworn he would. "Oh, of course!"

For that matter, Felipe laughed as well. "It's true. He came here from Spain after the war and taught geology and architecture at the university, but—"

"He discovered tango, and it changed his life," Daniel filled in solemnly.

Felipe rolled his eyes. "And I've never seen a man study anything as single-mindedly. When he turned fifty-five, he quit teaching about rocks, and even gave up some of his pension, and now he's our 'gran maestro,' the finest teacher in all of BA. In fact, wait here—" He jumped up and went to the hotel phone.

Daniel let himself close his eyes just for a moment. Almost forty hours without sleep. How he'd found the strength to tear into Luciano when he could barely hold his head up now, he'd never know.

When he heard Felipe say goodbye and hang up, he forced his eyes open. Felipe grabbed his jacket, sunglasses, and the camera case. "He's teaching tonight, but we can meet with him now if we hurry."

"That's very good of him." Daniel sighed inwardly as he pulled himself to his feet. "Giselle's suite is right over there." He gestured at the building beyond the garden. "I'll get her."

"But he said right away, and—"

"And if it weren't for her, we wouldn't be here right now."

Felipe shrugged but followed Daniel along the garden path toward the other building. Halfway across, he stopped.

Daniel turned to him. "What is it?"

Felipe was staring at a woman seated at a patio table next to the waterfall. Her head was bent over a sheet of paper on which she was writing. It was Giselle, so focused on her work at hand she was oblivious to everything around her. Daniel was about to call out to her, but Felipe looked so stupefied that he had to hold back a laugh. *Self-assured Felipe knocked off his feet after one glance at a woman he had never laid eyes on before?*

Through his haze, Felipe stuttered, "Are you . . . do you . . . need anything from your room before we leave?"

Daniel smothered a smile. "No, we just need to get Giselle. Remember?"

"And you said that way?"

Daniel could not resist. "Actually, she's right over there. But maybe you can't see her from here."

Felipe, still looking bewildered, glanced back over at her. She saw them and shielded her eyes against the glare of the late-afternoon sun blazing behind them. "I thought you'd still be sleeping!" she called.

As Daniel led the way toward her, the sun shifted, and she could see them more clearly. She froze when Felipe came into view. Daniel said to the younger man, "I need to give Guy a call before we leave."

"Yes, good, That's fine." Felipe's gaze was still fixed on Giselle, and hers on his.

"You *did* say right away."

"No, it'll be fine."

"Then I'll just let the two of you introduce yourselves."

As Felipe hurried past him toward Giselle, Daniel sighed. Yes, he needed to make sure Guy was keeping Luciano under control and also tell him about Maier. But when he opened the door to his suite, he looked back and saw Felipe and Giselle sitting together talking eagerly and looking both tentative and happy. The sight unlocked his own memories, long past but indelible, of his and Claudia's first meetings.

CHAPTER FIFTEEN

Daniel was pleased that Maier's home appeared to be an *estancia*, one of the region's rural smallholdings. The mile-long paved lane offered view after view of fields bordered by stands of trees, their leaves glimmering in the slow-setting sun. He tried to let the tranquil scene soothe his spirit, but the tentative yet intense whispers that Felipe and Giselle were exchanging in the front seat kept intruding.

Although he tried not to listen, their *coup de foudre* had rekindled the feelings of loss that had armored him against even the most fleeting relationships since Claudia had left him. And having at last seen her again, he no longer knew how he felt. Perhaps he would never know. But he felt trapped with the happy young couple in front of him. He envied them but could only wish them well and not begrudge them the happiness that he doubted he would ever know again.

The lane curved alongside a pasture where two horses and a foal were grazing. He glimpsed roof tiles beyond the trees and shifted in his seat to get a better look, but the damned camera case jabbed him in the side. *Would they ever learn what it meant?*

As Felipe pulled up in front of the house, the front door flew open, and Maier hurried down the tiled walkway toward them. He threw his arms around the younger man and, in keeping with an Argentinian tradition, they exchanged quick soundless pecks on one cheek.

"Welcome back, my boy!" Maier rumbled. "And these are your friends?"

He bowed to Giselle and kissed her hand, then turned to Daniel. As they shook hands, Daniel said, "It's very kind of you to see us on such short notice."

"But you are my boy's friends!" He turned back to Felipe. "And you? Do you think you've learned everything I have to offer in my classes?"

"Never!" Felipe laughed. "But—"

Maier shook his head and started to say something, but Felipe interrupted, "I know!" He mimicked Maier's rumbling voice, "'Too much business drains the joy out of life!' But so do empty pockets, Maestro!"

Daniel's line of work—and for that matter, Daniel's fraught personal affairs—had calloused him against strangers for the most part. That's not to say he didn't cooperate with them and even appreciate them case by case, on the basis of how willing they were to help him, how handy and uncommon their skillset, or what resources they brought to the table that he may never have secured on his own. Daniel, in other words, *respected* many of his colleagues when their professionalism warranted it. But he was finding it a rarer and rarer occurrence to *like* someone he'd just met, especially instantaneously. However, he didn't need to sort out the man's exact usefulness to know he liked Tomas Maier.

He had the happy, booming demeanor of a patriarch hosting his whole family for the holidays, and Daniel was sure that was part of it, but there was more. There was his impeccable but comfortable style of dress. His earnest smile. Daniel had no way of proving that this tango teacher was a kind, generous, even noble man—but he knew it all the same.

The older man hugged Felipe again and led them inside, along a tiled corridor softened with an array of rugs and into his studio. It was lined with bookcases and crowded with display cases full of architectural models, and its full wall of west-facing windows offered another view of the fields dappled with long, finger-like shadows from the trees.

"Please." Maier indicated four upholstered armchairs set around a large drafting table, its surface scratched and scarred from years of use.

After supplying them with coffee and small fruit pastries, he took his own seat and raised his cup. "It is always an honor when people seek me out to talk about architecture. Or dance." He shot a teasing glance at Felipe. "However dilatory their interest. And now . . ." He turned to Daniel and Giselle. ". . . he tells me that I may be able to help you."

Daniel hesitated, aware that he had to choose his words carefully because none of them knew whether or in what way Maier might be involved. The older man leaned forward. "*Así que esto se queda estrictamente entre nosotros.*"

Felipe translated, "It will remain strictly among us."

Daniel smiled his understanding, set the case on the table, and opened it. "It began with this."

"Ah, geology," Maier said. "One of my several past lifetimes." He picked up a fragment and rolled it between his fingers. "This is phosphate gravel. Also known as phosphate rock. Very important for agricultural purposes, but otherwise . . ." He shrugged.

"It came from a large shipment that we traced from mainland China to Hong Kong, where it was transferred to another ship and brought here. The shipping drums were labeled 'plant food' in Chinese."

Maier nodded. "A low-cost but very effective form of fertilizer. No doubt part of the international effort to support agricultural development in our hemisphere."

"Of course. But we've learned that it's being shipped here in huge quantities. *Not* through government channels, and with great secrecy."

"Smuggling."

"Yes. We want to find out where these shipments end up, and especially why."

Maier frowned. "This sounds rather far-fetched. And why is it even of interest to you?"

Giselle leaned forward. "Because for one thing, people linked to these shipments are dying. Being murdered. Four that we know of so far."

As she recounted the deaths of Gadicke and his secretary, Jaime, and Wong, Maier appeared more and more shocked.

"What's more," she added, "Daniel barely survived the most recent attack, just days ago."

"And you're investigating this because...?"

"Because when I accidentally got too close to the truth back home, it cost me my job, and much more. My apartment was ransacked. It was clear I wasn't safe any longer, so I had to leave my home, and move in with my uncle Daniel." She looked at him when she said this, her eyes gleaming with fresh appreciation. Redirecting her attention to Maier, she said, "We believe that a number of major international banks are parties to this smuggling scheme."

"But to what purpose?"

"That," she stated, "is what we are here to find out."

Maier turned to Felipe. "And you, my boy?"

"I believe that something suspicious is going on. Also, at the very least these conspirators may be stealing from our country and our people. And doing God knows what else."

Maier turned to Daniel. "Please tell me everything you know. Or suspect."

"Let Giselle start. If it hadn't been for her . . ."

After Giselle and Daniel finished recounting all that had happened since Giselle's firing from the Schmidts' Bank, Maier, who had been listening with complete attention, asked,

"So at this point you believe that Diessen is behind all of this. But again, to what purpose?"

"We're determined to find out," Daniel replied. "And the trail so far has led us here."

"To me?"

"Yes."

Maier pushed himself back from the table but indicated they should remain seated. Felipe, Giselle, and Daniel exchanged doubtful glances while he made a slow circuit around the room. Daniel felt as if he could see ideas clicking into place in Maier's head as he paced. At last, he returned to his chair. "I am reluctant to do so," he said, "but I feel I must offer you some information that you may find helpful . . . I too have had dealings with Diessen."

Quick glances were exchanged, but the three remained silent waiting for him to continue. Maier stirred the gravel fragments. After a long pause, he added, "And there could be consequences if they and their people learn that we have spoken." He paused again.

Maier turned to Felipe. "You have already told them how I came here after the war and established myself here as an architect?"

"Certainly, Maestro."

Maier nodded. "By 1949, I was well-settled here and being offered commissions. One day, I received a letter from Manfred Diessen, the head of their empire, asking to meet with me. When we met, he told me he wanted me to develop plans and architectural drawings for a large manufacturing complex—"

"Where? What kinds of plans?" Giselle burst out.

He mock-scowled at her. "Patience, my dear! To begin with, schematics to define the general scope and conceptual design. After he approved those, I created more than two hundred increasingly detailed plans. Everything had to proceed stage by stage because, in any project, the success of every stage depends on the quality and comprehensiveness of the previous ones. To omit anything is to invite disaster. I also provided drawings, notes, technical specifications."

"What about blueprints?" she pursued. "And the overall budget?"

"Blueprints would have been the next step. As for budget, it was never mentioned. I sensed that I had carte blanche as long as I did my best. One of his people would arrive here, give me my fee, and take the work I had done. Diessen would occasionally communicate with me by phone. It was obvious that he was telling me only the minimum that he felt I needed to know. But wherever the site was, it had either already been or would be graded and engineered for buildability."

"And its purpose?"

"As I've indicated, Diessen is a man accustomed to asking questions, not answering them. However, the plans were very large-scale. Three scientific laboratories, an airport hangar, runways that could accommodate large planes, a manufacturing and machining plant, fuel storage, agricultural equipment, and plumbing and electrical facilities. He also wanted several residential complexes with luxury accommodations, standard-quality apartments, and basic accommodations for, I estimated, as many as four hundred residents. The plans were also to include dining facilities, a small hospital, a gymnasium, and some recreational facilities."

"A totally self-sufficient town?" Daniel asked.

"More like a small city, in fact."

"But where? *Why*?"

"I was never told exactly where. And as for its purpose? More about that in a moment. For the moment, let me say it was of such scope . . . had he continued to retain me, you would be sitting here with a multi-millionaire." He shrugged again. "So it goes."

"He stopped using you? Why?"

"Perhaps because, although I was well aware that he was not one to accept an underling asking a question more than once, I told him not once but twice that it would be almost impossible for me to meet my professional obligations to him without seeing the site in person. He also waved away my offers to assist in planning the transport of the huge quantities of materials, supplies, and equipment that would be required. In any case, a few days after I had turned over all the materials that he had requested, he arrived in person, thanked me cordially, paid me twice what I had quoted, and took his leave. Perhaps he had judged me insubordinate and decided to turn my work over to others. In any case, I never heard from him again."

"Never?" Daniel asked.

"I can tell you that it was clearly a manufacturing facility of some kind. But I couldn't figure it out beyond that, and I didn't dare ask. And in the decade since, I have never heard even a whisper about any such project. However, two nights later, when I returned from teaching, all my files and copies of the plans were gone—with no attempt having been made to conceal that the theft had taken place. I could only take it as a warning to keep silent."

"You hadn't made copies for your own records?"

"I usually do, but I had many lessons scheduled that week. In any case, you now know everything that I know. And I must add that having told you even this much may mean that my life is now in your hands. Especially given what you have told me about the fate of others who have been involved in . . . whatever you have now involved yourselves in."

Daniel replied, "Then we are in this together. Which means we'll protect you as one of our own."

Giselle shifted in her chair, and Daniel felt sure she was about to ask the same question that had been nagging at him.

He hated to forestall her but felt he needed to play the "man-to-man" card if Maier were going to tell them what they needed to know. He caught her eye, and she nodded.

He turned back to Maier. "If I may, Professor, five years ago I built a new head office to house my business operations in Geneva. It took thirty-seven months from my first meeting with the architect to the day we opened our doors." He spoke reluctantly, fearing this might be his only chance to push Maier further. "And it could never have been accomplished without a site study—details of the elevations, the geography and geology, photographs . . . So either you are a wizard who was able to traverse time and space to learn what you needed to know, or—"

Maier raised his eyebrows. "Or I am not telling the truth? Or the whole truth?" He turned to Felipe. "My boy, your friend pulls no punches."

"That may be," Felipe replied, "but I trusted him with my life eighteen years ago, and I would again today, just as I trust you. And so should you trust him. And Giselle as well, of course."

Maier sighed. "I had hoped that my evasions would escape you. However, if Diessen ever . . ." He paused. "Of course, I was given all I needed. Geology, geography, elevations . . ."

"Photographs?"

"Yes."

"So you were able to locate the site," Daniel pressed.

Maier pushed himself back from the table and pulled a large book from a shelf behind him. He opened it to a page that had been marked with a slip of paper. "After the theft, I reconstructed as much as I could from memory, triangulated what geographical information I had, and concluded that the compound was to be located here." He pointed at a section far to the west of Buenos Aires. At least halfway across the Gran Chaco, near the border between Paraguay and Argentina. "And I would not be surprised if Diessen owns enough land in that region that he could create his own country should he wish to. Barges could move materials and supplies from Buenos Aires via the Parana and Paraguay rivers close enough to the site that land transport would be feasible from that point on. And flights with personnel would be possible from Asunción."

"Asunción!" Daniel exclaimed. "How many hours away is that?" He turned to Felipe. "Have you ever heard anything about anything like this?"

"No," Felipe replied, "but Jo handles the logistics at Asunción and knows most of what's going on there."

For a moment, Daniel couldn't put his finger on why *Asunción* sent his heart into a cold flutter. He still couldn't entirely explain it, not rationally, but he realized the word had renewed his fear for his boys. A look in Giselle's direction told him her mind had latched on to the same detail: they both knew that students, including his sons, were taken to the Buenos Aires airport and then flown to Asunción. It was from there they'd supposedly been taken to this "summer camp" from which they could not be withdrawn without risking their expulsion. A camp far away enough that Claudia now feared for their safety.

"I must apologize, my friends," Maier said, rising to his feet. "But I need to get ready for teaching now."

Even though Daniel's initial impression had not changed— he still believed Maier was a man of integrity—he also had an inkling the professor was not telling them everything. His desire to end the session seemed spurred by something weightier than needing to prepare for his next class. His eyes, previously brimming with such humor and warmth, now fixated on loose items on his desk. *Perhaps*, Daniel thought, *it was not that Maier was purposefully withholding part of the truth. Perhaps new pieces of it were dawning on him even now.*

Either way, Daniel did not want to leave without hearing everything on his mind.

But when Maier glanced at his watch, Daniel acceded that they needed to leave him to his preparations. He thanked the professor for his help. Maier, a gentleman even when pressed for time, walked the three of them toward Felipe's car.

Before they reached it, however, Felipe stopped short. Perhaps it was the sight of golden sunlight scintillating off his red car that reminded him of a beautiful vista he wished to share with the even more beautiful girl at his side. "Giselle." He said it breathlessly, as though this were a matter whose importance vied with the mystery in Asunción they had merely been discussing. "Come with me to see the horses in the sunset light."

She looked to Daniel expectantly, and he nodded. There was no rush so great that his niece, after all she'd been through, should not steal an extra moment of happiness. For the moment, Daniel had no reason to doubt this was true.

As he stood with Maier, observing the happy couple who were observing a scene that appeared borrowed from a postcard, something occurred to him for the first time. Something he felt sure Maier had time to answer before getting back to his life as a professor.

"Tomas, if you don't mind the question," he started, "you haven't said much about any amenities for the residents. If this was to be its own community of sorts, for whatever reason, surely there would be all means of services planned for their needs?"

Maier still appeared lost deep in thoughts heavier than any pertaining to geology or the tango. Still, he nodded. Then glanced in Daniel's direction. "Yes, there were to be provisions established for families."

"Provisions . . . such as recreational facilities, perhaps?"

"Yes. Recreational facilities were planned. And a school as well."

"So there were entire families there? Even children?"

Maier nodded. "Even a rather rough area of scrub trees where children were taught camping skills."

Daniel's mind reeled. Was it possible?

Maier gave him a puzzled look. "What is it?"

"No!" Daniel shook his head as if to rid himself of his sudden terror.

"My friend . . ." Maier persisted.

"Tomas, it seems impossible, but I fear that my boys are there! That their stepfather let their school send them there! After promising their mother that he wouldn't! What *is* this place? Have you told me *everything*? Or are you in on whatever this is yourself?"

"No. Never. I would never align myself with Diessen again. Especially after what you've told me today. But . . ."

Daniel felt his terror turning to anger. "But I *sensed*, and now I know, that you haven't told us everything!"

"Felipe," Maier called. "Miss Faber, please come over here."

Felipe and Giselle gave the horses and the foal reluctant farewell pats and, arms around each other, came over to Maier and Daniel.

Looking somber, he seated them and Daniel at some benches under the trees but remained standing.

"Your visit today has added a piece to a puzzle I had wondered about in passing ever since my work with Diessens ended." He bent over and picked up Jaime's camera case. "I now believe this small sample is the missing piece that will solve the mystery of the huge shipments of phosphate gravel and perhaps the deaths you've told me about. Because phosphate gravel is a rich source of uranium—and as the world witnessed twice in the summer of 1945, uranium is what makes nuclear weapons possible. And China has huge stores of it—for sale, no doubt, to the highest bidder."

Daniel had to struggle for words, but finally managed, "Are you saying that the compound that *you* designed may be producing nuclear bombs?"

When Giselle shivered, Felipe put his arm around her, as if this was a long-familiar habit with them.

"I fear so," Maier said.

"But why?"

"I don't know. However, for no rational reason, or perhaps my brain is just tricking me, but the word that keeps coming to me right now is 'cottonwoods.' Sometimes also called poplars."

"Cottonwoods?" Daniel echoed.

"Yes, my friend. And in retrospect, in my mind's eye, I can clearly see the resemblance between the plans I did for Diessen and the original place of the Cottonwoods."

"I still don't understand."

His face was somber. "In Spanish, the word for cottonwoods is *los alamos*. Los Alamos." He seated himself heavily on one of the benches and lowered his head. "The Hiroshima bomb was an atomic bomb, but the Nagasaki bomb was a plutonium bomb. And the Gran Chaco is a lot like Los Alamos—remote, underdeveloped, and easy to secure."

Daniel could not bear to open his eyes. It was too much to take in. *Was this where they were now? How had Giselle's knock on his door that rainy night led to this?* It was beyond his comprehension.

"Yes," Maier finally said, "I fear that the compound may be a new Los Alamos. With all that implies. Because bombs are only developed to attack targets."

"And you think that Matthew and Michael are there?" Giselle burst out.

Felipe took her hand and looked around at all of them. "Then there's only one thing to do. We need to find out whether this is true and try to get them back."

***

"Felipe," Daniel said, "how soon can you organize a flyover so we can find out for ourselves what's going on there?"

Felipe did not hesitate. "If we leave here tomorrow morning, we'll be in Asunción while there's still plenty of daylight. Jo will have everything ready for us to take off again for the Gran Chaco region immediately." He glanced over at Giselle. "It'll go faster tonight if you can help me." Even under the circumstances, she couldn't help but smile. Daniel surprised himself by briefly smiling as well. Their happiness was the only bright spot in his world at the moment. The rest was terror for his boys, anxiety about Claudia, the certainty that she must never hear one word about this crisis, and the comfort of knowing that he had made a new friend in Tomas Maier.

His musings and his gnawing anxious thoughts were both interrupted when Giselle answered her phone. It wasn't unusual for her to receive a call; God knows, she had a much greater affinity for the phone than Daniel ever had. However, it was unusual for her face to harden as it did just then.

"What is it, Giselle?" he asked bluntly. He knew if he was going to get a clear answer out of her, he needed to do so right then. Already her eyes were welling up and searching out Felipe's for comfort. Looking dazedly from her new love interest to her uncle, Giselle hung up the phone without saying goodbye.

"What's wrong? What have you learned?" He looked steadily into her eyes, trying to keep her there with him.

"That was Claudia," Giselle said, not whispering but still speaking so quietly Daniel had to strain to hear her.

"Claudia? Okay. What did she say to you, Giselle?" He could feel his own disquiet rising through his efforts to stay strong for his niece. Suddenly his neck felt clammy, and his thoughts raced, but he had enough self-control that the only sign detectable to anyone else would have been the swallowing of a lump in his throat. And his voice may have come out marginally higher than he intended when he asked, "Is it about the boys?"

"It's Luciano," she said quickly, seeming to realize that her stupor had given Daniel the chance to imagine unbearable atrocities. "He escaped."

At the same time, Daniel and Felipe began to ask, "What do you mean 'escaped'?" and at the same time each man stopped speaking in deference to the other. Even only partially spoken, though, their question hung there.

"I mean he got away." Her voice had turned into an intense whisper. "Luciano attacked Guy—he's recovering now from a head wound—and he got away."

CHAPTER SIXTEEN

D aniel stepped from the plane on arrival in Asunción. Few international flights landed or took off from Asunción other than from other Latin American countries. Most of the air traffic was domestic and comprised small planes, many of which Daniel could see on the tarmac as his plane landed. He guessed from their age that few would pass a mechanical inspection in a more developed country. He grabbed his carry-on and walked toward the bus waiting to take passengers to the terminal. The flight was only half-full, sixteen passengers at most, so they soon arrived at the drop-off point.

The day was so muggy that humidity would have seeped into the bus no matter what, but this one had no air conditioning to prevent the space from feeling claustrophobically damp and heavy. Daniel felt the perspiration on his brow and soaking through his white shirt.

He took his passport from his jacket pocket in readiness to produce it at Immigration. Since General Stroessner had taken control of the country a short while earlier, in 1954, martial law had taken over. Visas now were necessary, even from neighboring South American countries; there was a vast network of paid government spies throughout the country, and a gathering of three or more people could give rise to charges of an illegal meeting. Rumors of commonplace physical tortures in Paraguay circulated throughout South America. Daniel had considered bringing his Smith

& Wesson, but Felipe had advised against it. A search of his bag by customs would be sure to uncover it, and the best, but by no means certain, outcome would be his immediate departure on a plane back to Buenos Aires.

In the shabby terminal, Daniel followed crudely painted signs toward Immigration. Buenos Aires was barely five hundred miles away, less than a three-hour flight in a two-propeller pre-war Douglas DC3, but culturally it was a world apart.

A surly immigration officer—who looked as if he hadn't shaved, let alone washed, in days—took his passport and rummaged through the pages to locate the visa. Daniel wondered whether the man could even read. Paraguay had one of the world's highest rates of illiteracy.

"Why are you coming to Paraguay?" the man asked, in Spanish but with the strong influence of the local Guarani language.

"I am meeting with a company in Asunción that has invited me to discuss possible business opportunities." Daniel took out the letter he had procured. The officer took his time reading the few lines, to the obvious annoyance of other arriving passengers. Halfway turning to face them, Daniel shrugged in vague apology.

"Where are you staying in Asunción?"

"At the Grand Hotel del Paraguay," Daniel said flatly.

The man scribbled something on a pad, stamped Daniel's passport, and thrust it back into his hand.

He walked into the baggage hall. There was no carousel. Instead, bags were wheeled in on a cart by two rail-thin laborers who formed a row on the ground of all the cases. Daniel could spot at least three plainclothes government agents, lingering at different vantage points, checking out arriving passengers. He headed toward the customs area.

"Open up your bag," a uniformed woman demanded.

He complied. Apart from a change of clothes and toiletries, he had nothing.

With a chalk mark on his bag indicating he had passed inspection, he walked toward the exit. Outside, he made his way to the head of a line of dirty cabs.

From gouges in the black leather of the back seat, bits of yellow foam rubber found their way to Daniel's navy trousers. The driver habitually shifted from first gear to fourth, always skipping second and third, which let Daniel know there was something wrong with the gearbox. To his horror, he saw the sort of hole in the windscreen made too familiar to him in his Mossad days: a bullet hole. His own window presented him a streaming view of broken pavement, mangy strays, graffiti on crumbling stone walls, children and their mothers begging in the streets, men lying on the sidewalks, legs stretched toward the road and faces covered by their sombreros, empty beer bottles at their sides. The journey from the airport to the hotel in downtown Asunción took no longer than fifteen minutes. "Thank God," Daniel said to himself.

The Grand Hotel del Paraguay soon came into view. Once the stately home of the Irish mistress of a former president, it had turned to commercial enterprise years ago. It was German owned, but so were most of the better hotels in Paraguay. With one person out of sixty rumored to be of German descent, there was no avoiding the influence in this country. General Stroessner, a son of a Bavarian brewer had a place in his heart for Germans, especially Nazis who could line his pockets in exchange for a safe sanctuary.

The man at the front desk greeted him with a starched, "How do you do, sir?" and requested his passport, which he promised would be returned the next day. After handing over the room key, he pointed to an elegant staircase at the end of the lobby. As Daniel went to pick up his bag, however, the man called out that he had a message for him.

Envelope in hand, Daniel looked around the deserted lobby. The fact that it had once been a grand colonial home shone through dimly, if at all. After years of neglected maintenance, paint was peeling off the walls, cracks spidered across the surface of many floor tiles, and at least a few light bulbs had burned out and simply been left to gather dust.

He passed a pair of open double doors and glanced inside at an elegant room with floral murals and ornate chandeliers. Nonetheless, the restaurant was outfitted in cheap, drab chairs and tables. The best he could say for it was that clean-looking white linens and china waited at each place for a customer. As he turned away from the ghost room toward the staircase, a boy appeared out of nowhere. He wore black trousers and an ironed, collared shirt, but his feet were bare. Daniel got glimpses of the blackened and calloused soles as the boy, carrying Daniel's bag, led the way to his room.

After he'd tipped the boy, Daniel looked around the sparse bedroom. One single bed, low on the marble floor. An armoire to the side with a broken full-length mirror on one of its doors. A desk, with lamp and telephone. The brown curtains were drawn, and when he opened them, he was relieved that he had a view of the garden. The window was closed. He opened it to let in some fresh air in the hope that it would mitigate the mustiness of the room. The bathroom was basic but adequate. Above the bed was a large, framed color photograph of General Stroessner, looking serious and glum in military uniform, his chest adorned with an array of bright medals. The customary trimmings of a military dictator.

Sitting on the bed, he read his message. It was from Drew Adams, whom Felipe had advised of Daniel's arrival. They made plans to meet for a drink in the hotel lobby.

A secret service agent, past or present, could always recognize another. Drew Adams was standing in the lobby, reading the sports section of a week-old *New York Times*. He was tanned, blond, and athletic in a crumpled off-white linen suit with a pale blue shirt and thin, knitted navy tie.

"Let's grab a couple of beers and go sit in the garden," Adams suggested, shaking Daniel's hand.

When they'd procured their beers, they found a bench set in the middle of the garden, next to a fountain that looked as if it hadn't worked for years. Both men could see advantages in this arrangement that would have been invisible and irrelevant to most people: with all the spies around, they could talk here. They may not have been able to speak freely in bars, but on this bench, they were far enough away from any trees that their chances of encountering hidden microphones were dashed.

"Felipe told me to be helpful to you," Adams announced softly. Daniel knew he was thinking you could never be too careful out here. Yes, they were a respectable distance from the trees, but for all they knew, recording devices were hidden in the flower beds too. Even more quietly, he continued, "But he gave me no indication about the purpose of your trip."

Sipping his beer, Daniel recognized the taste as German. *A Munich brew*, he thought.

"Thank you," Daniel answered at a corresponding low volume. "I certainly would appreciate your assistance. I need to know more about the Diessen Family. Who they are and what they do. Their company, Panto, and their landholdings here in Paraguay. I'm here to find my two sons, who I believe have been kidnapped. I believe Diessens are involved. Why, God knows."

Adams stared out at the broken fountain. He then placed his glass down on the ground to retrieve a pack of cigarettes from his pocket. Daniel shook his head when offered one.

Adams didn't speak again until he'd found his lighter, lit the cigarette, and had taken a deep drag.

"I will tell you what we know, but I must caution you for your own safety. These people are dangerous. In many respects they own Paraguay. Many believe that Stroessner is their puppet. The Diess—"

"What about you?" Daniel interrupted. "What do you believe?"

"I believe they have bought Stroessner, body and soul. The Diessens are originally from Stuttgart. They may even be related."

"Go on."

"They are domiciled in Argentina, but their business interests are spread throughout Latin America. They are big in Peru, Ecuador, Bolivia, Argentina, and Brazil, as well as Paraguay. The company is run by three brothers. Their children and grandchildren are involved at all levels in their operations. Most Americans wouldn't believe it, but our mafia is nothing compared to the Diessen Empire."

Daniel thought he already knew what they had there in Paraguay: they were major stockholders in two of the largest breweries. They owned the largest newspaper in the country, not that it had meaningful circulation in a country where half the population was illiterate. And they owned a radio station. He probably should have been less surprised when Adams warned him, "They own this very hotel. So everyone you come across here—the bar tender, the waiters, the people at the front desk—are all likely spies. Don't ever forget that."

"What about their land holdings? I am told that they have a huge estancia somewhere in the Chaco region."

"It's a complete mystery. Before the war, they bought an estancia there, maybe one hundred thousand acres, give or take. They expanded it through land grabs and some legitimate acquisitions. Their holding is now close to two million acres. Maybe more. It's believed to be the largest contiguous landholding in private hands in South America, maybe the world. To put this in perspective, their area is larger than Connecticut. Most of it is fenced, but it is also patrolled by their private militia."

"Their militia?" He chided himself for registering surprise at anything to do with these people. Of course they had a militia, one equipped with old surplus tanks and heavy weaponry, from how Adams told it.

Daniel wanted to know what they were hiding there. "Do they have oil? Gold? What's so valuable? It can't just be for cattle." He held back that he already knew about the fortress.

"I'm embarrassed to say we don't know. Imagine, the CIA has no idea and nor do we make any attempt to find out. It would be reasonably simple to have aerial surveillance, but whenever it's suggested, the powers at HQ in Langley refuse to authorize it."

"Weird."

"Very weird, I agree. But you must remember what it was like working with some of those jerks from your own days working with Mossad. Felipe told me of your background."

"You bet."

"Let me give you an idea of how puzzling it actually is. A year ago, soon after I was posted here, a woman called the embassy one evening. Apart from a security guard, I was the only one in the building at the time. It was the start of the July 4th Holiday weekend. The woman telephoned from a hotel here in town and urgently wanted to speak to someone. As I said, I was the only one, so I agreed to see her.

"She arrived within the hour, an attractive American woman, maybe late thirties, from Kansas. She had been a nurse in the United States and had met a Paraguayan doctor who was doing a residency at a Kansas hospital. Evidently, he was something of an idealist. They got married. They left the States, and he brought her back with him to Paraguay—not to Asunción, mind you, but to a village in the middle of nowhere. The village is about forty or fifty miles from Mariscal. He established an office in the village there to look after the local Guarani natives. He had learned their dialect. The Paraguayan government paid him a modest retainer and he got some financial assistance from certain foundations around the world. The wife served as his nurse, secretary, and general factotum."

Daniel listened attentively as Adams continued.

"One day, a jeep pulled up outside his office, and two armed men in commando outfits burst in and demanded to see the doctor. They told him that his services were needed immediately at the Diessen Compound. They would take him to treat the person in need, and then they would bring him back.

"She said they spoke Spanish but with a foreign accent. She thought it was maybe German, maybe Scandinavian, or even Dutch. She couldn't say. When her husband finished with the wound he was currently dressing, he put his things together, kissed his wife goodbye, and then sped off in the back of a jeep."

Adams's story seemed to end there, but Daniel knew it didn't. He was also relatively sure he knew what came next. "And she never saw him again?"

"The woman, as I said, is American. She had reported it to the local police, and they'd done nothing, so she had come to the embassy for help. When the ambassador returned after the Fourth of July holiday, I told him what had occurred."

"Then what happened?" Daniel worded and even intoned it as a question, but he was confident he knew what came next here as well.

"Daniel, nothing. I asked the ambassador a couple of times after that if there was anything we were doing about her story, and he basically told me to drop it. It was embarrassing to me when the woman reached out, because I had to fob her off. The last I heard, she had moved back to Kansas."

"How long ago was this, again?" Daniel asked, trying unsuccessfully to hide his disgust.

"About a year." Adams dropped his cigarette and then ground it to an ashy stain under his boot. From how vigorously he had taken his first drag from it, he had nursed it along through all the twists and turns.

"Is it worth reopening the discussion with the ambassador?" Daniel knew it was not. He knew it, but he had to ask all the same. He had to pursue any possible route to help for his boys.

"Impossible. Shortly after this happened, the ambassador's term of office here came to an end, and he has been transferred to the Philippines. The charges d'affaires too is no longer in Paraguay. He's now in Costa Rica. The new ambassador is totally unapproachable."

Daniel thought for a moment. "So, this village must be close to the Diessen estancia?"

"Yes and no. Remember, their estancia is the size of Connecticut. Maybe the perimeter of it is about fifty miles from Mariscal Estigarribia, but their compound could well be in the middle of the estancia itself. No one, as far as I know, has ever penetrated that perimeter. It's guarded like Fort Knox or the Pentagon."

"I'm going to take a look. Felipe has arranged it."

Adams was shaking his head before the final words made it from Daniel's mouth. "I told Felipe when he called last night—going anywhere near it is ill-advised. You just heard my story about the missing doctor. If they catch you, you may never be seen again. And what's more, how would you propose to get there?"

"What do you mean? You said it was three hundred and seventy-five miles by air. Felipe has arranged it. Some young man he knows is picking me up tomorrow morning to fly me up there. Actually, I'd have preferred to have driven up."

"You haven't studied the geography, obviously." There was a hint of annoyance in Adams's voice as he patted himself down to see what he'd done with his cigarettes. He could keep track of the intricate dealings of spies, criminal family dynasties, and corrupt governments, but he couldn't, for the life of him, remember where he'd tucked his cigarette pack five minutes earlier.

"No road will take you from Asunción to Mariscal," he said. "They're talking about building one, but they talk about plenty. Boqueron is Paraguay's largest region, with an area of about forty thousand square miles. There are barely any paved roads and no opportunities to gas up. There is a landing strip for planes in Mariscal, but fueling options there are also limited."

"So how do people get around?"

"They walk, cycle, ride horses. Very few cars for all the obvious reasons. It's an agricultural area, mainly cattle so there are a few tractors. Remember it's not like Argentina and Brazil. Things there are . . . rustic."

"But they do have a landing strip?" Daniel couldn't, or maybe wouldn't, see why this piece of information was so quickly dismissed. A landing strip meant planes. Planes meant people did come and go from this region, even if they had to take a horse-drawn wagon to their next destination.

"Yes, but how the hell are you going to hop a flight to Mariscal without attracting attention? Maybe three planes land there every day, at most. And if you do manage to get there, how are you going to get from that little crappy airport to the perimeter of the compound? Where are you going to get a truck or a motor bike? Would a motor bike even have a big enough gas tank to get you to the perimeter of the fortress and back again? And if you somehow dealt with all that and reached the perimeter of the compound, you must keep in mind that the perimeter is only that. The compound itself may be one hundred miles away still. Never mind that you'd then have to go through barbed wire fencing and armed guards to get inside."

Daniel sipped his beer, making no attempt to answer his companion's frustrated questions. Which was just as well because Adams wasn't finished.

"And, if you do manage to get through—and it's a million to one chance you would—what the hell are you going to accomplish there anyway?"

Daniel may not have figured out all the logistics, but he trusted Felipe. He had to trust Felipe. And Adams may have saddled him with a fearsome view of reality there in Paraguay, but he had also given Daniel critical pieces of information, and he felt the man thereby deserved the truth.

"Once we're inside," Daniel said clearly, "I'm going to save my sons."

CHAPTER SEVENTEEN

Emilio was the name of the pilot Felipe had told him about. It was also one of the only pieces of information about the young man Daniel had been given. He certainly didn't have a way of knowing what Felipe meant when he said Emilio would be Daniel's kind of guy. This was one of so many areas where he placed his trust in Felipe—blindly and without concern that Felipe might one day let him down.

"This is perfect weather for flying," was the first thing Emilio said when Daniel met him on the tarmac, such as it were, beside his plane. "You bring the money?"

"Yes, of course," Daniel replied, smiling. Emilio *was* his type of guy. He could see the cigarette pack congesting the pocket of the young man's clean, white button-up. None fell out as Emilio checked over the two-engine plane.

From where he stood, Daniel had a clear view of the one runway, corrugated iron hangar, and parked planes; what he didn't see was any other person. A couple potholes in the runway looked menacing, as though they could easily burst a tire.

"Do you have to notify anyone that we're taking off?" Daniel asked.

"There's no control desk, if that's what you mean. There's also no runway lighting. That's why I'd like to be back before it gets dark."

"What about those potholes over there?"

"Don't worry about them. I know where they are." Emilio smiled again. "Climb aboard."

Daniel, in the copilot's seat, fastened his seat belt as Emilio started the engines. Daniel closed his window against the noise and the dry heat outside. It was a four-seater plane, provided no one weighed more than 175 pounds or had a waist size greater than thirty-six inches.

Emilio maneuvered the plane across the patchy grass toward the runway. He looked across at Daniel. "Don't be nervous. I fly this beauty three or four times every week. Relax and enjoy the flight."

Daniel nodded. "I'll try."

"These are great planes. Argentinean, Dinfia. We can get up to one hundred fifty miles per hour. We should arrive in Mariscal in about two and a half hours. Around ten thirty with luck. I'm going to fly this bird at about ten thousand feet, so you'll have a view of the landscape all the way. Unfortunately, you won't find it all that interesting. We fly over the most boring area in the whole of Latin America."

Daniel watched, holding his breath as Emilio accelerated down the runway, skillfully steering the plane around potholes.

The noise of the engines rendered it impossible to carry on a conversation, so Daniel contented himself with looking out of the window at the scenery. Emilio wasn't wrong. There was little to see. Endless miles of a deserted region, a few small streams but mostly dry riverbeds. Short trees, brushwood, cactus dunes, and some small hills. They flew over two or three large cattle farms. He reached to grab the binoculars from behind and saw the occasional Paraguayan cowboy.

Emilio shouted above the engines, "This area, the Chaco, is known as the Green Inferno. It's really desert. We're passing through the Tropic of Capricorn. There is hardly any rainfall here this time of the year. It's all scrubland."

"I see a few buildings down below to the left. What are those?"

"Simple wood hovels, for the cowboys. You notice those rusty corrugated iron roofs? They have those to accumulate rain, when it comes. In about twenty minutes, we will pass over one of the Mennonite communities. They've been here since the twenties. Good people. They say there is oil here, but no one has bothered to explore for it."

"What is that sweet smell?" Daniel asked.

"See those trees over there to the right? That's their bark you smell. They're some of the only trees that can survive in this area. If you were to touch one, it would be like touching leather."

After several minutes, Daniel was relieved to hear Emilio announce they were approaching the airfield and would soon be on the ground.

Emilio indicated that they would be veering to the left as they began the descent. He picked out two runways, several hangars, and what purported to be a modest control tower. As they descended, Daniel saw several men aimlessly walking outside one of the hangars but just one large, parked helicopter.

After the plane came to a complete stop at the end of the runway, Emilio waited for one of the men to drive over in a jeep to lead their plane toward a space earmarked for them. Having done so, the man stood waiting while Emilio killed the engines.

"*Buenos dias, Signor Emilio. Como estas?* Welcome to Mariscal."

"Thank you, Manu." Emilio looked at his watch. "I'm going to wait here while my friend attends to some business. Please would you refuel the plane?"

"Of course, Signor Emilio. No problem."

Daniel turned to look across the runway at Felipe's helicopter, which he had flown on from Buenos Aires with the photographers who would assist them, but his attention was drawn to a black cargo aircraft without any markings. It was overhead but beginning its descent.

Noting Daniel's interest, Emilio said, "It's a McDonnell Douglas. But the absence of markings is strange. I asked Manu, here, about it. He told me that plane flies over here about once every two weeks, probably lands at the compound, takes off again after a couple of hours."

"Interesting."

"And one other thing that was strange. Manu took a photograph of the plane one time, and he must have been spotted from the air with the camera because, within the hour, two soldiers drove over in military jeeps and confiscated his camera. He tried to reason with them, but they didn't speak any Spanish . . . just a language he didn't understand."

Daniel had many more questions about the unmarked McDonnell Douglas, but there was no time to ask them. Nodding toward the jeep, Emilio told Daniel, "Manu will take you to join your friend in the helicopter." As Daniel stood to deboard the plane, Emilio cleared his throat to get his passenger's attention.

"Daniel?" Emilio said, his voice much graver than it had been at any point during the flight. "Good luck."

Manu brought the jeep to a stop by the helicopter. Even though it hadn't been long at all since he'd last seen Felipe, Daniel felt a rush of relief upon seeing his friend alight from the shining, bulbous-looking copter. The first thing Daniel said to Felipe, upon joining him on the ground, was, "How come you got a helicopter and not a plane?"

"The Argentinean air force has a number of long-range Sikorski helicopters," his friend answered. "These choppers are ideal for aerial photography. They are used mostly for search and rescue operations. The doors open wide so a photographer can stand, strapped to the doorway of course, and lean out. The helicopters have stabilizers so there is little vibration. Aerial photographers dread vibration."

"Felipe, how the hell did you get your hands on an Argentinean air force helicopter, with a pilot, to fly into Paraguayan airspace without getting shot at and brought down?" He couldn't help comparing his worried tone to Adams's from the previous day.

Felipe smiled.

"Daniel, there is so much unrest in Argentina at the moment. The Perón regime is in trouble. The anti-Peronists are becoming more and more vocal. There are a lot of disgruntled people in the Argentinean air force. The anti-Peronists need a considerable amount of money for propaganda." He nodded toward the plane. "The photographers are ready for us to take off. We are paying them by the hour, so don't let's waste time."

"I sure as hell agree to that."

"We will be taking regular still photographs as well as 16 mm moving film."

"Sounds great, Felipe, but you still invaded Paraguayan airspace. Suppose they send up a fighter plane to shoot down our helicopter. This could become a serious international incident." Daniel didn't need to mention that five people had been killed already. He knew they were both thinking of it.

"That is true. I cannot argue against it. It's a calculated risk I thought was worth taking. It's unlikely that the Paraguayans have combat planes in this area. Their aircraft are all in Asunción. We should be safely back into Argentinean airspace before the Paraguayans get wind of what we're doing—let alone confront our chopper."

"Exactly how quick can we be?" Daniel asked.

"We should be able to get the photographs and drop you back off within forty-five minutes."

Daniel paused. "Why don't I pay off my pilot now and come back with you?"

Now it was Felipe's turn to pause.

"If you don't show up at the hotel to check out in the normal way, they would notify the police and God knows who else. It would look very suspicious, especially as you've probably left clothes and stuff there. If you're going to need a second trip, we need to keep this one as tidy as possible."

Daniel nodded. "I hope you've come clean with the photographers that this is a risky operation. I doubt they've had an assignment quite like this before."

"Of course I have. And believe me. They'll earn more for this one day than they otherwise would in six months."

Felipe explained to Daniel that the photographers were delighted they were using a helicopter and not a plane. With its secure straps and sliding platforms, they could work as far as three feet from the doors. While Daniel still worried about them—being connected to the deaths of five strangers would do that to a person—he felt comforted by their expertise. If what Felipe said was accurate, they should experience no hiccups once up in the air.

Perhaps Felipe sensed how concerned Daniel was getting for the innocent bystanders on this mission of theirs, because he suddenly gestured toward two men milling about the plane. "Look, Daniel. The crew have changed out of their uniforms into everyday shirts and shorts. Just in case, somehow, God forbid, we do get shot down."

Felipe's tone sounded as calming as a cool washrag against the forehead of a feverish child, but his words themselves sent a chill through Daniel. *Just in case . . . we get shot down.*

"Jesus."

Felipe said, "They've also covered up the Argentinean markings on the fuselage." Daniel hardly knew what to make of this news, whether he should classify it as a sign of how prepared they were or an omen that meant the dangers ahead were far more intense than they once imagined. When he hadn't responded for a long enough time that it bordered on awkward silence, Felipe said, "We better get aboard. Just one thing I must tell you . . . There will be two other men on board the chopper."

"Who, for God's sake? And why didn't you tell me before now."

While Daniel remained as convinced as ever that he could trust Felipe with his life, his sense of foreboding was increasing from a murmur to a roar. But what could he do with his misgivings? This was the only way he knew to gain insight into what was happening with his sons. He would voice no more objections to any path that led to them.

In fact, he had moved on so completely within that split second that it almost startled him when Felipe answered his question. "These men have rifles and machine guns." Felipe's eyes trailed down from the unmarked plane to the medley of rocks he was rearranging with the toe of his boot. Then he repeated a phrase he hoped, in vain, would somehow assuage both Daniel and himself. "Just in case."

"Shit," Daniel muttered.

The sky was clear, no clouds and just a slight breeze. Maybe 80 degrees, a little muggy. "These weather conditions are good, yes?" Daniel asked one of the pilots.

"Yes, we're lucky."

Fernando, the camera team's boss went to go over his needs again with the captain in the cockpit. They were straightforward. As long as there was no imminent threat of attack from the ground, the photographers needed to fly as low as possible, one hundred feet would be ideal. "If this could be arranged," Fernando said, "their telescopic lenses would do the rest."

"How long you reckon you need?" the captain asked.

"Five to ten minutes," Fernando answered with confidence.

"Just one thing," the captain said, stopping Ferando as he moved to rejoin his crew. "We head out and make our way back here as fast as we can. The *second* you've got your shots."

"Understood."

With that, Fernando rejoined the other photographers, where he conveyed instructions in a tone of hushed professionalism. His tanned, muscular hands formed efficient gestures. Daniel and Felipe relaxed in their seats behind the two pilots. Then, several stomach-churning seconds later, they were in the air.

Daniel and Felipe were seated behind the two pilots. Felipe opened his backpack and took out his binoculars. In the row behind, sat Fernando and his wife, the two lead photographers on the mission, and behind them their assistants. The two soldiers sat at the back, each by a window, with their loaded rifles and sub-machine guns placed on the adjacent empty seats.

The pilot passed them headsets, with microphones attached, so they could communicate more easily over the noise of the chopper's engines. Felipe turned around and saw that the others had already put earplugs in their ears as instructed by the copilot.

"You should tell the camera guys to get themselves ready now. And the soldiers in the back, don't forget them," the pilot added.

"God forbid we need their services," Daniel. He looked out of the window. Desolate and deserted arid land.

Felipe turned around and lifted himself a few inches from his seat and caught the attention of the two soldiers. He gave them a signal that they should keep their eyes focused and have their weapons at the ready but to hold off fire unless they were attacked.

Daniel looked across at the camera team. They were busy putting their equipment together. He admired their enthusiasm and professionalism. They strapped safety harnesses around their waists and held the bolts to secure themselves to the round steel hooks at the chopper's two doors.

"Listen to me all the time," the pilot announced.

"Of course," Daniel replied. Seconds later, he turned to give Felipe a thumbs up.

The pilot continued. "We are descending to three hundred feet. Your camera team should position themselves now at the two front doors which my colleague will open. They should make sure their harnesses are secure."

Felipe relayed the instructions to Fernando and the four team members stood and walked to the front. The copilot slid open the two front wide doors. The pilot turned around and gave out a second signal to the soldiers to open the rear two doors and secure themselves."

With the four doors open, the air inside the chopper became muggy, but fortunately the sky was clear and there was little wind. The conditions for good photography were ideal.

"We are approaching the compound in, I guess three or four minutes," Daniel surmised. He held Felipe's binoculars to his eyes.

The copilot looked over his shoulder and shouted to Felipe, "We are on track."

"Okay, we're over the wall now," Felipe shouted, his voice reflecting his excitement. The photographers were already focusing their cameras on the ground below, two photographers standing on each of the extension platforms. And, at the back, the security guards had their rifles at their side.

"We're down to two hundred feet. We see a large fortress ahead of us. At this speed we should be over it in about three minutes," the pilot shouted.

"Are there any other planes in the air? Are we being trailed?" Daniel shouted back.

"No, not so far."

The helicopter swooped down. There was clear and uninterrupted vision ahead, but that meant that they could easily be seen too. Daniel crossed his fingers that the operation could be wrapped up quickly before anyone on the ground could launch a missile or even worse a fighter plane. The photographers leaned far out in the open air, the sleeves of their shirts flapping in the wind.

Through a window Felipe focused his binoculars on the fortress. An ugly solid concrete building. Huge. The ugliness of the building was mitigated only marginally by the landscaping with a well-manicured lawn, tennis courts and swimming pool. Felipe had a clear view of twenty or thirty people, neatly dressed, relaxing, and enjoying a comfortable afternoon in the outdoors.

The chopper descended further, maybe to a little over one hundred feet. The noise of its propellers must have been deafening to those on the ground who ran en masse inside the building. In all likelihood, the sight of the two security guards with rifles filled them with surprised panic.

Felipe, from his position outside on the platform, turned to face the pilot and waved his hand and outstretched fingers clockwise above his head. The pilot beckoned to them to come back inside.

The copilot left the cockpit to help them unlock their harnesses and bring in their equipment. Meanwhile, the pilot accelerated and began the turn and ascent to a normal flight altitude.

"We should have some excellent photographs. We have really powerful lenses."

Within a little over ten minutes, the helicopter hovered over the tarmac back at Mariscal. When barely three feet off the ground, Daniel jumped out, and Mano and Emilio drove over to pick him up and drive him back to the small plane a few hundred yards away.

Daniel turned to look back at the helicopter as it started its ascent and through the window Felipe waved and gave him a thumbs up.

"Hell. Jumping off the helicopter wasn't the best thing to do. My leg is killing me."

CHAPTER EIGHTEEN

B y the grace of God—and some expert maneuvering on the part of his pilot—Daniel arrived back in Asunción safely. The moment he reached his shabby hotel room, he called Giselle.

"I have landed in Asunción, and I'm leaving for Buenos Aires right away. So is Felipe—he's returning with the photographers in his helicopter. When we arrive, Felipe will arrange for a technician to do a rush processing job on the reels and rolls of film we got. As soon as I arrive, I will come pick you up so that you can view the footage and images with us."

"Of course," Giselle said softly. He was not able to read the emotion behind her quiet tone.

"Is there any more word on Guy?" Daniel asked. "How is he doing?"

Giselle's voice found its volume as she answered, "He's in bed resting. He doesn't seem to have gotten better, but he's no worse, at least."

"And Claudia?"

Giselle's voice was on a roller coaster—down, up, then down again as she nearly whispered, "She's not doing well." She was so quiet Daniel might have assumed that Claudia was hovering nearby at that very moment, but he thought it was more likely his niece was speaking softly out of a fear all her own. "She's in such a panic about the boys, thinking they're still at that compound. She believes they're in trouble, and there's nothing she can do."

"I believe they are too, Giselle," Daniel replied. "But there is something we can do about it."

* * *

Back in Buenos Aires, Felipe had arranged for a car to take Daniel to his apartment, where Giselle was waiting. Felipe had said that he would see the initial images as they became available, and then, when Daniel arrived with Giselle, the three of them would review the remaining evidence of the compound together.

At the apartment, Giselle was ready except for slipping on her pearly beach-colored flats and applying a final coat of lip gloss. With these things taken care of, she hurried to join Daniel in the black Chevrolet idling in the building's front circular drive.

The two of them took their seats as the driver and his colleague threw their cigarettes onto the ground and stamped on them before getting into the car.

"Where are we going?" Daniel asked the driver.

"Signor Martinez is waiting for you at our barracks."

"Barracks?" Daniel asked.

There was no answer.

Within a half hour, they approached the barrier at the entrance to the military base. The driver flashed the lights five times. An armed sentry walked toward the driver's door. The driver lowered his window. With a salute, the sentry raised the barrier.

Steering the Chevrolet around a parade ground and between an alley of barracks and various buildings, he came to an abrupt halt outside the only building with its lights on.

At the sound of the car's approach, Felipe exploded out of the building. The driver was still shifting the Chevy into park when Giselle flew from it, rushing toward Felipe.

Daniel watched his niece throw her arms around her beau. He watched Felipe briefly get so swept up in the moment that he lifted her off the ground and whirled her, as a father sometimes will to the squealing delight of a small child. Just as quickly, though, Felipe seemed to remember himself. He set her down and took a step away from her, glancing toward the car that Daniel was just exiting. He considered telling them they needn't be formal on his account. He could hardly believe the bright spot their burgeoning romance was in all this gloom.

The photographers and their assistants had broad grins as they scurried past Daniel toward their parked vehicles to drive home. They'd had a long but profitable day.

Coming up to Felipe, Daniel said, "So tell me, what did you see from the photographs?"

"Daniel, it's amazing. They have practically a village within that compound. A large building that looks like a hotel or an apartment building, tennis courts, swimming pool, even a couple of tanks, countless jeeps and armored vehicles, a helicopter, an aircraft hangar. We couldn't see what was in the hangar. There's a runway and a control tower."

"My God. A fortress. It's a pity we couldn't see this ourselves from the helicopter."

"You're not kidding, but at least we have it on film. There was even a tennis match going on. They even had bleachers. Perhaps a couple of dozen spectators. When they looked up and heard us coming, they seemed bewildered. Some were dumbstruck and others jumped up from their seats and ran inside the building."

"Incredible."

"We have photographs of several anti-aircraft guns, but they had been covered up with tarpaulins, so we thankfully didn't have to contend with that danger."

"I'm amazed that we didn't encounter problems sooner than we did."

"We were flying low enough to avoid being picked up on radar for most of the time. The results will amaze you. The technicians are setting up the screening room to show you everything."

Daniel looked across at Giselle, who was shivering cold. She wore a flower-print dress with ruffled cap sleeves that fell like flower petals over her shoulders. Clearly had the intended effect on Felipe, who could not stop glancing at her. However, sensing her shivering beside him, he put his arm around her.

"What is this place?" Daniel asked.

It took Felipe a moment to return from Giselle's touch to the conversation.

"It's a photo lab used by the military to keep a track on all their reconnaissance work, but it's managed by a civilian. I'll introduce you to him when we go inside. It was good we used a helicopter, you know. Thankfully, they brought gyrostabilizers that they mounted to the cameras to reduce unavoidable camera movement when we hit bumps." Felipe turned in the direction of the lab, guiding Giselle gently by the shoulders. Daniel followed him. "They told me that they were shooting at a high shutter speed, maybe 1/1000th of a second and that too helped to prevent bumps from ruining the shots."

Daniel nodded, duly impressed by the photographers' professionalism in such extreme circumstances, but worried still. "Do you really think we'll have enough photographs?"

"Be prepared for what you're about to see. Come on, let's go in."

Signor Pereira, the owner, met them at the door and, after introductions, led them into the screening room. "Please make yourself at home. There's coffee and sandwiches in the kitchen. They're from the canteen here at the barracks. I'm sure you've had better, but please help yourself."

"Thank you, Signor Pereira," Felipe said. "You are most helpful."

"Not at all. Business has been bad. I am glad to have this opportunity of making a few extra dollars. When we're ready we can play the film you took, and we can pin on the walls some of the still photographs."

Felipe took Giselle's hand. "Are you tired?"

"Yes, very. It's been a long day. My goodness, it's three o'clock in the morning."

"It's all the hanging about that makes one tired. You'll soon wake up when you see the photographs."

The conference room was divided into two parts. One half was furnished with a long glass-top table surrounded by twelve leather and chrome seats. The other part served as the screening room with two rows of six velvet movie theater seats. On the cork walls that lined the room were black and white photographs pinned haphazardly. Giselle began her inspection at the nearest wall.

"Seems to me that Signor Pereira makes his money photographing nudes and making porn movies," she said with a smile. "Did you know that?"

"Well, I half expected so," Felipe replied as he stood next to her, admiring the stills.

Signor Pereira came out of the kitchen. "We're ready for you," he announced.

Felipe and Daniel took their seats side by side at the conference table while Giselle stole away to the kitchen for refreshments.

"We have about five hundred still photographs to show you and we can run the 16 mm afterward," Signor Pereira said.

"Daniel, we have something big here," Felipe reiterated. "Be prepared for a shock."

"If you say that once again, I'll deck you."

Felipe ignored him. "First, I want you to scan these photographs." Felipe pointed at the pile on the table and those on the walls. Daniel greedily took the mug of coffee and sandwich that Giselle placed in front of him. They watched in silence, studying Daniel's reaction, as he flipped through the pile, occasionally pausing over one for a few seconds.

"Okay, now what?"

Felipe called for Signor Pereira to start the projector and turn off the lights. They moved into the other part of the room. Daniel sat in the center of the front row, Giselle and Felipe took the two end seats in the row behind. It felt to Daniel distinctly as though he were waiting for a summertime blockbuster movie to begin.

Giselle's and Felipe's eyes focused on Daniel's reaction rather than on the screen. At first, he did not seem to manifest much interest, but he sat up and moved his head forward when the images of the building and the lawn came into view. He edged forward in his seat, his eyes fixed to the screen.

The film revealed a full-fledged weapons plant resembling Los Alamos, an airfield, and a residential complex with an area clearly intended for children, though none were visible. The next sequence focused on the area around a grand swimming pool . . . including unmistakable shots of—

Daniel screamed. And either his scream echoed, or his own terrified caterwaul was joined by Giselle's. For a moment, he could not tell the difference.

There, lounging by the pool as though whiling away a peaceful weekend, were Adolf Hitler and Eva Braun, alive and apparently thriving. They were surrounded by children.

"My boys . . ." Daniel could not bring himself to say the rest, but he knew they were all parsing this information to reach the same conclusion: some of these were clearly the children of Hitler and Eva, but many of them were not. The children formed such a mob that individual faces could not be made out, but Daniel felt certain his and Claudia's sons were among them.

"And look at the man sitting with Hitler," Giselle shouted. "That looks like Mengele."

Daniel stood, his body trembling, his hands shaking uncontrollably, tears flowing down his face. Giselle crossed the room to hug him. With her face brushing his, they held each other tightly. They then broke away in silence, their faces awash in their own and the other's tears. Felipe and Signor Pereira looked on in an embarrassed silence.

It was a couple minutes before uncle and niece dropped their arms to their sides.

"Imagine that monster is still alive," Daniel said, "living the life of the happy family man while he destroyed the lives of millions of innocent families, including my own. And the world all thought that he and that bitch had committed suicide in that fucking bunker. How the world was taken in."

"And maybe that was Mengele too?" Giselle again pointed out.

"That's the swine who performed those experiments on twins," Felipe said. "But we can't be so sure about that. I haven't seen too many photographs of Mengele to know one way or another, but that was certainly Hitler and Eva Braun."

Giselle watched Daniel as he slumped back into his seat, tears continuing to fall as he buried his head in his hands. "My God, what have we uncovered, Giselle? Who would have thought it would have led to this? And what do we do now?"

Felipe stepped away from where he had been standing and turned to face Signor Pereira.

"What you have just seen is to remain confidential, signor. You are not to breathe a word of this to any living soul. Is that understood? I will pay you an additional five thousand dollars tomorrow morning in return for your silence." He spoke firmly. "And if you remain silent until Signor Lavy allows you to discuss this with the press, or whoever, maybe in another few weeks, I'll see you receive a much larger figure. The sort of figure that may mean you never have to work again." Felipe looked at Daniel. "Is that okay with you?"

"Yes, of course." Daniel faced Signor Pereira and spoke in a manner less forceful and intimidating than Felipe's. "Signor, you have been very kind, gracious, and enormously helpful. What Felipe has offered you has my agreement. When this news breaks, and it will soon enough, be assured I will reward you handsomely. Very handsomely. But, if you should disclose any of what you have seen or heard just now, not one dime more. Do you understand?"

"I understand, Signor Lavy," he replied softly. "You can trust me. I will not let you down."

"Now, one more thing Signor. I want another set of prints as soon as possible and another copy of the film. I need them by noon. Okay?"

"Yes, you will have them."

Daniel sat down again. "I need to think."

"We all do," Giselle replied softly.

Daniel closed his eyes. His heart was beating fast. Since he'd given up smoking, he no longer carried his cigarette case. Now he missed it; he would've liked nothing more in this moment than to light one and allow his troubled thoughts to vanish into the curls of smoke.

CHAPTER NINETEEN

"We could hold a press conference and show the world what we have," Daniel was saying, "or head straight from here to the United States and show it to the president. This is a major historical event, to put it mildly." He, his niece, and Felipe were gathered back around the glass top conference room table.

The others nodded. "But how will that bring back your boys?" Giselle asked, wiping away her tears.

"We need to do something immediately before this information leaks. And it will assuredly leak. We need to rescue not just my boys but all the children."

"What do you propose?" Felipe asked.

"I'm going to do my best to get a meeting with the president of the United States. And if he doesn't want to do something about this, I'll go to London to see Harold Macmillan, or to Paris to see De Gaulle. After all, I served with both the RAF and the Free French just a few years ago, Goddammit."

"How are you going to get a meeting with the president, for goodness sake?" Felipe asked. On the table, he fanned out the photographs Daniel had requested.

"Listen, Felipe, I have friends in the US who owe me. We should all go back to your apartment right now. We'll get busy on the phone to the United States, and we'll charter a plane to fly us to DC tonight. Tell Pereira to come to the apartment and we'll pay him straight away. Keep him sweet. Okay?"

Daniel was back at the helm. All business, once again. Felipe had to admit, he liked seeing Daniel this way. It made him feel much more confident that everything would—somehow—work out in the end.

Back at the apartment, Giselle headed straight for her room like a commander in the armed forces striding toward the front of his troops. She immediately set on her mission of arranging for a charter plane to fly them to Miami that afternoon and for a second plane to take them from Miami to Washington, DC. After approximately two hours of speaking in assertive, even aggressive, tones to a spate of people, each of whom eventually agreed that what she wanted could be done—even on such short notice—she allowed herself a steamy shower.

Meanwhile, Daniel was busy on another line. Geneva was four hours ahead of Buenos Aires. He'd be able to reach, his personal assistant, Madame Coty.

"Good morning, Madame Coty. Please help me. I'm in a mad rush. I need to speak urgently with David Bass. You have all his telephone numbers—Cleveland, Washington, and Palm Beach. I'll stay on the line while you find them. Thank you."

David Bass was one of the few American Jews who had a real "in" with the president. He'd made his millions in real estate and convenience stores, and he'd devoted most of his life and resources to philanthropy in the United States and throughout the world. Along the way, he'd become involved in politics, majorly contributing to both political parties at various junctures. He believed in hedging his bets. He and the president had been golf and bridge buddies for decades. In addition to serving with Bass on the boards of two charities, Daniel had run into the man at a number of high-brow functions over the years.

"David," he said with relief as soon as the call went through. "It's Daniel Lavy. I'm sorry to disturb you so early in Florida, but what I have to discuss cannot wait a moment longer."

David Bass was a convivial man but nonetheless taken aback at receiving a call so early in the morning.

"What is it, Daniel? It has to be important for you to telephone me at barely seven o'clock. Where are you?"

"I'm in Argentina. I need your help. I must see the president within the next twenty-four hours. What I must discuss with him is of paramount importance. Believe me, David, this is something that is so big, so monumental, it will blow your mind and the minds of everyone in the world."

"Daniel, slow down. What could possibly be that important?"

"I cannot discuss this on the telephone. My assistant is trying to charter a plane for us to fly out from Buenos sometime today to Miami. I know you're in Palm Beach right now. We can fly there to discuss it face to face. But, in the meantime, please, I beseech you to speak to the president and get me an appointment with him. It has to be immediate. If the president is in the United States, I can meet him tomorrow. I only need a half-hour."

"Daniel, are you out of your mind? Do you think it's that easy to arrange a meeting with the president of the United States, especially on such short notice?"

Daniel heard the uptick of impatience in Bass's voice and knew it was time to turn on the pressure. He drew a long breath. "David, I'm going to give it to you straight. If I can't get a meeting with the president, I will fly to London and meet with the prime minister, Harold Macmillan, and have my discussion with him. Don't think I can't get to him. And believe me when I tell you the president would be livid to discover he'd been scooped. When he wants to know why he wasn't briefed on this matter first, your name will come up, and it will spell the end of your friendship with him."

Bass was not used to being spoken to in this way, nor had Daniel expected that he would have to resort to such a tone to address anyone as universally respected and admired as David Bass.

There was a long pause. Daniel was steaming. It had been a long night and his nerves were fraught. With his mind in turmoil, he had neither the patience nor the temperament to pussy-foot around the issues with anyone. He waited for a response. He knew the power of silence, and right now, David wielded it like a knife.

"If you will not discuss this on the telephone, let me know what time you will be arriving in Palm Beach, and I will meet you at the airport. You can tell me then what this is all about. *Then* I will decide if this is a matter which I am willing to call the president about. Got it?"

"As soon as I know when we will be leaving Buenos Aires, I'll call you. Goodbye . . . and thank you, David."

Daniel let out a long breath to decompress as soon as he'd hung up. *Where the hell had he gotten the balls to speak to David Bass like that?* He wandered into the living room, where he found a freshly showered, alert-looking Giselle.

"How are you doing?" he asked.

"I spoke to an air charter company," she replied. "They are calling me back after nine o'clock. They think they can have a plane that can leave at five this afternoon that will arrive in Miami around three in the morning. They'll let me know the cost when they call back."

"Tell them that we may need to fly to Palm Beach, assuming that we don't first need to clear customs and immigration in Miami. Ask them about that."

"I have it taken care of," she said matter-of-factly. "Have you been able to arrange a meeting with the president?"

"Not yet." Daniel explained the situation to her: how high David Bass's threshold for important news was, how they would have to prove themselves worthy of a meeting in Palm Beach before heading up to DC. "But Giselle," he started. "We will get our meeting. I still want you to go ahead and arrange our flight to Washington—"

"I have it taken care of it," Giselle repeated. And he could have been mistaken, but Daniel could've sworn she meant more than just information about customs or a chartered flight to Washington, DC. Something in her tone said, *Whatever you need to accomplish this mission—short of warfare—I have it covered.*

"I'll call Felipe at nine to see how it's going over at the lab with the copies," she said.

"Do you want to have some breakfast?"

"No thanks. I'd rather shower and change and just relax. I'm pretty drained."

"Tell me when you have some news."

He sat down in an armchair and fought unsuccessfully to stay awake. Only Giselle shaking his shoulders woke him up. Felipe stood beside her clutching a plain tan box, barely wider than a shoebox. Daniel spotted the edge of a negative peeking out from the side.

"Daniel, there's news," Giselle said. "We have a plane that will leave at seven tonight, not at five, which arrives in Palm Beach at six tomorrow morning. We can clear customs and immigration in Palm Beach. They're used to private planes flying in from South America. We could take another chartered flight from Palm Beach to Washington— I have one on standby. I have no idea when we'll be ready to leave Palm Beach. We need to pay for the plane to Florida now to complete the booking. I've given them your Diners Club card to keep on file. Okay?"

"Yes, of course. I'll call David Bass back and see how early he's prepared to meet with us. He's an early riser. We'll then need a hotel in DC."

"Listen," Felipe ordered, "don't let that box of photographs, the negatives, and the film out of your sight."

Giselle gave him a sober nod. "I'll get us a hotel in DC. Any preferences?"

"Something with a bed," Daniel said between yawns. "It's all we'll need. I have a feeling these will be exhausting days for us."

"We should leave here at five o'clock. I'll work on the hotel reservations."

"Thank you, Giselle, you're doing a great job."

Moments later, Daniel was on the phone again. "David, our plane leaves here at seven this evening. We should land at Palm Beach around six o'clock tomorrow morning. We have a plane on standby to leave from there to DC. When can you and I meet?"

"I'll be at the airport to meet you at seven. Believe me, Daniel, this had better be good. I've cancelled a game of golf with the chairman of IBM for this."

Bass uncharacteristically slammed down the phone before Daniel could respond. This didn't stop him from responding in his mind: *Fuck you and your golf with the chairman. You will rue the day if you can't deliver a meeting with the president.* Another part of his mind was already preparing for what he would do if it happened, taking mental notes of the things he would say to Clarissa Eden, the wife of Macmillan's predecessor who he felt could be helpful in securing a meeting with the prime minister.

How fortuitous that he had met Clarissa during the war, and how charmed he'd been by her beauty, her spontaneous wit, and her keen thoughts. They had remained in touch since the war, and he'd been thrilled to later run into her at a dinner party where she introduced him to her husband; they made an elegant couple. Eden was then prime minister.

He was packing, and still running through conversation starters with Clarissa in his thoughts, when Giselle knocked at his open bedroom door. Her face advertised pressing business. She didn't even let him greet her before saying, "We must invite Claudia to go with us."

"Giselle, she needs to be here in case Luciano—"

"Luciano is no longer our main concern, and I mean no offense, but you know it's true. It's not just for her own good, Daniel. She needs to be there for when we do get that meeting with the president. She can tell him things about Luciano and his involvement with the compound that we can't."

Daniel steadied himself for a moment, looking at his niece in all her quiet confidence. She was right. Even apart from the practicalities, Daniel knew that the boys were hers as much as they were his—and if he found out a mission to save his boys had excluded him, he would never forgive those responsible. He nodded.

"I agree. I'll call her right now."

CHAPTER TWENTY

D aniel strapped himself into his seat next to Felipe and stretched out. Giselle and Claudia sat behind him. They all desperately needed sleep, but none of them could get a wink.

"Suppose we're wrong, Daniel," Giselle said. "Just because we have a 16 mm film with a few seconds of a middle-aged man in a brown suit with a blond woman, it doesn't mean they're Hitler and Eva Braun."

"Giselle, there's no way—"

"And how can we be sure it's Mengele? Okay, yes, *something* is going on in that compound. There are Nazis for sure. But isn't it a stretch to say that we've found Hitler, his wife, and their two children, all alive and well in Paraguay?"

Daniel looked up. Giselle had left her seat and was now standing in the aisle next to him, peering down at him through bleary, nervous eyes. "We could look pretty foolish, if we're wrong."

He looked at her, his eyes affixed to hers for a few seconds. He bit his lower lip. "Giselle, I have no doubt in my mind whatsoever. It was Hitler."

"But, what about his suicide in the bunker in Berlin? Eva Braun too. I read that someone poured gasoline over their bodies and set them aflame. That's in all the history books."

"True, that's what the world has been led to believe for the last ten years. But maybe we were all fooled. Maybe that was the cover-up of all time. Maybe the bodies that were burned were of two suckers who had the misfortune to be in the bunker that night, and maybe Hitler and Braun were spirited away."

She paused. "But it's a long way from Berlin, a city practically destroyed in the war to the remotest part of Paraguay. How could that have been pulled off?"

"Giselle, I don't have that answer. Hitler still had friends. Somehow they could have got, for example, to Italy. Between the Vatican and the International Red Cross, God knows there were many possible escape routes. Remember too, the Nazis had millions in cash, gold, artwork. Money talks. You know that. I'm the living proof of that adage."

She nodded. "I just hope for all our sakes that we're going to be taken seriously and not treated as lunatics over all this. After all, all the evidence we have is photographs taken from a helicopter and a plane."

"True. But don't forget the high walls, the tanks, the unmarked plane, and the way everyone ran inside the building when they saw the helicopter. What did they have to hide?"

Giselle couldn't answer. Her eyes wandered back to where Claudia sat, fidgeting in her seat in a futile attempt to get comfortable enough to sleep. They both knew there was no way Claudia's mind would wind down enough for rest until her sons were back at her side.

The copilot poked his head around the cockpit door to announce that they would be landing at Palm Beach airport in about an hour. The middle-aged Argentinean flight attendant emerged from the galley with their simple breakfast trays.

"We will be landing away from the terminal in an area reserved for private planes," she explained to Daniel and Giselle. "We cannot disembark until US Customs and Immigration clear us. They will come aboard and attend to all the formalities here. A minibus will then take you all, with your baggage, to the terminal, and you'll be on your way."

Daniel had taken a bite of his blueberry muffin, crumbs appearing at the corners of his mouth, so Giselle answered. "Thank you. We have a meeting here at the terminal at seven o'clock, and then we're taking another chartered plane on from here."

As the flight attendant hurried on her way, Daniel grumbled, "It would have been nice if David Bass had invited us for breakfast and let us freshen up at his house. I believe he lives in a mansion on the coast with something like fifty rooms."

"You did say he was mighty pissed with you," Giselle answered.

"Everyone treats him as if he were God. What's worse— he believes it himself. To me he's just an old Jew who's made a lot of money."

"And you're a young Jew who has made a lot of money."

"Giselle, shut up," he snapped. "I can do without your insolence."

"Look, we're all tired and stressed by all of this," intervened Felipe, who had been listening to their conversation. "Giselle's comments about us possibly being wrong are fair. But I have to tell you, I'd bet the farm that we have found Hitler. Our job is to stay focused and professional enough to convince the world that we've found him. The suicide and cremation story is pure baloney."

"Don't forget that my name is on the line here too," Daniel pointed out. "I don't have too shabby a reputation around the world myself. I've neglected my business over these last few weeks to devote myself exclusively to this. And I reckon by now I'm out a few hundred thousand dollars. All that must mean something."

At exactly six o'clock, they landed. Shortly before seven they were escorted by a uniformed airport employee whose nametag read "Sebastian," and who appeared to be prematurely gray-haired, from the minibus to an executive VIP lounge. A porter with a baggage cart walked alongside with their cases, including the all-important steel box that contained their evidence.

"Your next plane, McDuff Airlines, is on the tarmac ready to fly you whenever you're ready. Just call me on that telephone over there," Sebastian pointed out. "Extension 317. I'll take care of everything."

Daniel nodded. "Thank you, Sebastian. We could be here for another hour or more. Please tell the crew in case they want to leave the plane and go for breakfast."

Fortunately, there was no one else in the lounge, apart from the lady who worked at the deli counter who brought them a fresh pot of coffee and inquired if they needed anything else. The clock on the wall read 7:15.

"Where the hell is he?" Daniel growled.

At 7:32, David Bass sauntered into the lounge. Thin, tan, and balding, he wore rimless glasses and held his mouth in a firm line that betrayed none of the kindness and generosity for which he was world-renowned. His bright apple-green trousers, white shoes, red belt, and open-necked short-sleeve yellow shirt suggested he hadn't canceled his golf match but merely postponed it.

"Okay, what's all this about?" he snapped as he approached Daniel. Introducing himself to the others, it appeared, was out of the question. He did take time to pour himself a cup of coffee.

"Thank you for coming, David. You won't regard this as a waste of time, I assure you."

Bass jabbed a finger in the direction of Daniel's company. "Who are these people?"

"They are my team. Let me introduce you to Giselle Faber, my executive assistant, and Felipe Martinez, my special projects consultant. And my former wife, Claudia."

Bass turned his back to them. "I have a few words that I want to address to you alone," he snapped. "Let's step outside."

Daniel did not hesitate. "These are my colleagues, and we have travelled halfway around the world together, working twenty-four/seven. We are a team. Anything you have to say to me, you can say in front of them."

"Okay then. First, I don't appreciate being woken up in the middle of the night and being addressed in the manner you spoke to me yesterday. I am old enough to be your father. I am a well-respected figure in this country and in yours too. You were rude and I don't have to take it." Daniel watched the man's nostrils flare and then relax. It would seem his rant had satisfied his indignation. "Now tell me what you've got."

Daniel was sorely tempted to tell the man he had no regrets about waking him up in the middle of the night and would not apologize for his tone, his supposed insubordination. He practically had to bite his lip to avoid repeating to Bass that he would get his information out to the appropriate channels—with or without his help. But Daniel swallowed those words, along with the words, *There's a plane on the tarmac awaiting my instructions. It can take us to Washington, DC, or it can take us to London. And you'll regret if it's the latter.*

David Bass, after all, had just calmed down. If Daniel put him on the defensive again, they could be there, locked in a pissing contest, for hours.

Daniel took a deep breath. "David, I count on your confidence. Your complete confidence."

"You have it. So continue."

"Madame Faber worked for a prominent bank in Geneva. She discovered regular monthly remittances over many years to an Argentinean account in favor of a Paraguayan company. We discovered through methods I don't wish to reveal that there were suspicious connections between the remitter of the funds and the beneficiary in Paraguay. We're talking amounts well in excess of twenty to thirty million dollars, David. And then there were the secretive imports to Paraguay of millions of dollars' worth of mysterious commodities. Maybe as much as a hundred million dollars' worth. Why?"

Bass's eyes dilated as he took in the figure. His defensiveness had fallen by the wayside and curiosity had taken over. He couldn't hide his eagerness as he nodded for Daniel to continue.

"We researched the Paraguayan company and learned that it owned a vast area of land in the undeveloped and unpopulated northern area of Paraguay. An American doctor was called to attend to a patient at the compound and was never seen or heard of again. We flew in an Argentinian military helicopter over the compound to photograph the area. That expense was considerable but so was the danger—flying unlawfully over Paraguayan airspace."

"And what exactly did you discover for your illegal escapades?"

"A Nazi compound." The phrase hit Bass like a stone, but Daniel wasn't about to stop, or even slow down, his story now. "We all know that many Nazis fled Europe after the war with the help of The Red Cross and the Vatican. We have located a lair where the top Nazis are living in what is tantamount to a private luxury resort, protected by high walls, a remote location, unmarked planes, tanks, heaven knows what."

"So why not just make a call to Simon Wiesenthal or that couple in France, the Klarsfelds, and let them get on with it?"

"David, this is too big for amateurs. This has to be handled by the very top person who gives orders down the pyramid. This can't be a bottom-up operation."

Bass leaned back and crossed his arms. They were at risk of his interest in the whole issue flagging. Daniel had hooked his interest initially, but he'd heard nothing tasty enough to warrant this meeting—much less a meeting with the president of the United States. "Why not? Who exactly is in the compound?"

"The very top, top, top."

"You mean Mengele, Borman? Who do you mean?"

"I'm not giving you names but I mean the top, top, *top*."

Bass drew breath as he eyed Daniel. Daniel watched the meaning of his words click. Bass's lips parted as though he were about to speak the name aloud, then gently closed again, as though he couldn't quite bring himself to do it. As though the name represented a curse.

"You must be crazy."

"No, we're not."

"For Christ's sake, you want me to go home now and call the president and get him to see you based on just what you have told me."

"Yes, I do. Based on what I have told you and the evidence that we have here," Daniel said pointing to the case on the floor by his right foot. "Evidence that has cost me at least half a million and for which lives have been risked and lost."

Bass took a sip of his coffee. The others watched him. He was in a bind. He looked as if he wanted to punch Daniel in the face, or at the very least tell him to go to hell. But the thought that Daniel might have something worth pursuing tugged at Bass's mind. His reputation would take a nosedive if Daniel did, in fact, take his evidence to London or Paris instead of Washington. After all, Daniel had no particular allegiance to the United States.

"Well, David?" Daniel pressed.

"Daniel, I don't like you. Frankly, I never did. I don't know whether what you have is for real or not. To tell you the truth, I don't buy it. But"—he paused so long it nearly became awkward—"I will put in a call to the White House. I cannot guarantee I can arrange an appointment for you. I will make that call, but on two conditions."

"There should be no conditions," Daniel spat.

"After your call yesterday morning, I telephoned the chairman of one of the boards on which you and I sit. He told me that last year you donated two hundred fifty thousand to that foundation. I want your pledge that if I make this call this morning, you will increase your pledge by fifty percent for this year."

Daniel smiled. The others raised their eyebrows.

"Another one hundred twenty-five thousand, okay. What about condition number two?"

"Very simple. After I made that call, I telephoned the chairman of the other board on which you and I sit. He told me that last year you donated a hundred grand. I want your pledge that if I am successful in getting you an appointment, you will double your pledge to that foundation for this year."

Daniel sighed. "I agree. You're a bastard but at least you're not lining your own pockets like some others I know."

"My pockets are lined enough already, Daniel."

"When will you make your call?"

Bass looked at his watch. "It's eight o'clock. I'll make the call when I get back to my house, within the hour."

"Okay, so we will fly now to Washington."

"Where can I reach you?"

"We'll be at The Hay-Adams," Giselle said.

Bass stood to leave. "Goodbye, Daniel and . . ." He had clearly forgotten the names of all Daniel's companions. When no one offered to help him out, Bass nodded, offered a modest salute, and left. His mostly full cup of coffee stayed behind.

"He's such a swine and the world thinks he's Jesus Christ," Daniel muttered the moment Bass had disappeared. "Look at how he was dressed. A circus clown."

"I have a question," Claudia said softly.

"Yes?"

"Why didn't you tell him we have photographs of Hitler and Eva Braun?"

"What, and have him think we're crazy?"

The three of them looked across at Daniel. They all burst out laughing.

"**W**elcome to the Hay-Adams, Mr. Lavy." The buxom receptionist, whose exquisite beauty was manifested by the narrow gap between her front teeth, smiled as she handed him the key to his suite. "And here are Ms. Faber's key and Mr. Martinez's and Signora's. Our bellboy will escort you to your rooms. Please let me know if there is anything you need."

"Thank you," Daniel replied. "Are there any messages for me? I was expecting one."

"No, I don't see anything, but I'll let you know the minute one arrives."

As they all shuffled into the elevator, Daniel cast a quick glance at Felipe to make sure he was still holding the steel box. There was the box, pinned to Felipe's side in a white-knuckle grip, while his other hand snaked out to grab Giselle's. Daniel watched his niece blush and look up at Felipe through her mascaraed lashes. Why he was paying for two rooms for them was a mystery. The only question about tonight was who would sneak into whose room.

The bellboy unlocked the door to Daniel's suite, which offered a bright, unobstructed view of the White House.

"Ms. Faber and Mr. Martinez are in rooms on either side of you, Mr. Lavy. They have connecting doors with this suite. Would you like me to open them up too?"

Before either Giselle or Felipe could answer, Daniel nodded that the doors should be opened. He suppressed a smile when he realized that, unless either of them walked back into the corridor, they would have to pass through his suite to get to each other. "How do you like that?" Daniel said with a chuckle. Giselle and Felipe ignored him. Claudia's room was on the opposite side of the corridor.

After the bellboy left, Daniel slumped into an armchair that was nearly the color of merlot. "There is one thing we have overlooked, Felipe. We need to separate the evidence. We have two copies of the film and two sets of prints plus negatives. Right now, everything's in one case. I don't trust Bass enough to leave it that way."

"What shall we do?" Giselle asked.

"We need an additional case. Find out from the concierge where you can pick one up. Then, come back here and we'll split the evidence between the two. Felipe, go downstairs and tell them we need a large safe in which to deposit both cases. They must have a strong room."

Felipe nodded. "Giselle and I can attend to that now."

"And have some lunch while you're at it. I'll stay here with Claudia and await Bass's call."

The hours ticked by with no call. Long after Felipe and Giselle had returned, having brought Daniel a Reuben sandwich and vegetable soup from the bistro where they'd stopped for lunch, they all sat around his suite. They passed the room service menu around and half listened to news on the television. At one point, Daniel stood at the window that provided a widescreen view of the White House. "So near and yet so far," he commented.

After he'd made versions of the same comment ten or more times, Giselle snapped, "Why don't you call Bass yourself? It's ten o'clock. He's already admonished you for calling him too early, so let him be angry if you call him too late."

She was right. "You have his Palm Beach number," Daniel said. "Please would you get him on the telephone?"

After a moment, she handed the phone to Daniel.

"It's good that you called me," Bass admitted after Daniel's terse greeting. "I'd forgotten where you said you'd be, and I wasn't prepared to waste time calling every goddam hotel in Washington. Expect a call from Wycliffe Jenkins at the White House. He'll probably be in touch tomorrow." Before Daniel could respond, the phone went dead.

"That man is a bastard," Daniel snapped. "Obviously there's nothing more we can do tonight so let's get a good night's sleep and get together for breakfast here at eight o'clock." It was a command, not an invitation. All three stood to leave. Daniel was beyond caring to which room or rooms they all went.

The next morning passed slowly. There was no call from the White House.

"Unless I've missed something in the news," Daniel growled, "there is no President Wycliffe Jenkins, so who the hell is he?"

"I've already called to find out," Felipe answered. "Wycliffe Jenkins is the assistant to the deputy chief of staff." He took a deep breath, anticipating Daniel's reaction.

"An assistant to the deputy chief of staff! I asked that bastard to get us a meeting with the president and pledged a small fortune for his trouble. And all he's succeeded in doing is asking some bloody underling to call me—which hasn't even happened."

"Daniel, he's not exactly a nobody. I think it's reasonable that this fellow, Jenkins, wants to speak to you before they schedule an appointment with the president," Giselle suggested.

"But he isn't speaking with him," Claudia said sharply from where she sat, curled in a ball on a coffee-colored couch. She had been there for hours now, but she'd been so silent Daniel had virtually forgotten her presence. Giselle and Felipe appeared similarly surprised to hear her speak.

"Can I get you something, Claudia?" Giselle asked. "Tea? A sandwich for lunch?"

"It's far past lunch time," Daniel muttered, returning his gaze from his ex-wife to the White House right outside his window. Claudia didn't answer Giselle at all. She tugged the blanket—the wooly one she'd taken from her room's linen closet—all the way up to her collar bone, gazed at the wall, and seemed to drift away from them.

More hours passed. "Giselle, it's five o'clock," Daniel said with all the composure he could muster. "Call the White House and ask to speak to Wycliffe Jenkins."

He watched her as she placed the call, which meant he saw her expression cloud over in response to whatever she was hearing. Daniel felt infuriated but not surprised at her news: "He's left for the day."

"Fuck. We have wasted an entire day. I'm going out for a walk. Imagine, *there* is the White House. So near and yet so far."

"If I hear you say that one more time, I'll pass out," Giselle said.

He ignored her.

"There's a decent looking bar downstairs. I'm going to check it out. Giselle, do you want to join me?" Felipe asked.

While Giselle's features betrayed her excitement at the idea, her eyes drifted to Claudia, who didn't appear to have moved for the past three hours. She looked shellshocked and stiff, the way a person tends to look immediately after receiving devastating news. Giselle began, "Claudia, would you like to join—"

"I'll be in my room." Her voice sounded like ice. Leaving her blanket in a rumpled pile on the couch, she left them.

On his walk, Daniel strode past the White House, but he couldn't bear to look at the building. He continued through the National Mall, the area between the Lincoln Memorial and the Washington Monument. Eventually he ended up, after about two hours, at the US Capitol Building and the Supreme Court. He'd had enough and was relieved to see an empty cab and return to the hotel.

***

The mood around the breakfast table the next morning was dark. They had grown tired of the lack of progress and were taking it out on each other. Daniel had several of the daily newspapers delivered along with breakfast but hadn't the patience to read any. Had he observed the surreptitious glances his niece and Felipe kept casting each other, it would have annoyed him, but he was too wrapped up in his own disgust to notice. He had no idea that Felipe and Giselle had, that morning, discussed how badly she wanted to see the city as a tourist. Felipe had encouraged her to tell Daniel she needed to get away and see the sites, but as much as Giselle wanted to, she worried that anything less than total commitment to their mission would make Daniel explode.

But at that moment, something else caused an explosion of sorts: a knock at the door. Daniel jumped from his seat.

He ran to it in expectation of a message being delivered from Mr. Jenkins or, better still, Mr. Jenkins himself. No such luck. It was the valet returning his laundry.

"Giselle, it's now eleven o'clock. Please would you check on flights to London. If we don't hear anything from Mr. Fucking Wycliffe Jenkins before the end of today, we'll fly to London tonight, tomorrow at the latest. Please call the office in Geneva and get me Clarissa Eden's telephone number. Madame Coty has it."

Shortly after twelve noon, the telephone rang. Daniel rushed to answer it.

"Mr. Lavy, this is Wycliffe Jenkins. I understand you would like to set up a meeting with the president. I do need to meet with you first. I can come to your hotel around three this afternoon?"

Daniel gave a thumbs up sign. "Yes, of course. I look forward to meeting you. Thank you."

As soon as Daniel hung up, he sprung into commander mode.

"Giselle and Felipe, I want you to go downstairs and book a meeting room for this afternoon. Arrange for a projector and screen. And unless one of you can operate a projector, we need a projectionist. And, at a quarter to two, get one of the cases out of the strong room."

"Do you think we should have the projectionist run the movie?" Felipe asked. "I think not. Let him show me how to work the projector, and then he can leave. We don't want any more people involved in this than absolutely necessary."

CHAPTER TWENTY-TWO

The atmosphere in the conference room was charged with anxiety. Felipe helped the projectionist, a man with glinting green eyes and a slight overbite, set up his equipment. A waiter with an annoying habit of frequently clearing his throat arranged a coffee maker, cups, and an assortment of soft drinks on a sideboard. Giselle tidied up the stack of photographs she'd just placed on the table. Daniel sat at the center, bristling with anger that the sum total of David Bass's intervention was a meeting with the assistant to the deputy to the White House chief of staff. Claudia sat grim-faced to his side, her eyes following none of the hustle and bustle around her.

"Giselle, it's now five minutes to three. Wait in the lobby for this Jenkins and bring him in. Don't expect to meet a decision-making senior executive. Imagine," he added, pointing out the window, "so near and yet so far."

Knowing they were finally getting somewhere—even if it wasn't as far as her uncle wanted to get—made Giselle feel just optimistic enough to ignore him. There was an end in sight. She might yet get to steal away for some sightseeing—her hand intertwined with Felipe's as they explored the nation's capital. "Sure, Daniel," she said and then left to wait for Jenkins.

"Are you set up, Felipe?" Daniel asked.

"Ready to roll. The projectionist has been most helpful. He'll wait outside in the lobby in case we need him again."

Daniel gave the projectionist a friendly smile and a wave as the man left the room.

The door opened a few minutes later, and Giselle followed Wycliffe Jenkins into the room.

Daniel stood and extended his hand.

"Thank you for coming to see us, Mr. Jenkins. I appreciate it. I'm confident that when you hear what we have to say, and see what we have to show you, you will realize the magnitude of what we've uncovered. Please take a seat."

Mr. Jenkins said nothing in reply, merely nodded without a smile. Giselle introduced him to Felipe and Claudia.

Daniel took an instant dislike to his visitor. He was tall and thin, and he'd brushed his long hair straight back to reveal an overlarge forehead. Daniel guessed he was forty. He had a disciplined bearing that suggested military service, maybe even a West Point education. He wore a simple striped tie with his dark gray suit and well-polished black shoes. Giselle poured him a coffee, for which he expressed no gratitude.

"What's all this about, Mr. Lavy?"

Daniel began by giving the floor to Giselle, who gave an account of her initial suspicions about the monthly remittances. All the while Daniel monitored Mr. Jenkins' body language and facial expression. He was not given to fidgeting or shifting his face out of neutral.

Felipe then took over to explain that the next step was to learn more about the account at Banque Debodiens and discover who managed it. He said they had obtained vital information through a lawyer in Switzerland.

Mr. Jenkins cleared his throat. "How did you do that? After all, files in a lawyer's office are confidential." He added, with a sneer, "They are in my country anyway."

"I assure you, Mr. Jenkins, that the Code of Ethics and Standards of Professional Conduct is every bit as correct in Switzerland as it is in your country," Daniel said.

"Then how did you get the information?" Jenkins looked directly at Felipe.

"Mr. Jenkins, I am a former CIA agent myself. I served in various offices around the world. I used methods that I learned in that capacity and during my training at Langley just a few miles away from here."

Jenkins nodded, seeming, for the first time, satisfied with the piece of information he had received.

"Once we had the information we needed," Daniel said, "we decided our next step was to go to Latin America. Felipe, please give Mr. Jenkins an account of where we went from there."

Felipe spoke uninterrupted for about ten minutes. Now and again, Jenkins sipped his coffee, raising an eyebrow occasionally, but in all other respects expressed no interest, nor did he ask any questions.

"Now, Mr. Jenkins, let's pause so you can look at the photographs you have in front of you. Giselle will explain what they are. And then we'll show you a 16 mm fifteen-minute movie."

Jenkins looked at his watch but said nothing.

After he had skimmed through the photographs, pausing on just a few of them, he turned to Daniel. "Interesting. Now let's see this movie."

Felipe moved toward the projector while Giselle pulled down the blinds. Jenkins turned his chair to face the screen. Daniel fixed his eyes directly on Jenkins to assess his reaction. He could not bear to look at the screen again for fear of becoming emotional at the sight of Hitler, Eva Braun, and the young children. He did venture a glance at Claudia, who he believed must feel the way he did: she had fixed her gaze on a point across from her, just above the tabletop. There were no tears, but her eyes were red-rimmed.

After a few minutes, Felipe and Giselle moved forward in their seats. They had reached the part in the film where the camera had shots of the tennis court and the game in progress. Any second the scene would begin with the children, the dog, and the blonde woman. It would show the man standing up, throwing the ball at the dog, and then gesticulating for everyone to run indoors. Giselle's hands trembled when these images came onto the screen. Felipe's reaction could not be seen, only imagined, as he stood behind the projector. Daniel never allowed his eyes to leave Mr. Jenkins.

The film came to an end. Felipe turned off the projector while Giselle opened the blinds.

It felt like thirty seconds passed before anyone spoke. It was Daniel who broke through the precarious silence.

"In a nutshell, Mr. Jenkins, we have unearthed a luxury lair for Nazi leaders. Not only leaders, but the ultimate architect of the evil regime. Adolf Hitler, his mistress or wife, whatever the hell she was. And, in all likelihood, their two children, probably born in that fortress. Bormann, Eichmann, Mengele. That is what your president needs to know. That's why I must see him at once."

There was no longer a hint of superiority or even standoffishness when Mr. Jenkins nodded. The man's eyes were still fastened to the screen, as though it might reveal more stunning atrocities.

Daniel continued. "Obviously that whole story of Hitler and Eva Braun committing suicide in the Berlin bunker and their bodies being burned is a myth. We have them."

They all looked at Jenkins, who tapped his finger on the table. He then let out a sigh.

"Drop it, Mr. Lavy. Maybe the man in the film is Hitler. Maybe he isn't. What does it matter anymore? You people have had your day in court—the Nuremburg War Trials. You have the United States government's guarantee that Israel will survive. Why do you want to open up old wounds?"

Daniel and the others could not believe the words that were coming from Jenkins's mouth. Daniel's fists were clenched. Giselle fought to hold back her tears. Felipe stared at Jenkins, his eyes wide open and nostrils flaring. Claudia sat motionless, still looking at that imaginary point just above the table across from her.

Jenkins folded his hands tidily in front of him. "We're busy rebuilding Europe. Germany is finally our ally instead of foe. We stand shoulder to shoulder with West Germany against the Soviet Union and East Germany. It is no secret that many German scientists who worked for the Nazis during the war, developing the bomb and rockets and such-like, are now working for us. The brilliant Werner von Braun is working with us, for heaven's sake. I repeat, Mr. Lavy—why open old wounds?"

Daniel's face contorted in anger. He opened his mouth to fire at Jenkins with the speech that sat bullet-like in his throat, but the other man was not finished.

"If it is Hitler there in that fortress, along with the others, they are effectively prisoners. They're not going anywhere. Leave it alone. And something else—what about those two young children? If indeed Hitler and Eva Braun are their parents, then what? If we execute the parents, what the hell do we do with the children?"

In a tone that announced this was the final word on the matter, Jenkins said, "Who cares anymore?"

Daniel could bear it no more. He stood directly over Jenkins, pointing at the man with a tremulous finger. "I care," he shouted, "*I* care. At least sixty-five million people perished in the war started by that monster, including my parents, my brother and sister, and God knows how many other relatives of mine. You tell your fucking president that I'm here to represent them."

Jenkins shuffled in his chair and attempted to get up, but Daniel blocked him.

"And what's more, you insensitive stupid piece of contemptible shit, you ask me to consider what would happen to Hitler's children. How dare you? Have you forgotten the one and a half million Jewish children who were slaughtered in concentration camps? Did the US Courts and your fucking president consider the fate of the Rosenberg children when their parents were executed two years ago?"

For the first time, Claudia seemed to come alive from her stupor. She looked up at Daniel and unthinkingly nodded along with his words. Her fingers braided together as though she were holding her own hand for comfort. The change in her demeanor did not go unnoticed; Giselle seemed to float over to Claudia. She placed her hands lightly on her aunt's slender shoulders.

Before Mr. Jenkins could dream of answering, Daniel barreled ahead. "You are either a complete fool or a total swine. Either way, you're a horrible human being. I'm never going to forget this conversation." Daniel paused long enough to meet his ex-wife's eyes. Felipe and Giselle both took note of the look that passed between them; it was a look of mutual encouragement, of comfort.

"I no longer care about meeting your president. You can both go to hell. But I'm going to make sure the whole world knows about your comments. By noon tomorrow, you will be reviled throughout the world. And should your president be as dumb as many people already think he is, and he backs you up, he'll be impeached so help me God. Now get the hell out of this hotel."

Daniel moved back to allow the man to stand. Jenkins moved toward the door hesitantly, either giving Daniel the chance to berate him further or giving himself the chance to come up with words of self-defense. By any account, he was stopped by Felipe's sharp but composed voice.

"Just one thing Mr. Jenkins. I recorded our meeting. One of the little tricks I learned at Langley. I also learned to do my homework. One other thing I learned about you is that your wife is Jewish and it's her family's money that allows you to live where you live and how you live. I can only imagine she would take issue with some of your remarks."

A look of horror spread across Mr. Jenkins' face. He was about to utter something, but words failed him.

"Giselle, bring over the phone," Daniel said. "Mr. Jenkins is going to call the White House and speak with the president to arrange the appointment for us this afternoon."

After Giselle handed Jenkins the phone, Daniel whispered to her, "Do you think anyone has ever spoken to that man like that before?"

Giselle just smiled. "While I was buying the case for the photographs, Felipe went out and bought a tape recorder. He thought it might come to using the man's words against him."

"That was a brain-wave. Why didn't you tell me?"

"We also bought that big basket of fruit. I hid the tape recorder in the basket over there." She pointed to the sideboard.

Daniel allowed himself a half smile, then a whole one, which expanded to a beam. "Well done. Well done. Now we must think about our next step. If I'd known that the meeting was being recorded, I'd have been careful not to use so many fucks and other expletives."

"That's one of the reasons I didn't tell you."

Daniel smiled again. "Pass me a banana from the basket."

"The president will see you at half-past four," Jenkins said, barely able to contain his trembling. "Can I go now?"

"No way, you're coming with us."

Daniel waved his finger at Felipe and beckoned him to the door.

"I deliberately didn't mention the uranium and lead deals. These were managed by that CIA outfit in Hong Kong. We didn't need to alert Jenkins that we knew about them," Daniel whispered.

"He probably already knows," Felipe replied. "Remember two people were killed—that journalist, Monteverde, and his Chinese colleague close to the uranium mine."

The smile that had just stretched Daniel's face faded immediately. "How could I forget?"

CHAPTER TWENTY-THREE

Two black Lincoln Town cars drove in convoy the half mile from the hotel to the White House. Jenkins, Daniel, and Felipe sat in the first car, followed by Claudia, Giselle, and the projectionist in the second. Neither Daniel nor Felipe gave any appearance of being in awe of their surroundings as the guard at the main outer gate waved them in.

Jenkins led them all into the building and pointed to a reception desk where they were all obliged to sign their names and provide identification. The receptionist dialed an internal number, after which a security guard appeared to escort them to an elevator at the end of a long corridor.

"Are we meeting in the Oval Office?" Daniel asked. "No stunts, Jenkins. This meeting is with the *president*, yes?"

"That's what I arranged." Turning to the security guard, Jenkins asked, "Where are you taking us?"

"To a conference room near the Oval Office."

A secretary greeted them at the elevator and then took them into a large conference room overlooking the gardens. They took their seats at a table. The projectionist sought out an outlet for his equipment, after which he set up a screen at the far end of the room. A Stars and Stripes flag hung above a cadenza on which was placed a bust of what Daniel guessed was a former president, though he didn't recognize the face.

"Can I bring you coffee or anything?" the secretary asked. "The president will be with you in a few minutes."

The projectionist gave Felipe some additional instructions before leaving the room to take a seat outside. Daniel smiled as he saw the man pocket a White House ashtray as a souvenir.

Minutes later, they all stood as President Kyle Denning entered the room, accompanied by Bennett Simmons, his chief of staff. The president wasted no time on pleasantries.

"What's this all about, Mr. Lavy? Mr. Jenkins seemed almost hysterical about setting up this meeting. I can give you a half hour at the most." Despite the fact that he was not a physically imposing man, Kyle Denning's presence commanded attention. He was of medium build with a nose and eyebrows just a little too large for his face. He didn't pay careful attention to his clothing, which meant his sleeves were always a little too long and therefore needed to be rolled up, as they were today. Combined with these other factors, his gray hair should have made him look grandfatherly, approachable, but he only looked stately. He entered the room with the energy of a college student and the confidence of a CEO. He was rarely interrupted or questioned; when he talked, everyone around him listened.

"Mr. President, thank you for seeing us. Once you hear what we have to say and see the photographs and the film we have brought with us, you will appreciate the urgency and importance of our visit."

"Mr. President," Felipe interrupted, "We're also talking about the kidnaping of many children, including Mr. Lavy and his former wife's"—he pointed at Claudia—"young sons."

"Before you show the film, I'd like an explanation." The president's voice was firm but not unfriendly.

The voice of Mr. Simmons, on the other hand, had a gruff edge to it that made him sound suspicious of everyone. "Let me see the photographs." He was a large man with eagle-like features and close-cropped dark, wavy hair. Giselle handed the stack of photos to him and then withdrew her hand quickly, as though she'd just fed a dangerous animal that might bite.

Mr. Simmons went through them in silence while Daniel outlined all that had taken place since Giselle had burst into his apartment mere weeks earlier.

The president listened attentively, even as Mr. Simmons leaned across the table to hand him certain photographs that had captured his eye.

"Okay, Mr. Lavy, run the film for me."

"Certainly, Mr. President, but before doing so, I want you to listen to the last five minutes of a recording we made earlier this afternoon during our meeting with your Mr. Jenkins, here."

This whole time, Jenkins had been acting in the manner of a man with a gun to his head. Now he went as stiff and white as though he'd heard the trigger cocked. "Must you?" Jenkins's voice came out high, feeble.

"Carry on, Mr. Lavy," the president responded.

No one said a word as they listened to the tape. The only sound, in fact, was Jenkins's frequent swallowing and staggered breathing.

The president paused. "I can understand why you didn't want that played, Jenkins. Now let's see the film."

Giselle stood to close the drapes as Felipe turned on the projector.

The president moved forward in his seat, his eyes wide open, his face turning to surprise and anger and his fists firmly placed on the table.

The film came to an end and Giselle went to open the curtains. Claudia began to tear up. "Mr. President, did you see the young children? My twins were among them."

The president did not reply. His eyes remained fixed on the blank screen.

The others looked at him, awaiting some reaction. It didn't take long in coming.

"Bennett, cancel all my appointments for the rest of today. Call my brother immediately over at Langley and get him here immediately. I don't give a damn what he's doing. I want him here within a half hour. "

Simmons was about to open the door to leave the conference room when the president called after him, "And get hold of the chairman of the Joint Chiefs of Staff and whoever is in the Pentagon right now at the highest level in the marines and air force. While you're at it, call Harris at the State Department. I want to meet with all of them in the Cabinet Room one hour from now. Okay?"

With a solemn half nod, Simmons left the room.

"Why does he want his brother involved?" Giselle whispered to Felipe.

"The president's brother is head of the CIA," Felipe answered. He looked at her, playfully brushing her hair behind her shoulder. "The Dennings are a powerful family."

"We're going to get to the bottom of this, Mr. Lavy," President Denning said. Then he turned his attention to Claudia. "And we will do our best to rescue all the children."

"Thank you, Mr. President," Daniel responded.

The president stood to open the door to call in one of the secretaries.

"Have them set up the Cabinet Room. And have these photographs and the film taken down to the conference room."

He returned to his seat at the table.

"Jenkins, what do you know about this?"

Jenkins had not returned to a normal posture, skin tone, or breathing pattern since the tape had been played. Even now, his face looked slick with sweat and his voice wavered. "Until I met with these people this afternoon, I knew nothing at all."

The president grunted, "I don't know who to believe any more. I'm going back to my office, and I'll see you all downstairs in the cabinet room in an hour. My secretary will escort you there."

"Thank you, Mr. President," Daniel replied.

"Mr. Lavy, I am shocked by what I have seen. The enormity of all this is historic."

"Mr. President." Claudia trembled as she spoke. This meeting already represented the most she had spoken in the past week. "There is something else that has not been mentioned. My husband is the Italian ambassador to Argentina. There have been top secret meetings in Bariloche, Argentina attended by members of the German community in Buenos Aires, many of them former high-ranking Nazis as well as senior Italian fascists."

"Unfortunately, they are everywhere, my dear," he said.

"Also some Americans, I believe."

All the president could manage in response was, "Oh."

"From what I gathered while listening to conversations my husband had with his brother, there is something being planned. Something . . . big. I don't know what it is, but I know it's serious."

The president turned to face Jenkins.

"Do you know what she's talking about?"

"No sir. I'm sure your brother may be able to shed some light on this."

"I sure hope so." He glanced up at the clock on the wall. "I'll have some tea brought in, although I'd guess all of you would prefer something stronger. I damn well know I do."

CHAPTER TWENTY-FOUR

They paused to take in the room and the people who had assembled. Even Daniel was overcome as he looked up at the neoclassical molding and then at the fireplace flanked by busts of George Washington and Benjamin Franklin. Above the mantel, a large painting of the signing of the Declaration of Independence. Portraits lined the walls. Seated around the table on chairs engraved with the names of the cabinet positions were at least twelve people, some of whom Daniel and Felipe recognized from photographs in newspapers. A chair at the center of the table, its back a few inches taller than the others, was reserved for the president.

Everyone stood to turn toward the door when Daniel and his team entered. Mr. Simmons, the chief of staff, whom they had met earlier in the conference room, came forward. He announced their names and then introduced the men standing. The secretary of state, Terrence Crosby; the head of the CIA and the president's brother, George Denning; the head of the FBI, J. Edgar Hoover; together with various military personnel whose titles of joint chiefs of staff meant more to Daniel than their names. Some of them nodded by way of a greeting. One or two gave out half-smiles, but most remained expressionless.

Mr. Simmons led them toward a row of chairs along the wall that faced the president's empty chair.

"Wycliffe, please sit directly behind Mr. Denning," Mr. Simmons instructed his subordinate. Daniel winked at Felipe, gratified not to be seated next to Jenkins. Giselle pointed out to Claudia the unique design of the carpet, with its deep reds, golds, sapphires, and greens.

Mr. Simmons knocked on the door that connected with the Oval Office, and they heard him say, "We're ready for you, Mr. President."

When Kyle Denning entered, everyone stood.

"Thank you all for coming on such short notice," he began, motioning for everyone to sit. "I will ask our visitors to pledge that, once they leave this room, they will reveal no details of this meeting."

Mr. Simmons stepped forward and instructed Daniel, Felipe, Giselle, and Claudia to stand and confirm that they understood and would abide by the president's direction.

"Gentlemen, I have invited our visitors to attend this meeting in view of what they have to discuss and its significant impact not only on the United States but on the entire world. I am sure they will be willing to answer any questions you may have."

All eyes turned towards Daniel and the others.

"Now, Mr. Lavy, please will you explain what all this is about?"

Daniel stood. "First, I want to express my appreciation and gratitude to you, Mr. President, and to all of you who are here in this room for the speedy attention you are devoting to the issues we will present to you. In addition, I want to convey, on behalf of the four of us, we are especially grateful to you, given that none of us are citizens of the United States, for honoring us and receiving us in this way."

"Please continue, Mr. Lavy."

For the next twenty minutes, Daniel gave an account of all the developments that began in Geneva when Giselle first arrived at his apartment and which led to their presence at the White House.

George Denning, the head of the CIA, raised his hand to ask a question. When he held it aloft this way, it was obvious how imposing and gnarled the man's hand was. Judging by his hands, a person might have thought George Denning worked as a lumberjack. For that matter, the only thing about his appearance that served as a counterpoint to that assessment was his manner of dress. He wore a crisp double-breasted navy suit. His cufflinks gleamed and his American flag pin stood perfectly upright on his lapel.

"Mr. Lavy," he began. "You have traveled from Geneva to Hong Kong, to China and Tibet, to Argentina and Paraguay, and now to Washington, DC. You have flown on private planes. Traveled with three people, stayed in five-star hotels. You have incurred huge expenses. Who is paying for all this? Which foreign power is supporting you?"

"Mr. Denning. No foreign power is financing this. Nor is any other individual. I am paying every expense from my personal bank account."

"Can you prove that?" It was clear from Mr. Denning's tone it was a threat, not a question.

"Absolutely," Daniel answered, piqued and surprised by Denning's hostility. He sat.

The president turned to Felipe. "Mr. Martinez, please explain your involvement in all this."

When Felipe finished with his part, George Denning again indicated he had a question. Again, his massive paw reached into the air.

"Mr. Martinez, when I was advised by the president you would be in attendance, I ran a background check on you."

Felipe's eyes opened wide. It wasn't so much the prospect of having been investigated; he knew to expect they would be diligent at this level of security clearance. It was, again, Denning's open hostility. He wasn't being cautious. He was being belligerent.

"I discovered that, at one time, you were a CIA operative but resigned to set up your own company in Buenos Aires. Correct?"

"Yes. That is true."

"Were there any other reasons why you resigned?"

"No."

"Are you sure?"

"I am sure."

"When you resigned from the service, you were obliged to return equipment that had been loaned to you. You did not."

"Of course I did. What are you alleging I did not return?"

Denning did not respond.

"Mr. Martinez, your name was originally Mandelbaum. I am assuming you are of German Jewish origin. Are you in the pocket of the Israelis? I know their Mossad organization has a history of recruiting former CIA agents."

"Mr. Denning." Felipe did his best to remain calm. "First, you have accused me of being a thief without providing any evidence. And in answer to your question, I am not in the pocket of the Israelis, nor have I ever been. But, yes, I am Jewish. What has my religion got to do with this?" Felipe's voice rose. "If you have evidence I stole property of the United States, produce it. Furthermore, Mr. Denning, when I resigned, I received a letter from your predecessor acknowledging my years of service to the agency. That letter is framed and hangs in my office."

Denning again responded to none of this. He merely braided his sausage-like fingers together in a way that made him appear to be plotting his next attack.

"Let's all try to stay calm," the president said. "Now, Miss Faber, it all began with you. Please give us your account, but just tell us anything that Mr. Lavy may have left out inadvertently." He smiled at her, thinking of his two daughters around her age.

"Truly, Mr. President, I have nothing to add."

He nodded and smiled again.

"And, please, Madame, what have you to tell us?"

Claudia stood. When she looked down, she noticed a small sepia-colored stain on her blouse from the English breakfast tea she had spilled earlier that day. Her hands had been shaky all day, and she couldn't stop them even now. She tried pressing her palms firmly to her sides.

"Please forgive me. My English is not so good. And I am nervous."

"Please don't be." The president now offered his warm smile to her. "Just tell us what you know."

"Thank you, Mr. President. My priority is to have my twin sons returned to me as quickly as possible. I fear for their lives, and when you gentlemen see the film and the photographs, you will understand why."

"We understand that, perfectly. And I want you to know that not only are you here among friends, but you are also here among twins." He gave her a broad smile. "I have twin daughters myself and my brother, George, well he and I are fraternal twins. People forget that don't they, George?"

George Denning remained expressionless but nodded.

"We are fully mindful of your distress and concern for your sons. Now, please tell us specifically what you know about this meeting in Bariloche and what gives you reason to believe that something major and dramatic is about to happen?"

"Mr. President, my husband's family was prominent in the Italian fascist movement and very close to Mussolini. They are extreme right-wing even to this day. My brother-in-law is married to a member of the Diessen family that has close ties to the Nazis in Argentina."

"What does that prove?" George Denning shouted.

If Claudia had been holding a cup of tea just then, she would have spilled the whole thing down her front. As it was, she couldn't help but flinch at the man's outburst. How different he was from his softspoken, quick-to-smile twin brother.

"Mr. Denning, it was Giovanni, my brother-in-law, who kidnapped my sons to take them to Paraguay to that fortress."

"We have heard about your sons. I'm now only concerned about this nonsense about some secret event that is going to devastate the world," the CIA director shouted.

"George, please," his brother interrupted.

"I can only tell you what I heard," Claudia offered. It took all her resolve to keep speaking while being shouted down by this bear of a man. "My husband and my brother-in-law were discussing the meeting they attended in Bariloche. They said they were pleased with the progress being made at Mariscal. That's where the fortress is. They also said they would be ready by the time the meeting between the Russians and the Chinese took place."

"And what meeting is that?" the secretary of state asked.

"I am not a politician, sir," Claudia answered. "But from what I heard, and my husband mentioned to me, the Russians and the Chinese have had their differences for a long time on Marxist ideology, so much so that it could lead to a war between the two countries."

"Yes, we know about that," the president said.

"Well, what I believe was being discussed in Bariloche with the right-wing Fascists and the Nazis was that when this meeting took place between Mr. Kruschev and Chairman Mao, the site of their summit would be bombed. Chaos would break out, and a right-wing dictator would be installed over both Russia and China. He would effectively rule the world."

"I have never heard such rubbish in all my life," George Denning shouted in rage. "Are we being asked to believe the hysterical ramblings of this woman whose only concern is to trick us into some sort of action to rescue her damned children and place the entire world into chaos?"

Daniel stood. "I will not remain in this room and hear my ex-wife insulted in this way or have our boys referred to as 'damned children' by that man."

"Mr. Lavy, I understand. Please accept my apologies for what my brother has said." The president pointed to the head of the CIA. "You are not the chairman of this meeting. You will speak only when I allow you to speak, and you will apologize to the Lavys forthwith."

George Denning stood and murmured an inaudible apology.

Mr. Hoover, the head of the FBI could not resist a smirk at Denning's embarrassment.

"President Denning, I can only tell you what I heard. My husband and I are not on good terms, for obvious reasons, but nonetheless he is a former ambassador and a highly educated man. His brother is an influential businessman in Argentina. I know their friends and the circles in which they operate. They are capable of anything."

"Please go on, Madame," the president said.

"I also heard my brother-in-law ask my husband if the United States was fully informed."

There was a gasp around the room.

"And what was the answer?"

"He said that they were."

The room fell silent. It was left to Daniel to stand to suggest that they run the movie and examine the still photographs.

"I agree," the president replied. "First the photographs."

"You may need a magnifying glass, sir. May I come and stand beside you with mine?"

"Yes, of course."

The photographs went around the table. Giselle had already placed all the ones with the young children at the end of the stack, and with a red pen had drawn a circle around a man's image on each of them.

When the president came to the last photograph, he passed the magnifying glass around the table along with the photographs that bore the red circle.

"Gentlemen," Daniel said, still standing next to the seated president, "I urge you to look closely at the man's face. It could be the infamous Dr. Mengele, the physician who escaped Europe after the war. He is the monster who performed medical experiments on twins at various concentration camps. He evaded capture at the end of the war and fled to South America."

"What utter nonsense," George Denning shouted.

The president drew a breath. "I've told you to keep your mouth shut, George."

"How long are we going to have to sit here and listen to all this?"

"For as long as I say so," the president replied. "Okay, Mr. Lavy, let's see the film."

Someone stood to turn off the lights.

Daniel could not see the expressions on everyone's faces, but he felt the tension around the table. He put the projector on pause when the first shot of the man they suspected of being Mengele came into view; he adjusted the lens to get a close up. Allowing that enlarged image to stay on the screen for half a minute, he restarted the film. He paused the film again when the unmistakable faces of Hitler and Eva Braun appeared on the screen. Daniel swore he could hear the president's breathing slow down at the sight.

After the film had ended, the president blinked heavily as his eyes readjusted to the light. "Well, everyone?"

"I say, we've had enough of this. Let's go home," George offered in the same surly tone he'd used for the whole meeting. If the content of the film had given him the slightest pause, he didn't show it.

For the first time that afternoon, the president changed his own tone, matching his brother in volume and aggression: "George, you're being rude and tiresome. Now shut your damned mouth."

"I have some questions," the secretary of state said. A tall man in his late sixties, Marcus Silverton always dressed as immaculately as he had that day, with his cornflower blue tie matching his pocket square. He was a man who did not have to speak loudly to command a room's attention. He stood and walked to stand behind the president, facing the head of the CIA.

"My questions are for George Denning, not for you, Madame. Please relax and sit. We are all sympathetic of your situation, as a mother, and appreciate you being here this afternoon." Then he turned back to Denning.

"You have been very defensive and obstreperous, George. I, for one, believe you have something to hide."

"Absolutely not. Don't be fooled by these people," he replied, pointing at Daniel and the others.

"What did she mean when she reported that she had heard her husband say that the Americans knew what was going on?"

"I haven't any idea."

"Mr. Lavy spoke earlier about a laboratory at the fortress. What do you know about that?"

"Nothing."

"And what about the huge imports of uranium to Paraguay that had been brokered by a company in Hong Kong, managed by a CIA agent of yours."

For the first time, George Denning appeared stymied. His eyes were temporarily those of a cornered animal. Swallowing deeply, he managed to recover. "I've told you that that's nonsense. Do you choose to believe that Italian woman or me?"

"Right now, George, I believe the lady," Marcus Silverton answered.

"You're all fools."

The president stood and asked his secretary of state to step aside and sit down.

"So, George, we have a situation whereby a CIA agent, Singleton, on the payroll of the US Government, is arranging huge amounts of uranium to be exported from China to Paraguay, and you know nothing about it. Was the United States paying for this? For Christ's sake, George, tell us what the hell was going on!"

George Denning looked down at the table, where his overlarge hands were folded messily. From a distance, his hands resembled one large, tan knot.

"We're waiting for an answer, George."

Finally, after what must have been more than a minute, George Denning cleared his throat and addressed the room.

"Yes, I knew about this summit meeting between Chairman Mao and President Khrushchev. Yes, it was and remains my opinion that the interests of the United States would be well-served if both these despots were annihilated and we could put in our own man to run those countries. We would then control the world. No other country on the planet could threaten us in any way."

One of the military men shuffled uneasily in his seat. The others remained cold-faced.

The president's voice came out like ice. "And you never discussed this with me?"

"You wouldn't listen. You and your leftist friends on Capitol Hill. None of you."

"And how many American dollars have been spent on this whole nonsense?" Silverton asked.

"I don't have that figure in front of me," George Denning snarled.

"Did you have any approval to incur that level of expenditure?"

"No. I had applied for annual increases in my budget, and I had no need to give a detailed account. My applications were always accepted. I used those funds."

"And you never stated, nor were ever asked why you needed additional funds? I don't believe it." Seemingly unaware of his own actions, the president rose again. With his knuckles flattened against the oak top, he leaned heavily into the table. He blinked in the same way he had when the lights had flicked on after the movie. The movie that established Hitler wasn't gone.

George Denning said nothing.

"I believe you must have lied on these applications."

One of the joint chiefs of staff stood.

"A question. Once you had eliminated Chairman Mao and Premier Khrushchev, who had you in mind to install as leader of those two countries?"

No answer.

"George," the president began, "you are to return to your office immediately, and I demand by noon tomorrow morning a detailed memorandum setting out exactly what sums were paid by your office from the very beginning toward this outrageous scheme, including every dime on that damned fortress. I want to know names, names, names, George." The president's voice grew louder. "And I want to know about this cockamamie scheme to assassinate Khrushchev and Chairman Mao. Got it?"

George Denning stood, his face reddening. "You'll have it tomorrow, Kyle."

"There'll be severe consequences if I don't have it on my desk by noon tomorrow. Now, get the hell out of here."

Everyone remained silent, motionless, and embarrassed, as the president's brother left the room.

"Gentlemen, bear with me. This is devastating, and I can only leave it to your imagination to appreciate my humiliation and shame that my brother has brought this on himself and this country. He has let us all down."

Then turning to face Claudia, he said, "And I want to apologize to you again for the way he spoke, and indeed to his rudeness to you too, Mr. Lavy and Mr. Martinez."

"Of course," Felipe muttered.

"But now we must discuss what we do next."

"Mr. Jenkins," the president said. "I didn't want everyone here to have to listen to your insensitive and ill-judged remarks on the tape recording that was made earlier this afternoon. But you have demonstrated that you are not the sort of person I want in my White House. You're fired."

Jenkins stood. "But sir . . ."

The president turned to his chief of staff. "Take him out of here and have security and the personnel department do what they have to do to strip him of his White House and government credentials."

The president looked at his watch. "It's six o'clock. We're not going to leave this room until we've formulated an action plan. Okay? And that includes you, Mr. Lavy, and your colleagues. We're going to move on this—right now."

CHAPTER TWENTY-FIVE

"Unless George can come up with a fully comprehensive explanation," the president began, "and a detailed account of all the millions of taxpayers' money expended on this ludicrous and unauthorized project, clearly a new head of the CIA will have to be appointed. But I demand that nothing of what you have just heard be discussed outside this room. Understood? And that applies to you, Mr. Lavy, Mr. Martinez, and the ladies."

"Of course," was the unanimous response.

"Are you going to wait for your brother's resignation? Why not just fire him?" Mr. Hoover asked. Despite a somewhat off-center nose and the concentration line deeply embedded between his eyebrows, J. Edgar Hoover had a perpetually harmless, almost friendly look. It was a combination of his tone of voice and his bulk that convinced everyone around him to take him so seriously.

"I may well do that, Edgar, but first I want to see the memorandum I've demanded he produce by noon tomorrow. We must now decide our next move."

No one immediately offered any thoughts. Figuring out a next move felt nearly impossible, even for the nation's top strategists.

"My thinking is that we should go into that fortress right now. Seize everyone there, bring them back to the United States, cross-examine them."

"And the children?" Claudia called out. "Forgive me, President Denning, but please, please rescue my children—and all the children."

"Of course, we will, my dear," he assured. "So, what do we do? What are the logistics of flying there and taking the place over?" He turned to the three joint chiefs of staff. "What do you think, gentlemen?"

The army chief of staff, Willard Bonom, looked at his two colleagues before beginning. Those who worked with Bonom were accustomed to his courtesy and softspoken voice, both of which belied how authoritative he could become when the situation called for it. He ran one hand through his thinning, sand-colored hair and took a deep breath.

"First, based upon Mr. Lavy's description of the fortress and what we have seen in the film, in my opinion, we could complete the mission with a hundred marines and the necessary equipment."

The colleague to Bonom's right, a young man with gelled blond hair and eyes the color of a clear April afternoon, suggested, "We should take interpreters and photographers too. As well as medical personnel, of course."

"How many planes will we need?" the president asked.

"If we are going to bring back all those people who live and work there, maybe four?" Bonom ventured.

"How long will it take for you gentlemen to get this together and be in the air?"

The joint chiefs of staff talked among themselves in hushed tones.

"About six hours," one of them answered.

"Too long. Make it four."

Daniel reached out for Claudia's hand. "We're getting somewhere."

She nodded and gave a nervous half-smile. Daniel couldn't help noting how natural her hand felt clasped in his, and he wondered if she was thinking the same thing.

The secretary of state, Marcus Silverton, stood. He smoothed his cornflower blue tie before proceeding.

"Gentlemen, you are all overlooking one important fact. An operation such as this will involve flying over the airspace of several friendly countries. We should ask their consent."

"Sit *down*, Marcus."

Silverton returned to his seat, his cheeks red in response to the president's rebuke.

"Obtaining all the consents will take too long and there is a huge risk of leaks. This operation must be swift and secret. Period. There is no other way."

"But Paraguay, for one, will have the right to bring this blatant violation to the attention of the Security Council?" Silverton pleaded.

"Marcus, do you think despite all the requests that we, Germany, and Israel have made over the years to those damned South American countries to extradite the Nazi criminals in their midst that they want to draw attention to either their complicity in shielding them or their incompetence in not being able to find them?"

Felipe nudged Daniel and gave a thumbs up.

"And one other thing. When we wrap up this meeting, you are to summon the Chinese and Soviet ambassadors. You're going to tell them that we believe there is an assassination plot afoot to bomb the site of their upcoming secret summit, which would place their two countries in total chaos. I'm going to put in a call to Kruschev too."

Silverton nodded.

"Make sure they express their gratitude to us for sharing this information with them and make it clear that we expect them to veto any resolution at the UN that Paraguay brings to complain about us. Okay? Do that now. There is no time to lose."

Daniel stood. "Mr. President, forgive me. We appreciate very much what you are doing and for allowing us to remain in the room. Be assured we will keep everything we have heard confidential. But, speaking for myself, I would like to travel with the marines on this operation. I have had combat duty and was an officer in the 1948 Israeli War of Independence."

"Me too," Felipe stood. "I also request permission."

Giselle and Claudia stood.

"We would like to go too," Giselle said. "We can assist the medics, and I want to be there to be part of the rescue team."

"Please sit down, all of you. I understand your request. I must defer to the joint chiefs of staff, who will have responsibility for this mission. What do you think, gentlemen?"

Willard Bonom looked at Daniel and each of them in turn. "There is no guarantee this mission will be successful. There could be injuries and even fatalities." He waited to see both men nod before he continued. "I have no problem with Mr. Lavy and Mr. Martinez traveling with us, provided they appreciate the dangers involved and that they agree to take orders from our officers as if they were full-fledged members of the United States Armed Services. As for the two ladies . . ."

Claudia interrupted his hesitant trail-off. "President Denning, I beseech you to allow us to go," she pleaded, her voice louder and stronger than she'd spoken in days.

The president ignored her. "Mr. Lavy and Mr. Martinez, I am assuming from your backgrounds that you both speak fluent German. Yes?"

"Indeed we do, sir," Felipe answered.

"In that case, you will be traveling as interpreters. And"— he turned to Giselle and Claudia—"you can travel as auxiliary medics and emotional counselors in the event that the children need the security of a woman's involvement amidst the pandemonium of a hundred or so armed marines suddenly landing in their midst."

Claudia exhaled heavily and Giselle stood up straighter. "Thank you, sir."

"Do we need to bring in parachutists?"

"I'd rather not," Bonom said in his ever-gentle voice. "In the film we saw many anti-aircraft guns on the ground. It would be too risky."

"Gentlemen, it's now seven o'clock. Get busy and be in the air by eleven. Good luck. And good luck to you wonderful brave people," the president said, turning to Claudia and Giselle. "Now I must prepare myself to deal with my duplicitous bastard brother. We will pick all of you up from your hotel at ten o'clock. Please, all of you, be ready."

"Hurry, you all have a long night ahead of you," the president said as he left the Cabinet Room to return to the Oval Office.

***

"Thank you, Tom for getting here so quickly," the president said to his senior advisor as they stepped into the Oval Office. "I want you here when I telephone George. When this whole saga gets out, my role as the brother of this swine will be examined under the microscope, so your role here is to be an honest witness."

"Understood," Tom Buxton replied. He'd been a member of the New York and Washington, DC Bars for ten years, but had quit private practice to serve as counselor and advisor to the president with a view to eventually launch his own political career. His short, perfectly coifed hair was the color of a walnut, and his shoulders were perpetually squared.

"He should be back at his desk by now," the president said, glancing at his watch and simultaneously dialing the direct line to his brother.

"George, what the hell is going on? You're in serious trouble, and you've put me in an embarrassing situation."

"That may be, Kyle, but it's nothing compared with what you and your weak administration are doing. For heaven's sakes, man, can't you see you're allowing the Russians and the Chinese to take over the world? Democracy and western civilization are not going to last another five years at the rate you're spearheading their decline."

"Tom is here as witness to this conversation. Be aware that if he decides he should report this to the attorney general or the Justice Department, that is his decision, and I will not intervene. Do you understand?"

"Perfectly," George Denning snapped back. "I would welcome it. It would give me an opportunity to tell the world of the danger we're facing and that my own brother is the worst, the weakest, and the stupidest president in the history of the United States."

"I don't know if you have committed treason. That will be for the courts to decide. What I do know is you have operated behind my back and misappropriated countless millions of taxpayers' dollars in pursuing your own agenda. An agenda you shared with neither me nor anyone else on Capitol Hill."

"Fuck you, Kyle."

The president paused. Tom Buxton remained standing.

"And I want a detailed memorandum from you by noon tomorrow about this whole project. Got it?"

"What if I don't comply?"

"Don't test me, George."

"You might as well know there is no way I'm going to let you have that memorandum tomorrow, the day after, next week, or next month. So go to hell. I'm spending the evening with Madge tonight. She's having surgery in a couple of days. Remember?"

"I remember. But I'm ordering you to let me have that memo by noon tomorrow."

"Madge is our sister. I live with her, have you forgotten?—"

"George," the president began slowly, "how long has this nonsense been going on?"

"I'm not answering any of your damned questions."

"How many German scientists are working for us?"

"You yourself approved several, Wernher von Braun and a few of his colleagues. You know that."

"How many more?"

No answer.

"Is this notorious Dr. Mengele at the fortress?"

"I have no idea."

"George, for God's sake, you and I are twins. There are confirmed accounts of that man's monstrous medical experiments on twins. Don't you have any feelings at all?" The president's voice rose. "Tell me about these huge imports of uranium and lead."

No answer.

"George, we all know that you are virulently anti-Communist, as we all are, but are you so right wing that you would risk a third world war?"

"I'll do whatever it takes to restore some sanity in the world."

"How could you possibly hope to do that when *you're* insane?"

"Kyle, you are a weak, stupid fool. You've brought shame onto our family."

"No, George. If anyone has brought shame on us, it's not me."

***

Kyle Denning had never cared much for his elder sister, Madge. A sharp-tongued woman whose hair always looked cottony no matter how she styled it, she had always struck Kyle as secretive. He had ignored his misgivings, long ago, when she and George had moved in together. The two of them had always gotten along quite well, and as Madge's health suffered, Kyle told himself it was good that George was there to watch after her—after all, he couldn't bring himself to care about her various surgeries and doctor's appointments. Now those initial misgivings roared back stronger than ever. He found himself wanting to know what was going on with his big sister. Immediately.

***

"I need a drink, what about you, Tom?"

"Sure."

The president went to a sideboard and poured two glasses of cognac, handed one to Buxton and took his seat behind his desk.

"If you don't mind me saying so, Mr. President, your sister is somewhat of a cold fish. I've met her a few times and in fact, sat next to her at last year's State Dinner for the president of France. What's her background?"

"You're right there. She is a hard bitch. I was never close to her, not like George. She and George were always very tight. As they grew older, both of them were unmarried, so she moved in with him when she came back from Germany when we entered the war."

"She was in Germany? Why?"

"She majored in German at Yale and then, with our father's help, got a job in Berlin at the *New York Times* bureau there. I had little contact with her for many years and then, when war broke out, I was in the navy. When we finally met up again in 1947, it had been thirteen years since I'd seen her. Not that I had missed her."

"When she came back to the States, did she stay with the *New York Times*?"

"Oh no, she'd left them around 1936. She'd been head-hunted by the Reich Ministry of Public Enlightenment and Entertainment."

"In what capacity?"

The president thought. "I believe it was something in the foreign press department."

"And she came back to the States in 1941?"

"She managed to get out of Berlin and into Switzerland and then somehow got herself back here."

"What did she do then?"

"She arrived in Washington and got a position at Georgetown University in the modern language department. She is fluent in French and German."

Tom Buxton sipped his cognac and stared out of the window, his mind racing.

"Mr. President, you do know, don't you, that the Reich Ministry of Public Enlightenment and Entertainment was headed by Dr. Goebbels, Hitler's right-hand man."

Not for the first time that day, the president felt at a loss for words. His throat went dry. He could barely get out the words, "Oh my God."

CHAPTER TWENTY-SIX

Whenever Kyle Denning sat behind this desk by himself, no one else in the room, he found the Oval Office lonely and overwhelming. Now he poured himself another cognac and stared across the room. He thought of his difficulties with his brother beginning in childhood, when George had been the family favorite due to his academic successes. George had proven himself at Princeton, Oxford, and the Sorbonne while Kyle's accomplishments had largely been extracurricular: he had captained the University of Virginia's football team and debate club. Even when he had been elected to the senate, his family had been preoccupied gushing over a recent article of George's in the *Washington Post*. His parents were both deceased by the time he was elected president. If they hadn't been, he was sure, they would've overlooked his win on account of George having obtained a new pair of socks or parted his hair the other way.

His thoughts were interrupted by a gentle knock. The White House head of security along with his chief of staff, Bennett Simmons, entered the room. The head of security, Bert Lannister, was a tall Black man, six feet four with close-cropped hair just beginning to gray at the temples. The president was accustomed to seeing *him* in a somber mood—it came with the territory of the job. But both men approached him as if tiptoeing across a minefield.

"Mr. President," Simmons began as he neared the desk. "Bert and I have some devastating and tragic news."

"What is it, Ben?" he asked softly.

"It's about George. He's dead."

The word meant nothing to the president at first, even as he echoed it back: "Dead. What are you talking about? I just talked to him. I—" *I was just reminiscing about what an asshole he's always been, how he's always stolen my thunder. I was just blaming him for souring my relationship with my parents.*

"His secretary went into his room to ask him a question and to see if he needed anything and she found him dead on the floor. She called me and security five minutes ago."

"Oh my God. What was it? A heart attack?"

Bennett Simmons paused. "No, Mr. President. Suicide. There was an empty vial next to him on the floor. It must have been poison. Cyanide, maybe."

"Jesus Christ." When Kyle Denning stood, his hand knocked over the mostly empty glass of cognac on his desk. Simmons lurched forward to set the glass upright before its amber liquid could stain the many papers fanned out across that surface. "Apart from the security guard, does anyone else know?"

"I'm sure the guard will have said something and that the word is out downstairs that the president's brother and head of the CIA has committed suicide."

"I suppose there's no way we can avoid an autopsy?"

"Definitely not," Simmons answered firmly.

"Fuck!" Denning shouted as he reached out for the dregs of his cognac.

"If I may suggest something, Mr. President," Bert began, "we should call in the police. After all, it could be a crime scene."

"I agree. There must be no cover-up. Get the attorney general over here ASAP, Ben. And Tom Buxton."

"Yes, sir."

"I'm going over to see Madge to tell her. Get me an unmarked car and a driver, and instead of Buxton coming here, give him Madge's address and I'll meet him there. You stay here with the AG and police, keep everyone calm." He strode across the room to where his jacket hung.

"Mr. President, do you think it's wise for you to go over to see Madge right now?"

"Hell with that Ben. After all, she is our sister, and she and George lived together. It's only right she hears it from me, not the newspaper."

"But—"

"Fuck, Ben, I'm going. Get me that damned car and tell Buxton to be there in fifteen minutes."

***

"Stop here, please." The president told the driver. "And wait."

He stepped out of the Ford Taurus and walked briskly toward his sister's house. Tom Buxton had arrived already and was standing by his car.

"Are you sure you want me here, Mr. President? After all, this really is a private family matter."

He didn't even glance up at Tom as he answered. "I want you here."

They walked up the pathway to the front door.

"Madge and George lived together in this house for close to forty years. She bought it for about five thousand dollars after the War. God knows what the house is worth now. Arlington real estate has soared."

He rang the bell. It was a cold night and Buxton crossed his arms against his chest.

The president rang the bell again.

"Oh hell. She probably can't hear it. She's deaf but won't admit it. There's a side door she leaves open for George when he invariably forgets his key. Let's walk round the back."

Buxton followed the president around to the back of the house. An outside light, styled to look like an old-fashioned lantern, illuminated the path to the door.

"Madge, it's me, Kyle. Are you there?"

They walked through the kitchen, awash in yellows, oranges, and browns, into a dining room with an antique formal dining table, eggshell-colored cloth napkins folded at every seat, and finally into the L-shaped living room. This room made it evident that the dining table was the house's big bragging point.

"As you can see," the president explained quietly, "my sister doesn't spend much on furniture. All this stuff belonged to my parents. Christ, the sofa has to be a hundred years old. It still smells of cat piss."

As they turned the corner into the part of the room hidden from them in the first leg of the "L," the president and Buxton stopped in their tracks. Madge Denning sat in the leather large club chair that had once belonged to her father, her chin dropped to her chest, eyes open but vacant. Clearly dead.

"Mr. President. Don't move or touch anything," Buxton whispered urgently.

For a moment, the president just stood there, speechless. If it hadn't been for the preceding day's events, he may have remained in shock much longer as he absorbed the sight of his deceased sister. But the day had delivered one blow after another, and now he felt inured. He wore the previous surprises and tragedies like armor. He blinked rapidly. He forced his breathing to steady. And he noticed something.

"Look over there, Tom, in the corner."

The rug had been rolled up partially and revealed an open trap door that had not been closed.

"Call the police," he instructed Buxton.

"Mr. President. You go back to the White House immediately. I'll wait for the police to arrive. I'll take care of everythig."

The president nodded and muttered that Tom was right. It had been quite a day. "Only God knows what tomorrow would bring."

***

It was close to midnight when the president, who had been thinking only of how low the brandy bottle was getting, received a call.

"Yes, Tom, what's the situation?"

"It was suicide, Mr. President. Cyanide. Just like George. The police and the coroner are here right now . . . Also, the CIA."

"CIA. What the hell is that all about? Who called them in?"

"You remember that open trap door in the living room? FBI agents discovered your sister had a whole room down there. Desk, chair, typewriter, filing cabinet. The cabinet was locked, but the FBI is in the process of taking it away."

"So she had a home office in the basement."

"She also had a telex machine down there."

"Why the hell would *she* have a telex machine? Remember, George lived with her. Maybe it was his office? We now know he was a fifth columnist working against the United States."

Buxton paused. Sue, the president's night-time secretary, knocked and came into the room with a fresh bottle of cognac. He raised his eyebrows and nodded in appreciation.

"Mr. President. It gets more complicated. You know how a telex machine works. Your sister's anyway. First you make a tape of what you want to send. It's a narrow white tape, perforated and it comes out looking like braille. Then you check it over, and if it's okay, you feed it back into the machine and dial the number you want to send it to, and press 'send' and off it goes. And then the tape falls onto the floor or into a wastepaper basket at the side of the machine."

"So?"

"Your sister sent the tape, but in her rush and emotional distress, she didn't destroy the tape. It was sitting on the floor by the telex machine."

"And . . ."

"The FBI ran the tape through the machine to see what she had sent. It was a short message sent a few hours ago to someone in Geneva, a Guy Broussard. She wrote him to advise that by the time he saw this telex, George would be dead. She also wrote that the operation planned for later this month was in jeopardy. 'Mariscal needs to be evacuated urgently.' That was the last line."

"So, Madge was in on it. Christ. She must have been indoctrinated all those years ago when she was working for Goebbels."

"It looks like that, Mr. President."

"Now what?"

"When the FBI agent read the tape, he said it was now a matter for the CIA. Three of their agents arrived within a half hour. By the time they were at the house, an incoming telex came in from this Broussard saying he was en route immediately to Paraguay and would revert on his arrival there. He also said he'd got what he needed from the rue du Rhone office." Tom paused. "Madge probably never saw that telex."

"So, who is this Broussard?"

"The FBI had nothing on him, but the CIA confirmed he was one of their operatives, based in Geneva, and that he reported only to your brother, George. That's all they knew."

"Did they know George was dead?"

"None of the guys I was with seemed to know."

"At least there's that," the president mumbled. It was small consolation, but it was something. And at a time like this, focusing on the positive was essential: not everyone knew about his brother's suicide yet, and he had a fresh bottle of cognac.

***

Daniel glanced around the plane. It was half-full. Apart from Giselle, Claudia, Felipe, and himself, there were maybe fifty uniformed marines. The four planes were flying in convoy, so he surmised there would be additional military personnel as well as nurses and interpreters in the other planes. Claudia was already asleep in the row behind him, and Giselle and Felipe had dozed off in the seats across the aisle. On boarding, Daniel had placed his jacket in the overhead locker. Now, with it having turned cold inside the cabin, he got up to retrieve it. As he put it on, he felt the envelopes sticking out from the inside pocket. Along with hotel receipts, there was a message he'd been given by the front desk as he left for the airport. There had been so much on his mind, he'd forgotten all about it until now.

He opened the envelope and saw that it was a telex from his secretary, Madame Coty.

Dear Mr. Lavy,

I have terrible news. I had to leave the office early yesterday afternoon to go to the dentist. I left Jacqueline in charge and told her to lock up at the end of the day. When I arrived this morning, Jacqueline was dead. She'd been murdered. Shot. And one of the drawers in the filing cabinet in your office had been prized open and files removed. That was your personal filing cabinet, so I had

*no way of knowing what was removed. I called the police
immediately and they have sealed the office. If I hadn't
had to leave for the dentist, that girl would be alive now.
When are you coming back, Mr. Lavy?*

Coty

Daniel's hands shook as he reread the telex. He beckoned to
Felipe to come to sit with him. Once Felipe extricated himself
from Giselle, now in a deep sleep with her head on his shoulder, sat beside Daniel and took the telex.

Jacqueline had been working for him for three or four
years. In her mid-thirties, she was a single woman who lived
with her sister and parents in Geneva. She'd worked for an
attorney but decided that the world of international finance
and trading might be more interesting, let alone rewarding.
She had not been disappointed. But now the poor girl was
dead.

"This is terrible, Daniel. What do you think all this is
about?"

"I must get back to Geneva, or at least get hold of Madame
Coty. But we're stuck for another nine hours in this plane.
And even when we're on the ground, I feel like reaching her
is going to be nearly impossible."

***

"Mr. President, I'm leaving now," Sue said as she approached
the desk. "Lucy has arrived. Can I order you something from
the kitchen?"

Kyle Denning stirred in his chair. He glanced at the
clock on his desk. Seven-thirty. He'd fallen asleep. He ran
his fingers across his face. "Coffee, please, and then I'm going upstairs to shower and change."

"Mr. Buxton has arrived. Shall I show him in, or shall I tell him to wait until you have changed?"

"Show him in."

"Mr. President, I hope you feel better than you look," Buxton said as he strode into the Oval Office.

"I could say the same about you, Tom. What's the latest?"

"Gets weirder by the minute. Between the CIA, the FBI, and Interpol, with help from the Swiss police, we have an interesting development."

Denning took a gulp of coffee and Buxton waited before continuing while the daytime secretary, Lucy, poured him a cup too.

"A murder and break-in was reported earlier today in Geneva. The local police went to the scene of the crime. A woman, in her thirties, was found by a colleague dead when she arrived at work this morning. The indications are that the woman was murdered sometime last night."

"Tom, forgive me, I'm exhausted. What the hell has this got to do with us? This is a local Swiss matter, tragic as it may be, of nil importance to me."

"Mr. President, the murder took place at an office in rue du Rhone in Geneva."

"So?"

"It was at Daniel Lavy's office."

"My God."

"And, Mr. President, Madge's incoming telex was from a Mr. Broussard, who informed Madge he'd collected what they needed from an office, without naming what office. And indeed Mr. Lavy's personal filing cabinet had been broken into."

The president fell silent.

"We need to talk with Lavy."

"That's not going to be easy. He's about to land in Paraguay and he may already be there."

"Then, this Broussard—"

"In his letter to Madge, he said he was also en route to Paraguay."

CHAPTER TWENTY-SEVEN

The marine colonel in charge of the mission, a man with a jaw like a shovel, left his seat and walked toward the cockpit. Felipe nudged Daniel and pointed out of the window.

"We're below the clouds so I guess we're close to our destination."

"Maybe, or maybe they want to fly low to avoid being picked up by radar," Daniel replied. He knew the prospect of arriving should have meant more to him, but between what was going on at the fortress, his children, and now the tragedy at his office, his mind was bouncing all over the place. He turned around to see if Giselle and Claudia had awakened, but they were still asleep.

"Colonel Judd here," came a gravelly voice from the cockpit. "Listen to me carefully. We are going to descend rapidly. We are approaching Paraguayan airspace and must avoid being detected by radar. We expect to land in about twenty-five minutes. We will open the doors even before we land, and you are to exit with your rifles at the ready and encircle the plane. Captain Brennan and Sergeant Nelson will be in charge of this unit. Your preliminary mission is to ensure the safe landing of the plane that is following us. Remember, there are four aircraft on this mission. The one behind us should be on the ground within two minutes of us, so move quickly. Then the third and fourth within two minutes of each other. We do not know the defenses at this fortress, so be on your guard. Do not open fire until ordered to do so—and good luck. This could turn out to be a historic mission. Something to talk about with your children and grandchildren."

Leaving the cockpit, Judd approached Daniel and Felipe.

"You are to stay on the plane, and the two women with you, until I give you the go-ahead to disembark. Understand? We must secure the place first and deal with any resistance before we can let you guys get off the plane. Okay?" Despite the fact that he ended with a question, his tone left no room for discussion.

When Daniel turned around, he saw that Giselle and Claudia appeared wide awake. Certain they'd listened attentively to the colonel's announcement, Daniel gave them an encouraging wave. Then, staring out the window, he took in the landscape below. Barren scrubland. "I guess we're below a thousand feet," he murmured to Felipe.

The marines on the plane stood to stretch their legs and grab their weapons, fasten their ammunition belts, and put on their helmets. No one spoke.

"Daniel, there's the outer wall of the fortress, remember?"

"I see it."

"This is Captain Reed from the cockpit. We're about two hundred feet and we'll be on the ground in a little over a minute. We're opening the doors at fifty feet. Good luck, gentlemen. May God go with you."

"Okay men, prepare to exit the plane," the colonel shouted.

The doors burst open with a resounding *thud*.

Less than a minute later, the men rushed from the plane and took their positions on the ground, rifles at the ready, some with machine guns. Felipe moved to a window seat behind Daniel to get a better view.

The roar of the planes behind them, preparing to land, was deafening. One of them pulled up to the side of the first aircraft with its cargo bay doors already open. Four armored vehicles and a Land Rover drove off. Two armed guards rushed toward the vehicles. A marine shot them using a silenced pistol but failed to kill them. As a third guard appeared, one of the US marines in the Land Rover aimed an unsuppressed rifle. The shot rang out, echoing even inside the plane where Daniel, Felipe, Claudia, and Giselle waited. The guard's limbs splayed. His weapon hit the earth. Then he fell alongside it.

The two remaining planes were now on the ground. Led by Colonel Judd, the marines charged toward the fortress. The occupants gazed in shock, confusion, and fear as they stood petrified. Entering the fortress, Colonel Judd used a megaphone to shout first in English, then in Spanish, "We are United States marines. Put your hands above your head." He paused. "And throw your weapons onto the ground."

Most of the occupants, both men and women, were well-dressed and seemingly civilians. Along with a number of Paraguayan workers in navy overalls, there were perhaps twenty or thirty European men in their thirties; by their uniform haircuts, blond hair, and Teutonic features, they appeared to be military personnel. This was corroborated when they were the only ones who had weapons to throw onto the ground.

Claudia was biting her nails, watching the marines' every move but thinking only of her children. Giselle did not know where to look first. Felipe and Daniel stood by one of the open doors, watching the activity, frustrated that they could not participate.

After close to an hour, Colonel Judd came aboard. Giselle and Claudia moved to the front of the plane. Judd removed his beret and wiped his brow.

"Thank you for being patient. We've secured the ground command and their communications capability. Our assault unit has sealed the building and has ensured that it has been evacuated. The occupants have been divided between Germans, Americans, Paraguayans, and others. We will start the interrogation process immediately. We believe that no one is still armed, so it will be safe for you to leave the plane. Sergeant Taylor is in charge of the unit that will secure the runways to enable us to leave. I'm not sure when we will actually be ready to leave. It may not be for a few hours. We will need to refuel and will make a stop on our way back in Caracas for this purpose."

"What about the children?" Claudia practically shouted.

"We have learned that the children are held in another building about a half mile from here but, of course, still in the compound. Two of our men are there now, and as soon as I hear back from them that it's safe, you will be taken there in one of the vehicles we have commandeered. A military doctor and two of his nurses will be going too."

"Thank you, Colonel," Claudia said softly. "We are praying that the children will be safe."

"Mr. Lavy, I am sure that you want to go, too, to see if your boys are safe, but afterward, I want you to come back to the main building and work with Mr. Martinez here and our other interpreters to interrogate the Germans we're presently holding captive."

"Can I help too?" Giselle asked. "I speak German and Spanish."

"That would be helpful. Thank you. You may come back with Mr. Lavy."

"How many captives have you, Colonel?" Felipe asked.

"Approximately one hundred forty Germans, twenty Italians, seventeen Americans, and about seventy-five locals—Paraguayan, Argentinean, and Bolivian."

"One hundred forty Germans?" Daniel could not contain his surprise at the number.

"But we don't yet know anything about who is in the building where the children are being housed. Just a minute, I may have news on that now. I'll try to reach my men there." He jumped from the plane as his walkie-talkie crackled and spit static.

He couldn't have been gone more than a minute or so, but it was long enough for Claudia to start twisting strands of her hair into a tight braid. Giselle was still thinking of how to comfort her, amid thoughts of dusting off her German for the interrogations ahead, when the colonel climbed back onto the plane.

"We have a vehicle coming to pick you up now to take you to the children. The doctor and his team are already there. The building is safe. Thirty-six children. All twins. Ten German women, one Argentinean and English, two guards, and four German men."

"Are the children okay?" Daniel asked.

"I can't answer that question, Mr. Lavy. Let us hope so."

CHAPTER TWENTY-EIGHT

A jeep pulled up alongside the plane, driven by a marine. "Climb aboard, please," the colonel ordered. "I pray you will find your children in good health and unharmed." Turning to Felipe, he said, "Mr. Martinez, follow me. I'll walk you over to the fortress, where you can assist with interrogations. My fellow officer, Major Comer, has a list of questions you will be required to ask each of the captives. Try to keep the interviews quick, say maximum fifteen minutes each. We want to begin our return before nightfall. Those we can't interrogate by then, we'll continue on the flight back."

"You mentioned that we would stop for refueling in Caracas. Do we really have enough fuel to get us there?"

"Mr. Martinez, the people on the ground here had two planes. They were tipped off about us flying in. Those planes have taken off, maybe two hours or so before we arrived. We're not sure yet who was on those planes. But there's still fuel here that we are going to use and certainly sufficient to get us all to Caracas where we can refuel all four planes."

"Colonel, I know that after Daniel has satisfied himself knowing his boys are okay, he'll need to be in touch with his office. It appears one of his staff members was murdered yesterday. Is there any way he'll be able to talk to his office?"

"That's terrible news, Mr. Martinez. There's no way he'll be able to reach Switzerland from here. From Caracas maybe, but not from here."

***

After a quick drive down an asphalt road leading from the main building, the jeep pulled up outside a self-contained two-story building. Daniel helped Giselle and then Claudia out of the jeep and onto the dusty ground. A soldier with auburn hair and a smattering of freckles stood waiting.

"The children are all outside at the back. They are bewildered. Our doctor and nurses are with them now. Everyone else, all the personnel we encountered, are being held under armed guard in the first room on the left as you enter. We have vehicles coming over to take everyone to the main building, but we want to keep the children separate."

"Can we see them now?" Daniel asked.

"Follow me."

"I'm scared, Daniel," Claudia whispered.

"So am I," he replied.

Giselle took Claudia's hand as the three of them followed the marine around the building to a play area at the back. The children were all seated on the ground as the doctor and nurses examined them, talking to them all the while in low, soothing tones.

Giselle, Claudia, and Daniel stood at the edge of the lawn, all three straining their eyes in search of Matthew and Michael. Their lines of vision whipped toward a shriek. "Michael, look, it's Mama and Papa, and Giselle is with them too."

The boys jumped up from the ground and sprinted to their parents. Claudia and Daniel burst into tears as they hugged their children. Beside them, Giselle wept softly as she ran tremulous fingers through Matthew's hair, then Michael's. When they could be pried away from their parents, she enveloped them in a hug of her own. Holding their lean, sunburned bodies in her arms and seeing Claudia and Daniel with smiles of pure ecstasy, Giselle could not help reflecting on the night she'd knocked on her uncle's door. How terribly nervous to approach him she'd been. *What if she and Daniel hadn't reconnected? What if she'd been too scared . . .*

She embraced the boys until Matthew cried, "Too tight, Giselle!"

She let go as they all laughed. Claudia was laughing and crying at once, but her joy was clearly the predominant emotion. She beamed and stood up straighter than she had in weeks. She wouldn't allow her eyes to flicker away from her boys for a second.

Daniel led the boys, Claudia, and Gisele, to an empty part of the play area and sat down on the ground with them.

"Tell me boys, are you okay?"

"Yes, Papa. We're okay. Are we going home now?" Matthew asked.

"Very soon," Claudia replied.

When Daniel reached out to take Matthew's hand, something on the child's arm grabbed his attention like a thunderbolt. It was a tattoo. It bore a number and the word "Jude."

"Oh my God," Daniel whispered before bursting into tears all over again. "I never thought I'd live to see the day when another member of my family would bear such a tattoo." Weeping, he stood and then walked around to the side of the building, where he buried his head against the stone wall, his sobs audible to everyone.

Because they were both gazing in Daniel's direction, Claudia and Giselle were startled to see the doctor and one of the nurses in front of them. The doctor was a reedy man with thin silver hair and a slack face; if it weren't for his clunky brown shoes, he would appear capable of blowing off in the wind. The nurse beside him was much more substantial, with thick red curls and even thicker glasses.

"I'm Doctor Everdeen," the man said. "This must have been a terrible shock for you, but you don't know how lucky you are. I don't want to go into it all now, but believe me, you are very fortunate."

"Tell us about the children here, Doctor," Claudia pleaded. "Are they all safe?"

"Yes, thankfully. We will work with the local authorities to trace their parents and find out how they arrived here. After we've examined them medically and psychiatrically, we'll ensure they're returned home."

"And our boys?"

"We haven't gotten around to examining them yet," the nurse said, "but we will, of course."

Dr. Everdeen added, "I'll need to ask you what you know about how and when they were kidnapped. You see, your sons are the only Europeans here. All the other children are Latin American."

Claudia hugged her boys and Giselle ruffled their hair playfully.

The doctor excused himself to go speak with Daniel, but the nurse stayed behind to answer Claudia's and Giselle's questions. As Dr. Everdeen approached him, Daniel's head was still buried against the wall, his body shaking with his sobbing. He heard the doctor approach and turned toward him.

"Doctor, forgive me for being so emotional, but the sight of those tattoos on their arms brought the horrors of the concentration camps right back. My family, you understand, was destroyed. I was the lucky one."

"Mr. Lavy, your children were lucky too. I do not believe they have suffered any harm, but you should know that they, along with all the other children, were in extreme danger."

"Tell me, Doctor."

"The children being held here, as you may have noticed when you arrived, are all twins. Eighteen sets. They were held captive because a doctor, a man who can only be described as a monster, was conducting medical experiments on them. Many children died here as a result of these experiments, and their bodies were cremated."

"And were experiments conducted on my boys?" Daniel asked, feeling his heart beating in his throat.

"I don't think so, but I can't be certain until I have examined them."

"And the other children here?"

"We need to interrogate the doctor and his staff to get these answers."

"Where are they?"

"Inside, under armed guard."

Daniel nodded. "Can I see this monster? This doctor. Can I interrogate him?"

"No, Mr. Lavy, it will be too emotional for you. My orders are to see you taken back to the main building, to Colonel Judd, and the women who are with you back to the plane."

"And my boys?"

"After I have examined them, they will be taken to their mother."

"I see," Daniel said, finally regaining control of his breath. "Thank you, Doctor."

***

Daniel, Claudia, and Giselle were led back into the building by a marine with wavy, pumpkin-colored hair.

"The children will come to you in the plane as soon as the doctor has finished examining them. Please, when we enter the building, keep your eyes fixed straight ahead of you. We have armed guards outside holding captive the twelve women and six men who worked here," the officer instructed.

They nodded as they quickened their pace. Even Daniel, who had expressed a wish so recently to interview the doctor involved in the medical experiments, felt nauseated at the thought of establishing any eye contact with these people.

A soldier held the door open so they could all pass into what pretended to be a garden with a lawn that was more brown than green, and a few bushes planted as a fence.

"Shit," the marine snapped. "The jeep isn't here yet."

"He's on his way," the soldier at the door answered.

Ignoring the officer's instructions, Giselle looked across at the female captives, lined up in front of guards who pointed machine guns at them.

"Giselle!" a woman shouted from the middle of the row of captives.

Giselle, in shock, turned quickly to see which woman was calling out her name.

"Antonia!" she shouted back. "My God, what are you doing here?" She rushed toward her friend, but her way was blocked by one of the guards.

"Get away from me, you fucking Jewish bitch. Look what havoc you have caused! When I got you that job in Geneva, I never thought it would lead to this."

The guard tried to pull Giselle back but without success. Claudia and Daniel looked at each other, then across at Giselle and the row of female captives, confused.

"My father told me that when you and your fucking colleagues were in Hong Kong, you were sniffing around and that one of them even went to China to check out the uranium. You idiotic bastards," Antonia snapped.

Giselle stood motionless. "What are you talking about, Antonia? I don't understand. What have you got to do with all this?"

"You stupid bitch. You've ruined the plan to save the world. The fuehrer's work wasn't finished in 1945, but at last, we were going to see it succeed. And now it's all in ruins."

The men, lined up on the opposite side, began chanting with their right arms outstretched, "*Heil* Hitler! *Heil* Hitler! *Heil* Hitler!" One shouted, "Well said, Antonia!"

Just then the marine with the pumpkin-colored hair whipped his head around. "The jeep is here! C'mon! Hurry!"

CHAPTER TWENTY-NINE

C olonel Judd jumped from the driver's side of the Jeep. "Hurry," he said softly.

Giselle trembled as she climbed up next to Claudia, who had already taken her seat in the back.

"Slight change of plan," the colonel addressed Daniel as he U-turned toward the parked planes. "I'm taking your wife back to the plane. As soon as the doctor has finished examining your children, someone will bring them to their mother. We will see that you will be brought food and drinks, and hopefully we'll be ready to set off back to the States within a few hours. Try to get some sleep."

"Thank you, Colonel," Claudia replied.

"Now a change of plans for you." He turned around to face Giselle. "We have very limited time and many people to interrogate. We want your help with the interviewing process. Your colleague Mr. Martinez is already conducting interviews, and we need your help too."

"Of course, sir. Anything I can do. I also speak some Italian and Spanish, if it will help."

The colonel sounded weary but admiring as he said, "Clever girl."

***

After dropping Claudia off at the plane and seeing her safely escorted up the steps by a soldier, Judd drove the few hundred yards to the main building, a massive concrete structure devoid of architectural detail. In its simplicity, it reminded Giselle of a child's drawing of a building: a blunt square with a row of squares for windows and a rectangle door and nothing else.

"The interview process is taking place in what was used as a gymnasium," Judd informed Daniel and Giselle. "Ten interpreters came with us. With the two of you and Mr. Martinez, we have thirteen. With a bit of luck, we'll be able to handle around fifty interviews every hour."

"How many people altogether need to be questioned?" Daniel asked.

"About two hundred fifty. But just the basics. Look at it like the triage formalities in a hospital. We're getting together the basic information from each of the captives, and then we'll decide what to do with them."

"I'd like to see them all shot."

"Mr. Lavy, there'll be no shooting here under my watch."

Daniel nodded, but the look in his eyes remained murderous.

They stood at the entrance to the gymnasium. All exercise equipment had been pushed to the back. Interrogations were taking place at tables set up along the other three sides of the capacious room. Giselle and Daniel watched as the uniformed interpreters—all men—fired questions at their captives and entered their answers on the forms provided.

"There's Felipe," Giselle pointed out, her hand still trembling after her encounter with Antonia. Felipe was easy to pick out, as he was the only one in the room not wearing a uniform.

"Okay, please, find a couple of spare seats and get started," Judd ordered. "I'll be popping in and out during the next few hours. Later we'll all have a meeting to share our findings."

***

Six hours later, the last interviewee was escorted under armed guard out of the gymnasium. The room stank of sweat and cigarette smoke. An orderly had periodically brought in rations and coffee, as well as packs of cigarettes, to the interpreters. In the air hung a sense of both exhilaration and exhaustion.

All interpreters had piles of completed interview forms stacked in front of them.

"So, in a nutshell what have we got here? Let's go round the room and tell us in a couple of minutes what you've learned. Let's start with you here, Sergeant?" Judd pointed to the man seated behind the first table to his right.

The sergeant stood. A tall man, clearly spent, mid-thirties. His hair was cropped so short he appeared bald from a distance.

"There is no need to stand, Sergeant."

"Thank you, sir," he replied with a deep southern accent.

"This fortress was used as a science laboratory to manufacture a bomb. I couldn't determine from the interviews I had why they needed to produce a bomb. But that was the ultimate objective."

Judd turned his attention to a corporal, a man whose baby face belied his true age and whose eyes were the color of clover.

"In addition to the science laboratory, there was also a medical research lab in another part of the complex. A separate building where experiments were conducted on twins. Horrible experiments like injecting dyes into the kids' eyes, cruel spinal cord taps, transferring typhus and other diseases to perfectly healthy children."

"Yes, we know about that. Thank you, Corporal."

The corporal continued. "A few of the people I interviewed said they saw a bulldozer dig a hole in the ground a few hundred yards from the medical research lab into which bodies were thrown. Another man I interviewed said he saw two doctors personally shoot any of the children who survived the experiments to get rid of what they referred to as 'the scientific materials.'"

Daniel flinched.

Another interpreter, with a midwestern accent and a dimple on only the right side of his face, said, "I interviewed not only German and Italian scientists but also some American."

"Me too," another contributed.

"I managed to get out of two of my interviewees that the objective of this place was to manufacture a bomb," the baby-faced corporal said. "They were racing around the clock to do this because the objective was to blow up a place in remote Tibet where Khrushchev and Chairman Mao were meeting to resolve their differences. With those two despots out of the way, Russia and China would be in chaos and their governments would be replaced by right-wing leaders."

"Did anyone tell you who they reported to?" Colonel Judd asked.

"There was a hierarchy," an interpreter with a gruff voice and a thick beard answered. "The Americans reported to one man here, and he reported to a woman in Washington, a Lucinda Hayworth."

Another interpreter, whom everyone could tell was remarkably tall even as he sat, spoke up. "And the Italians here, they reported to a Giuseppe . . . who is based in Rome but who also has an office in Buenos Aires."

Felipe and Daniel exchanged glances across the room.

"And the German scientists," Colonel Judd said. "Who did they report to?"

Silence.

"I couldn't get that answer," the tall interpreter replied.

"Could *anyone* get that answer?" Judd shouted out in anger.

Around the room, interpreters chorused versions of the same reply: "I tried, but I got nowhere."

Finally, a young interpreter with curly auburn hair that seemed hellbent on speaking up said, "I interviewed a German scientist who spent a lot of time in Tibet, procuring uranium."

He was interrupted by rapid fire from another part of the building.

"What the hell's that?" the corporal with the bright green eyes shouted.

"You interpreters stay here," Judd shouted. "Seal this gym," he ordered a soldier. "All other men, follow me."

***

Leaving just one marine to protect the thirteen interpreters, Colonel Judd rushed from the gymnasium followed by five of his men.

"I want you all to remain calm," the marine began. "Just remain in your places and this will be settled quickly."

"I thought you people had disarmed everyone," shouted an interpreter with a prominent Adam's apple, now bobbing as he swallowed heavily.

"We thought so too."

More shots from behind the closed door.

"This is ridiculous," Daniel spat as he approached the marine, a compact, muscular man with dark skin. "There are thirteen of us in this room, fourteen with you, and only one of us has a weapon. If anyone breaks in through that door, you're a dead man and we will be too. For Christ's sake, man, tell your fucking Colonel Judd to give us weapons. I can't speak for the others, but Martinez and I have seen combat duty."

The soldier bristled with embarrassment and anger. He nodded in silent agreement with Daniel.

More gunshots. This time from outside the building as well as from the adjacent part of the fortress.

Giselle sat anxious; her eyes affixed on Daniel across the room. The scientists sat grim-faced and quiet.

The door suddenly sprang open as Colonel Judd reentered.

"Okay, everyone. The shooting is not yet over but will soon be contained. There's been a breakout. The Argentinean guards retrieved a cache of rifles and revolvers that had been hidden. They've distributed these among their colleagues. As far as we can tell, they have limited ammunition. We are in control of the situation."

"Is anyone guarding the planes? My wife and children are on one of them." Daniel snapped. There was far too much going on at the moment for Giselle, Felipe, or even Daniel himself to pick up on the fact that he hadn't said "my ex-wife."

"Yes, the planes are being guarded."

"All these gunshots," muttered the short-haired sergeant, the first who'd given his report. "What are the casualties?"

"Five dead. Including two of our own men."

"Colonel Judd, my colleague and I are former military men. We've seen armed combat. You must allow us to do something. One marine with one revolver isn't going to save us if any one of the bastards breaks in here. Give us guns."

The colonel hesitated, but only for a moment.

"Okay," he ordered the marine. Take the revolvers from the dead guards and bring them to these two. Move quickly."

He then turned to the others. "I want you all to form a single line and follow me. When the marine returns, we will run to the first plane."

"Does that include me?" Giselle asked.

"No, I want you to remain here until we can take you over to the children's building in case you're needed there."

The marine rushed back into the gym and handed Daniel and Felipe each a revolver with additional ammunition, which he had taken from the remaining dead on the ground.

"The medical people over at the lab," Judd said aloud. "We need to keep them under guard before any of them drives right out of this compound and disappears."

Daniel shot Felipe a glance.

***

The marine appeared bewildered as Daniel stood uncomfortably close to him and shouted. "Give Giselle a gun too, for God's sake, man. If she's to remain here, she needs to be armed." Judd, having disappeared into the bowels of the building, was not there to approve or disapprove. Intimidated by Daniel's display of pretend authority and chutzpah, the marine rushed to grab another revolver.

It was the first time in her life Giselle had ever held a weapon. Her eyes, wide with confusion and uncertainty, flickered between Daniel and Felipe.

Amid the sound of more gunshots, a different noise filled the room.

"What is that?" Giselle asked. The three of them ran to the window.

There they saw a helicopter about to land. It hovered over the fortress before descending in the direction of the children's building.

"Felipe, go find Judd," Daniel ordered. "Tell him about the helicopter in case he hasn't heard it. Maybe it's here because he summoned it. But why the hell is it landing here where all the action is? We need to find out who's on board."

Felipe nodded vigorously. He ran out of the gym to join up with the other marines.

"Giselle, it's just you and me. Judd's jeep is outside. We're going to make a dash for it and drive to that other building. When we get into the jeep, sit in the back and keep your head down. There may be snipers on the roof here."

"Daniel, Judd is going to kill you. It's his jeep."

"What's he going to do? Court martial me?"

Through the window they could both clearly see the jeep was no more than fifty feet away. Straining their eyes, they could also make out three men jumping from the helicopter then walking purposefully toward the children's building.

More gunshots.

"Come on. Let's hope he left the keys in the jeep or else I'll have to hot-wire it."

They turned toward the door then ran in the direction of the parked vehicle. "Thank God, he left the keys," Daniel muttered to himself. "For Christ's sake keep down," he ordered Giselle. He turned the ignition and stomped the pedal. He drove them full speed the short distance to the smaller building, pulling up with a jerk alongside the unmarked helicopter.

Even this far from the fortress, they could hear the metallic echo of bullets being fired.

"Okay, Giselle, let's calmly walk inside and find out what the hell is going on here. Don't let them see you're scared. Okay?"

She nodded as she slid out of the jeep.

"Walk alongside me. Don't hide the gun. Let them see we're armed."

They walked through what purported to be the front garden and into the building. There wasn't a sound coming from the two rooms on either side of the open front door. Carefully turning the knobs, Daniel peered into the empty rooms, closed the doors back softly, and then pointed with his revolver that they should move on.

They came to the end of the corridor and joined up with another that led both to the left and right, seemingly covered the full width of the building. They heard voices, men's and women's. They peered behind the corner and saw a man with cropped, jet-black hair hurrying out from the building and into the back garden carrying bundles of files.

"Okay, Giselle, this is it. As soon as that man comes back, we're going to walk down this corridor into that room to find out what the hell is going on here."

A couple minutes later, the man returned from the garden, empty-handed, and went back into the room.

"Okay, let's go."

The voices from within the room grew louder as they approached. The door was wide open.

"Everyone, drop what you're holding and put your hands in the air," Daniel ordered. "Giselle, keep your gun pointed and don't shoot until I tell you." Turning his attention back to his hostages, Daniel spoke louder: "Make a line. Stand close together."

There were seven of them, Daniel surmised: three men from the helicopter, the man who had just come in from the garden, a woman, two middle-aged men—one who stooped slightly as though from back pain, the other one who looked oddly familiar. He and Giselle assessed the people quickly before turning their attention to the layout of the room. It was clearly a laboratory, rife with the usual chemical apparatuses and odors, with a couple of desks and three steel filing cabinets, the drawers of which were open.

"My God," Giselle shouted. "It's you!"

The young woman, whose sandy hair was disheveled and beginning to knot, growled, "Giselle, you bitch. You're not going to get out of here alive. You know that don't you?"

"Antonia, I don't understand."

"Don't move. Any of you!" Daniel shouted.

"Daniel, she's right. Drop your gun," a man said in a firm, strong voice.

Daniel turned to face the man who stood at the end of the line, whose hands were still in the air. Out of context, he hadn't immediately recognized him.

"Guy. What the hell? What are you doing here?"

"You fool, Daniel. For a former Mossad guy, you really are stupid. You should have known all along I was still CIA. When I got word that you idiots were en route here from DC, I came here straight away to rescue Antonia and the others here and see that you were killed before you could mess up our plans."

Daniel felt the perspiration drip down his face.

He could only make himself utter a one-syllable word: "Why?"

"Because you stupid liberals and commies are going to destroy the universe. We need a new world order. We must destroy communism by whatever means at our disposal. And until you idiots got into the act, we had those means, and we were close—very close—to accomplishing our objective."

Guy lowered his arms.

"Keep your hands above your head," Daniel menaced.

"Don't be foolish, Daniel," Guy replied softly.

"I said, keep your hands above your head."

Guy continued to lower them, smiling as he did.

"That's it, Guy."

One shot and Guy slumped to the ground, blood squirting from his chest.

Giselle's mouth fell open, but before she could form a sound, Daniel commanded her to stay calm.

The remaining captives stood in silence, shaken by the death of their comrade, whose blood was seeping beyond his chest, out onto the floor. For a fraction of a second, Daniel registered that he, too, might have been shaken by the event—but he wasn't. His military training had taken over. He had just slain an enemy solider, and it emboldened him. Daniel turned toward two older men, who stood across the room from him.

"And which one of you is Mengele?" Daniel asked calmly.

"Neither of us is Dr. Mengele," one of them replied. "I'm Dr. Josef Hofstetter," he said in a voice proud and arrogant, with a strong Bavarian accent. "I was Dr. Mengele's assistant. What are you going to do with us?"

"Then you're as evil as Mengele. Your time is up, Hofstetter. You've escaped justice for too long. You and your boss will go down in history as two of the cruelest, most vile and despicable people who ever lived. I'm not going to waste my time talking to you or taking you away to face trial. In the name of justice for all the men, women, and children you have tortured and on whom you committed the most shameful and horrendous experiments, and all the people you have killed—in their name, I am going to rid the world of your presence." One gun shot and Hofstetter's body slumped to the ground.

"Oh my God!" Antonia shrieked, her eyes watering as she dropped on the floor beside the doctor. Like a nurse on a battlefield, she placed her hand gently under his head. Stooping farther, she kissed him on the lips. Then she turned to Daniel.

"You bastard!" she screamed.

Giselle watched Antonia closely. Her left hand scurried down Hofstetter's body, where it flicked aside his white coat. Giselle could see that, tucked in his trouser belt, was a gleaming revolver. Antonia snatched it free.

"She's got his gun!" Giselle shouted.

"Shoot her!" Daniel ordered.

"I can't," she stammered.

Without repeating his command, without waiting another second, Daniel fired his next shot. Hofstetter's head fell with a *thump* onto the tiled floor as Antonia's fell on top of his chest.

"Giselle, keep me covered." Daniel strode to the five-remaining people in line. He patted each one down. Satisfied that none were armed, he ordered them to march outside and form a line in front of the jeep.

"Giselle, we're going back to the fortress. These jokers will walk ahead of us. If any one of them should be so foolish as to try to break away, for God's sake, shoot!"

She shuddered at his anger.

It was now sweltering heat. The captives walked in single file back to the fortress, from which gunfire still rang. Daniel drove at snail's pace behind the group. Deliberately, he parked in the same spot where Judd had parked earlier.

With his revolver, and Giselle's, still pointed at the group, Daniel ordered them to the gym.

"Sit down and remain seated with your hands on the table in front of you. And don't move." Turning to Giselle, Daniel lowered his voice. "Giselle, stay and watch these men. Don't let them out of your sight and shoot to kill if any of them move. Okay?"

"I won't let you down this time."

"Good," Daniel answered curtly. "I'm going to find Judd."

Daniel headed in the direction of the spasmodic exchange of fire. One of the captives, a middle-aged thin man with thinning grey hair and heavy, black horn-rimmed spectacles, stood.

"Excuse me, sir," he said in a soft and frightened voice. "Please may I speak to you in confidence?"

"It'll have to wait. I'm going to find the guy who is supposed to be in charge of this mayhem."

"It's important, sir."

"Then save it till I get back."

***

The captives sat in silence opposite Giselle. Her eyes scanned the line, from left to right and then back. None of them, apart from the thin man who wanted to speak with Daniel, seemed to have any fight left. They wore the blank expressions of people resolved to their fates. The gunfire had abated, but Giselle forced herself to stay alert, conscious of her promise to not let Daniel down.

"Can we smoke?" asked the man with the stoop, which was noticeable even as he sat.

"Yes," Giselle replied.

At that moment, Judd, Daniel, and Felipe stormed back into in the room.

"I am confident that finally everything is contained here," Judd announced, mopping the sweat from his brow, and placing his revolver back in his holster. "I'm hopeful that we can get three planes up in the air within a couple hours. We're going to leave maybe fifty men here until we get back. Replacement commandos arrive maybe tomorrow."

"Gentlemen." The man who had wanted a few words with Daniel earlier stood. "It is important I speak with you. I have information of vital importance. Trust me."

Daniel and Judd exchanged a look, after which each shrugged his shoulders.

"What is it? Judd demanded.

"I need to talk with you in confidence."

"Traitor!" snapped the man with the short black hair. "If I had a gun, I'd kill you now."

"Okay," Judd said. "Come."

The man left his position and walked across the room to join Judd, Daniel, and Felipe.

"You cowardly swine! Judas!" his former colleague shouted after him.

Once they had retreated to the corner of the room, well out of earshot of the others, Judd said in a low but firm voice, "Who are you?"

"Ludwig Jager. I was a professor at Heidelberg University before the war. I had nothing really to do here at this fortress. Of course, I knew exactly what was going on. My cousin told me. She arranged for me to come here after the war. I knew about Hofstetter and Mengele and their experiments on twins. I also knew of the work the German and American scientists were doing to manufacture a bomb to rid the world of the communist threat. And I knew about their work on chemical weapons, but I wasn't directly involved in that."

"So, Jager, what *did* you do here?" Judd snapped.

"You must understand that Germany, unlike France and England, didn't have colonies that could provide stimulants like coffee and tea to its people. How do you think German soldiers and pilots were able to stay awake for days on end as they stormed through Europe?"

Daniel shrugged. "They were motivated by hate."

"Not so. We manufactured a methamphetamine pill that swept the country in 1938. Everyone from the highest in the land to the lowliest laborer was hooked on it."

"And you were involved in that?" Felipe asked.

"That was my specialty. Even the methamphetamine pill Pervitin, which people rushed to buy as soon as it came to market. It was doled out to the military without restrictions. Our athletes in the 1936 Olympics flourished on it."

"So, what you're telling us is that you are totally innocent of any of the criminal activities taking place here," Daniel said.

"My job was to ensure that everyone here had access to as much Pervitin as they needed. In the '20s, I was one of the scientists involved in the manufacture of synthesized heroin. Please, if you would allow me, I want to take you somewhere now that will explain everything."

"Okay, Professor, show us what you want us to see." Judd moved aside so Jager could lead the way. "But be quick about it."

"Professor," Daniel asked. "You mentioned your cousin was instrumental in getting you here."

"Without her help, I would have been rounded up by the Russians when Berlin fell."

"Who was your cousin?" Judd asked.

The professor paused. "Eva Braun," he answered in barely a whisper.

They stood in silence, stunned.

"I don't understand," Felipe said. "Hitler and Eva Braun, we were all told that they committed suicide in 1945. How the hell could she have helped you escape from Germany after the War?"

The man simply repeated his request. "Follow me."

CHAPTER THIRTY

L eading the way, the professor left the room and then turned left down a long corridor.

"Professor, I know that Hitler and Eva Braun allegedly committed suicide on April 30th," Felipe said with an edge in his voice. "It's my birthday—I remember it well. And the Soviet army captured Berlin a few days later. So how the hell could Eva Braun have helped you escape from Berlin? We have reason to believe they were here at this damned fortress."

Rather than answer, the professor continued shuffling quickly down the hall. They passed several rooms, their doors open, where armed American soldiers watched over their demoralized captives. At the end of the corridor, the professor stopped in front of a steel door. The professor punched numbers into a panel on the wall, and the door opened automatically.

As they passed through, the area in which they found themselves became illuminated by a row of ceiling lights. A table with a telephone and a chair were the only fixtures.

"What's this room, all about, professor?"

Jager moved toward another steel door and, again, punched numbers into a control panel. The door slid open with less sound than a whisper, as the first had. They followed the professor into this room. At the far end there was a staircase leading down.

"We have quite a long way down, I'm afraid, gentlemen. Three levels, and at each, I have to repeat the process of unlocking doors."

Judd removed his revolver from his holster.

"Is this a trick?" Daniel asked.

Jager did not answer.

The only sound was of their footsteps on the concrete floor.

Daniel began to feel the pain in his leg. "Christ, and we have to climb back up afterward? Did anyone think of putting in an elevator when they built this fucking place?"

"We are descending to approximately one hundred feet below the ground, gentlemen."

"Thank God it's lit up."

When they reached the bottom, the professor paused to take something from his wallet. It was a thin plastic card.

"No code to punch into the wall this time," he explained. "Only a handful of people here have this card."

They watched as he slid the card in a slot in the panel. When a light flashed green above the door, he pushed it open.

They walked in slowly behind him. It was an entry hall to what appeared to be an apartment. The floor was covered with Persian carpet. A console stood against a wall, a number of framed photographs arranged neatly on it. Two oil paintings hung on the wall. A wide, ornate staircase led upstairs.

"Who the hell lives here?" Daniel asked. "This seems very luxurious compared with what we've seen elsewhere."

"Before we go upstairs, take a look at the photographs on the console. And the paintings on the wall."

The professor seemed too pleased with himself, like a tour guide flaunting the trivia he'd memorized for tourists willing to pay him too much. It annoyed Daniel, but his annoyance couldn't compete with his curiosity.

Daniel, Felipe, and Judd approached the photographs. "My God!" Daniel exclaimed as he picked one up to show to Felipe.

"Please don't touch anything," Judd said. "We may need to fingerprint this place."

"The painting on the left is by Carl Spitzweg. The one on the right, by Adolph Ziegler."

"Hitler's two favorites," Daniel muttered.

"Follow me," Jager said as he moved toward the staircase, passing two flags on either side of the wall, one the Swastika flag and the other the Reicheskriegsflaggg of World War II.

***

A large wooden chandelier illuminated the staircase as they walked up. At the top of the staircase, an oversize living room, again brilliantly lit, awaited them.

"The lights are on all the time," the professor explained, "so it's easy to forget that we are underground. This part of the complex was constructed as a bomb shelter, able to sustain even a nuclear bomb."

"Look at this photograph, Felipe." Daniel pointed to a framed photograph of Hitler sitting on a balcony, probably at the Berghof, his mountain retreat, reading a newspaper. Another showed him smiling in front of a crowd of children in lederhosen, all saluting him.

"This place is sickening me. I'm going downstairs," Daniel announced.

"No, Mr. Lavy," the colonel ordered. "We must stay as a group."

Daniel grunted, his eyes welling up with emotion.

The room, furnished with heavy Bavarian furniture, featured in the corner a desk with a leather blotter that had been in use for some time, as the blotting paper had not been replenished. A silver inkstand also graced the desktop, engraved with a swastika on top of the inscription, "To our beloved fuehrer, Adolf Hitler, on the occasion of his fiftieth birthday, April 20, 1939 —Joseph and Magda Goebbels."

"The painting on this wall came from Poland." Jager pointed to a portrait of a young man. "It is by Raphael. It is probably a self-portrait."

Daniel couldn't prevent a gasp from escaping. "That painting is priceless."

"Eva has a Klimt in her bedroom and the Fuehrer, in his room, has a Metzinger. These two came from the Rothschilds in Vienna."

"You say 'came,' professor. Do you not mean 'were plundered,'" Daniel snapped.

"My English, forgive me," Jager replied insincerely.

Felipe bent to inspect a radiogram next to the desk. A record was on the turntable. The Berlin Philharmonic conducted by von Karajan playing Wagner.

Double doors led into a square dining room, with a large round table, and eight chairs. Another Spitzweg painting—cows and sheep—hung on the wall. A door opened onto the kitchen, and from there, a narrow corridor led to two small bedrooms and a bathroom.

"This is where the cook and housekeeper slept," the professor pointed out. "Now let me show you the other bedrooms."

They followed him out of the corridor, through the narrow galley kitchen and back into the dining room and living room. Another door opened onto a wide corridor.

"That photograph in the wall over there," the professor pointed out, "is of their apartment building in Munich. 16 Princeregentstrasse. I used to visit my mother there after my father died. Eva Braun arranged for her to live there until she moved to her house in Tegernsee. On the small table by the door, you'll see Eva's album full of photographs taken by the Fuehrer's favorite photographer, Heinrich Hoffmann. Eva had worked for him years ago."

Felipe moved toward it.

"Don't touch it," Judd reminded him. "Everything here must be fingerprinted."

"Most of the photographs here are of the Old Chancellery in Berlin after it was renovated by that horrible woman, Gerdy Troost."

"Look, Felipe, here's one of Hitler with Neville Chamberlain." Daniel pointed to another framed photograph. "Who's the man with them?"

"That's Paul Schmidt, the interpreter."

"It makes me vomit when I see these photographs of the bastard stroking his dogs and feeding these deer, all while millions were being slaughtered, including your family and mine," Daniel said to Felipe.

"That's Hitler with Leni Riefenstahl. She was a regular guest at the house in Obersalzberg," the professor continued in his oily, tour-guide voice. "You see the porcelain in the glass-fronted display cabinet?" The professor pointed with an age-spotted finger. "Gerdy designed that too. A place setting was displayed at the Haus der Kunst in 1938. I was at the opening of the exhibition. If you want, I can show you the monogrammed linen and silver in the butler's pantry."

"Believe me," Daniel replied, "I've seen enough."

"There are two master suites here. My cousin's was this one on the right and the Fuehrer's was on the left."

"For God's sake, Colonel, I can't take any more of this," Daniel pleaded.

His words of protest didn't dissuade the professor, who powered forward with his recitation. "Their bedrooms are a mess. They packed very quickly, and they had to leave lots of clothes. She even forgot to pack all her perfumes, some of her jewelry, and her silver hairbrushes, a present from the fuehrer."

"I understand how you must feel, Mr. Lavy," Judd interrupted. "Let's go downstairs, professor. I want you to give me your entry card and the codes so we can return here later. I'm going to telex Washington to request they send a team of photographers and fingerprint experts immediately. Meanwhile this place needs to be sealed."

The professor opened his wallet to hand Judd the card.

"How many people here know the codes and have cards?"

"A few."

"I'm going to post guards on all the doors to seal this place until the photographers and fingerprint team gets here," Judd announced. "There mustn't be any looting by souvenir hunters."

"Professor, your colleagues in the gymnasium yelled 'traitor' at you." Daniel concentrated on keeping his voice even and moderate in volume. "Why did you bring us here?"

"I am innocent of everything that took place here. I wanted an opportunity to establish that fact. But I am angry and hurt, very hurt. My cousin brought me here. Yes, she saved me from being taken by the Russians, who would probably have executed me. But when we realized that something potentially dangerous to us was taking place—when we first saw a plane flying low over us, with photographers leaning out—everyone began to panic. Our telex operator conveyed our concern to our contacts in Washington and Buenos Aires, but no one here told us how they responded."

They stared at the professor as he continued.

"We can only assume that an answer did come in on the Fuehrer's private telex machine, which is in his bedroom, and that he was told to evacuate immediately."

"And when did this happen?"

"Just two or three hours before you all arrived."

"You still haven't explained why you are telling us all of this."

"My cousin brought me here." The professor's voice had finally risen from tour-guide mode to a disgruntled tone. He seemed to be telling the truth; he was genuinely offended by the events he described to these men. "Do you not think she should have found a place for me on the plane on which they all fled? Eva and the Fuehrer left, with the children, their governess, the cook, and housekeeper, their two dogs, Mengele, Martin Bormann, and a few others. The Fuehrer was too busy dealing with overall strategy and the assassination of Khrushchev and Mao. Bormann had day-to-day responsibility for this place. By any account, when they all escaped, God knows where to, there was no room for me on the plane." He shook his head in anger.

"This is truly earth-shattering," Daniel said softly. "It's hard to believe. And the whole world thought Hitler and Eva Braun died in the bunker."

There was a brief pause.

"We fooled you all," the professor said with a sinister half-smile.

"**D**amn it!"

Daniel Lavy slammed his mug of Lowenbrau down on the coffee table in front of him, levered himself up from the black leather couch, stomped over to the television set, and turned down the volume. He'd had the game up full blast against the sound of a howling summer windstorm, and just taken his first sip of ice-cold beer when he'd heard the sound: a gentle rapping at his front door.

With the TV volume turned down now, he could hear the insistent but soft knock more clearly. For a moment, his heart froze. He wasn't expecting anyone, certainly not at this hour, and he couldn't help but think back to the last time his evening had been waylaid by an unexpected guest at the door. In fact, he could've sworn he recognized the knock—and that it was, yet again, Giselle.

When Daniel flung the door open, he saw that he was partially right. Standing there were his niece—wearing a fashionable tea-length jacket and smiling warmly—and Felipe, whose beam matched Giselle's. Their expressions instantly put Daniel at ease. Surely, they wouldn't be smiling this way if they'd come to warn him that the world was again on the brink of mass destruction and an international fascist regime. He welcomed them.

Noticing the game nearly silenced on Daniel's TV, Felipe said, "I hope we didn't interrupt you."

Daniel felt so relieved by Felipe's and Giselle's happy comportment he had forgotten about the game entirely. He turned the TV set off so there would be no distractions. "What brings you two to see me?" he asked.

"Well . . ." Felipe began.

"We're engaged!" Giselle burst out before he could continue. Daniel was still making sense of the words as she whipped her left hand out of her jacket pocket and showed her uncle the glittering diamond ring. "He asked me this weekend at dinner, and we couldn't wait to tell you. You're the first one who knows."

"We know it's fast," Felipe said cautiously. The way he looked at Daniel made it clear how much he wanted his approval. "But our courtship hasn't exactly been normal. We were thrown off the deep end right away, and we've already been through more together than most couples will in a lifetime."

Daniel placed reassuring hands on Felipe's shoulders. "Not to mention," he said, "we've all just seen how fragile life is. I don't blame you for moving forward with the person you love." He nodded at his niece, who grinned.

"I knew you'd be happy for us!" Giselle cried, bouncing on her toes in her excitement. "Have you already eaten dinner?" she asked Daniel. When he shook his head, Giselle said, "I'm going to cook us a special dinner to celebrate," as she rushed off to the kitchen.

When Daniel was alone with Felipe, he said, "I have to admit, while I'm very happy for you two, I'm also simply relieved. Whenever I hear a knock on the door, it worries me. For a minute there, I was concerned you were here to tell me there was more activity from Hitler."

Saying the name was like tossing a bucket of ice water over the happy mood that had merely filled the room. Daniel had to imagine it was this way for everyone. Yes, initially Claudia had been ecstatic just to be reunited with their boys, but he had to imagine that she now spent many nights tossing and turning in the sheets she had nervously sweat through, dreading the day that Hitler reared his head and again put their sons in danger. He imagined that even their young, exuberant love couldn't prevent Giselle and Felipe from having flashbacks to the horrors they'd witnessed in Paraguay. They were all deeply scarred.

Not so long ago, when the name "Hitler" had been uttered, it had certainly been unsettling, but it had also been past tense; it had referred to a monster who could never again terrorize because he was gone forever. Now, even with all they'd accomplished, Hitler was back. He had fled to God knows where to formulate a new plan, which no doubt could be bigger and harder to thwart than this one.

Felipe nodded silently. For a moment, the only sounds were those of Giselle clanging pots and pans as she prepared their celebration feast. Finally, Felipe confirmed what Daniel suspected: "I think about him out there all the time. And I know it means that none of us are safe."

"How soon do you two plan on marrying?" Daniel asked quietly.

"*Soon*." Felipe said it with an urgency that made it sound as though he and Giselle would walk down the aisle the next day. It was the urgency of a man who knew that he could lose everything he loved in a heartbeat.

"What do you say if afterward . . ." Daniel's voice trailed off as he looked toward the kitchen, making sure Giselle couldn't hear him. The last thing he wanted was to ruin such a joyous occasion for her.

"We go after Hitler?" Felipe finished for him.

Daniel raised his eyebrows, proposing the question. He knew he was talking about a mission that would take all their energy, their time, their resources. They would be putting themselves in constant danger for a world that would never have a clue of their sacrifices. But he was ready if his nephew-to-be was, and he knew he would need Felipe's help.

Without a moment's hesitation, Felipe nodded vigorously. Looking Daniel in the eye, he said, "I'll be ready."

photo credit: Darien Photographic

S tephen Maitland-Lewis is an award-winning author, a British attorney, and a former international investment banker. He has held senior executive positions in London, Kuwait, Paris, Munich, and on Wall Street prior to moving to California in 1991.

He has owned a luxury hotel and a world-renowned restaurant and was also Director of Marketing of a Los Angeles daily newspaper. Maitland-Lewis is a jazz aficionado and a Board Trustee of the Louis Armstrong House Museum in New York. In 2014, he received the Museum's prestigious Louie Award.

A member of PEN, The Authors Guild and The Dramatists Guild of America, Maitland-Lewis is also on the Executive

Committee of the International Mystery Writers Festival. In addition, he is on the Advisory Board of the California Jazz Foundation and is a former Board member.

His short stories have appeared in various magazines and his first collection, *Mr. Simpson and Other Short Stories*, was recently published. His novels, including the latest suspense thriller *Duped*, have received numerous accolades. Other titles include *Hero on Three Continents, Emeralds Never Fade, Ambition,* and *Botticelli's Bastard.*

Maitland-Lewis' short story, *Mr. Simpson*, was developed as a play and has been performed by various theatre companies. He divides his time between Beverly Hills, California and New Orleans, Louisiana.

Made in the USA
Columbia, SC
13 August 2023

21516981R00169